WHITE GOLD

DAVID BARKER

ALSO BY DAVID BARKER

Gaia Trilogy

Blue Gold (Book 1)

Rose Gold (Book 2)

For Fiona, who deserves platinum

PROLOGUE

NORSAR's Finnmark station, Norway, June 2034

The Earth shook and somebody was listening. Six times already this century, NORSAR's team had detected nuclear tests carried out by the North Korean military and reported it to the United Nations. By coincidence, that very morning, the Finnmark station was being visited by the newly appointed minister for science, keen to show herself associated with one of Norway's success stories.

"So that mad dictator has broken his promise again?" asked the minister.

The man, whose screens had flashed and pinged an alert, turned to face the visiting dignitary. He looked puzzled. "Actually Minister, I'm not sure. It's a strange signal. I don't believe it was a nuclear bomb."

The minister breathed a sigh. Her husband was in Japan on a business trip. Not a great place to be if the North Koreans were rattling their swords again. "You use seismology to detect these bombs, is that correct? Could it be a regular earthquake?"

"Hmm, it's the wrong profile for that. I think it's a shift in the magma chamber of a volcano getting ready to blow."

"Big deal."

The man scratched his head. "Have you ever heard of the Volcanic Explosivity Index?"

The minster shook her head.

"It's like the Richter scale they use for earthquakes. Every point higher on the VEI represents a ten-fold increase in the volcano's eruption."

"And?"

"Paektu is on the border between North Korea and China. When it blew its top over a thousand years ago, it scored a seven. A thousand times bigger than Eyjafjallajökull. Ten times bigger even than Krakatoa. If it's getting ready to go again, forget about monitoring for some squitty underground nuclear test. The whole world is going to notice this explosion."

PART I

———

'Twas brillig, and the slithy toves
  Did gyre and gimble in the wabe

1

Freda Brightwell awoke in a strange bed, wondering if she had done something foolish the night before. For a moment, she was twenty-one again. But there was no hangover and no fellow student lying next to her. As the disorientation faded, she remembered where she was and groaned. The guard had banged on the cell door, just after 6am, as usual. The routine of the maximum-security Russian prison was starting to imprint itself onto Freda's brain, if not her body clock yet.

She had been awake for most of the night, fearing that Overseas Division had abandoned Gopal, Rabten and herself. Agents left to rot in a Russian dungeon? Surely not. At the very least, her boss Wardle ought to be worried about 'enhanced interrogation.' How long could the three of them be expected to resist torture once it began? She thought it odd that they had been in this prison already for a week and nobody had bothered yet to question them. Though perhaps she should be grateful for small mercies.

Freda hoped that the Russian and British Intelligence services might be negotiating some sort of trade. But during the darkest hours, with nothing but insects for company and deranged screams for a listening track, Freda's optimism scuttled off to hide in the corner. She worried that perhaps everybody was too busy with more important matters to concern themselves about three OFWAT agents. She knew from years of experience how meticulous the department was at preparing false identities. Her attempt to extract Gopal and Rabten must have been leaked to the Russian border police somehow. There was no way their IDs would have been spotted as fakes.

Freda had finally fallen asleep just as the summer dawn had started to chase away the shadows from her tiny cell. And then the guard with his stupid bloody baton. She could visualise his grinning face, set into his thick neck and massive frame. A walking walrus, with a moustache to match. An image popped into Freda's head: she was sitting up in bed as a child while her dad read an Asterix book to her. She realised that the guard outside her door bore an uncanny resemblance to Unhygienix, the fishmonger. The little smile did not last long.

Will I ever see my father again?

It was Freda's first pang of homesickness since she had joined OFWAT nearly twenty years ago. An eight-foot by eight-foot cell with a bucket of piss for company can do that to a person. She swallowed her weakness and got up, jogging on the spot to get the blood pumping. The door to the cell pushed open and she stood to attention, waiting to be called to the breakfast hall. She ducked through the under-sized door and started walking along the metal grating that formed the corridor towards the canteen. Another prisoner, on the floor above hers, shouted something in Russia and spat through the grating of his walkway. A glob of mucus landed next to Freda's foot. She hunched her neck in case more phlegm was flying her way but refused to look up.

The breakfast offering was not dissimilar to the mucus. She wouldn't be giving this hotel five stars on Trip Advisor. Freda shuffled along in the queue, barely looking at the food as she tried to keep her attention on fellow inmates next to her. The knife-attack a few days earlier had been a close thing. Waiting for the next strike was almost worse.

Freda sat down next to Gopal and Rabten. Able to relax a little with extra pairs of eyes on alert, spending a little time with her fellow agents at least helped to chase away the night-time gloom. An ex-Gurkha with a dry wit and a Buddhist monk whose glass was always half full. Hardly the usual recruits to Overseas Division, but then, the Himalayas mission six years earlier had hardly been a typical assignment. Freda wondered how her other partner on that mission, Sim Atkins, was getting on. He had been sent undercover to work at the moon base a few weeks ago. There had been no updates on his progress before her capture. Another source of anxiety.

God, what is this food? Dumplings laced with downers?

Back in her cell at the end of a monotonous day, Freda lay on her wafer-thin mattress trying to recite to herself *The Jabberwocky*. The nonsense poem she had memorised for a school talent show a very long time ago. The mental distraction, and the lack of sleep from the previous night, were helping her to drift off when a loud insect buzzed into her cell. Freda tutted, wondering if the Russian pests around here were biters. And then she realised that this was the first bug she had heard all week. She sat up and tried to locate the insect. No chance in this darkness.

The buzzing stopped and a message appeared on the wall opposite Freda's bed. Her heart lifted as if it had been pumped full of helium and a broad smile spread across her face. Her vision went blurry as she tried to read the words, tears starting to form.

The insect must be a nano-drone sent from Wardle, shining a beam across the room. Not forgotten after all!

Three Hydras on their way tomorrow.

Rendezvous exercise courtyard 11am local.

Freda slept well for the first time in a week and for once was grateful for the guard's wake-up call. She hurried to breakfast and sat down with Gopal and Rabten, whispering the news when nobody else was near. Freda's legs jigged up and down beneath the table. The questions flowed.

"What if we can't get out to the courtyard?" said Gopal.

"How do you mean?" said Freda, her optimism taking a step backwards.

"Say there's a fight breaks out. It's the only thing that passes the time for some of these knuckleheads. Exercise privileges are normally cancelled for the rest of the day when that happens."

"We pray," said Freda, clasping her hands together.

Rabten's face lit up and he mirrored Freda's gesture. "Namaste." The discussion continued. Hydras – hypersonic drones – were too small and light to carry a human more than a very short distance. So even once out of the prison, how were they going to get out of Russia? And if they were dangling below the drones as they escaped, surely the marksmen in the guard towers would be able to pick them off with ease? Wardle must have thought of all this, he must have this figured out. That was Freda's mantra all morning as the minutes ticked down, with all the pace of a classroom clock, to showtime.

The buzzers on the door out to the exercise yard sounded on schedule and the prisoners filed through for a daily dose of vitamin D and the freedom of an open sky above their heads.

Freda muttered a thank you to the heavens as she, Gopal and Rabten gathered near the middle of the yard, keeping an eye on the guards' towers and the other prisoners around them. Three sides around the courtyard were exterior walls, about fifteen feet tall, with the fourth side made up of the main prison building. An armed guard was at each corner of the yard, perched high in a tower. Freda couldn't help thinking of an old classic film, *The Shawshank Redemption*. She just hoped they were heading for the same happy ending.

But eleven o'clock came and went. Nothing happened. After the euphoria of thinking that a rescue operation was underway, Freda sank into an even deeper slough than before. The prison walls seemed to lean in towards her, the barbed wire reaching out to snag her clothes.

At lunchtime, the three agents assessed their options. "Something must have gone wrong," Freda said. "Maybe the hydras were intercepted."

"Maybe tomorrow meant tomorrow," said Gopal.

Freda played with her stew. "What's that supposed to mean?"

Gopal shrugged. "If the nano-bot came after midnight, then strictly speaking, when it said hydras arriving tomorrow, it did not mean in a few hours' time, but the day after."

"Well I wish they'd write some clearer instruction." She put her spoon down and a faint smile appeared. "You could be right."

The waiting was even worse second time around. All those fears about an interruption to the routine seemed more real now. They had been lucky yesterday. Surely their luck would run out today. But the buzzer sounded for morning exercise on schedule. The three agents stepped into the courtyard hoping for the best, fearing the worst.

A high-pitched whine alerted Freda to the approach of the drones. She grabbed Gopal's hand and gave it a squeeze. Three missile-like aircraft, with grey stubby wings, flashed past three of the guard towers and released a vapour. A trio of guards slumped to the floor. But the fourth tower was alert. A claxon sounded out and the guard managed to loose a hasty shot at one of the hydras before he too was overcome by gas. The three hydras descended to the middle of the courtyard and handle grips unfolded from the belly of the small drones. But only from two of them. The third hydra had been damaged by the guard's lucky shot. An acrid smell and dark smoke drifted out of the back of the wounded drone and the grip would not descend.

"Grab hold of those two," Freda shouted to her colleagues.

"We're not leaving you behind," said Gopal.

One of the hydras fired a burst of shots over the heads of other prisoners who were approaching.

Freda shook her head. "No time to argue."

"Grab hold of us. Three bodies, two hydras," the Gurkha suggested.

Freda thought for a moment, then shook her head again. "They're on their limit as it is."

Gopal folded his arms. "Then we wait for another rescue attempt."

"There won't be one." Freda looked at the smoking hydra and then bent down to the ground. "Help me find a stone, quick."

Gopal's top lip curled and then he started scrabbling through the thin layer of dirt, searching for something larger than gravel. A small prisoner at the back of the courtyard was directing his entourage towards the hovering drones. But it's not that easy to get past a *White Crane* martial arts expert. Despite being much smaller, Rabten was too fast and accurate for the lumbering muscle men headed his way. After a head-kick, a jab to the solar plexus and a leg sweep, three giants lay dazed on their backs.

"Here," said Gopal tossing a plum-sized stone to Freda. She caught it and rammed it into the tailpipe of the damaged hydra. Gopal looked bemused as the drone sputtered and then dropped to the ground.

"Fourth protocol," said Freda. "An immobilised hydra will self-destruct in thirty seconds to avoid being captured. Quick, help me place it against the outside wall."

Between them, Gopal and Freda dragged the heavy drone across the courtyard to the foot of an exterior wall. The small prisoner gesticulated towards the hydra and some of his entourage started running towards the machine.

"Get back!" she yelled, running to the furthest corner of the yard with Gopal and Rabten, waving her arms in gesture to the other prisoners. Some understood and followed suit. Others, maybe distrustful of orders or unable to understand, approached the damaged hydra just as the explosion ripped a hole in the wall. Bodies and debris went flying across the courtyard.

Freda was knocked to the ground by the shockwave. As she staggered to her feet, a blanket of silence seemed to have descended on the yard. Smoke billowed across the quad as armed guards in riot gear burst out of the main prison building. She could see people were shouting but nothing was registering in her ears. A trickle of blood found its way into her left eye and blurred her vision.

The guards began to attack the prisoners with riot sticks, who fought back with bare hands, their only hope in weight of numbers. One prisoner had his front teeth knocked out and his nose broken by a flailing baton. But his two friends exacted terrible revenge on the baton-wielding prison guard, pinning him to the ground and pressing the weapon into his windpipe.

Freda looked up to see more guards, armed with rifles and respirators, appearing in the lookout towers. Two of the men in the towers fired cannisters into the centre of the courtyard. Tear gas began to mingle with the smoke of the detonation. A gust of wind pushed through the hole in the outside wall and the cloud began to dissipate. The path to freedom became visible to those who had not been overcome by the gas. The three agents bolted for the hole along with numerous other prisoners. Bullets bit into the ground near the breached wall and then stopped. The still-functioning hydras had opened fire at the guards in the towers.

Once outside the prison the fugitives began to fan out. They faced another obstacle: a wire fence, at least three meters tall, topped with razor wire. Some prisoners risked lacerations and started scaling the fence, their dark blue prison robes showing flashes of bloodied skin beneath as the blades cut through their clothes. The three OFWAT agents crouched down as one of the hydras emerged through the hole in the stone wall and fired a missile at the chain-linked barrier. A section of the fence disintegrated into a twisted heap of wire. Prisoners surged through the second breach, pushing and shoving each other to be the first out. They staggered onto a road. A passing car broke sharply and skidded, trying to avoid the human obstacles. One of the prisoners was clipped by the front wheel arch of the vehicle and went spinning to the ground in a howl of pain. None of his fellow prisoners stopped for him, but instead sprinted towards the trees on the far side of the road.

Freda and Gopal did the same. Rabten wanted to stop to help the man who had been knocked down, but the other two dragged him away, into the forest. The pair of remaining hydras followed the agents until they were safely in the woods, and then the drones disappeared into the azure summer sky with a scream of their engines. Freda looked around at the dozens of prisoners in distinctive blue uniforms as they scattered in all directions.

At least these lot should keep the authorities busy for a while.

But still, the three of them were also in prison uniforms, stuck somewhere in Russia with no weapons, no equipment or money and no IDs. Part two of Wardle's escape plan had better be more fool proof than the first part.

"Relax, kid, we got you."

Sim Atkins was being helped on board the orbital rocket that had picked up his moon-base craft. The other escape pod, containing Doctor Payne, had already been collected. But the lifeless body inside had told of a man wanting the easy way out rather than the rest of his life behind bars. Sim cursed when he had heard this news. He had wanted to question the doctor further. The plan to blow up the moon base that Sim had helped foil – who was behind that? Was there any remorse for those murdered workers? And was it connected to his son's death? A deadly disease let loose upon the residents of Moon Lab One. It had claimed only two victims: Sim's son and the host body, Yusuf. A new form of suicide bomber. How had that even been possible? Was there a secret agent working at NASA? Moon Lab One was supposed to be a shining example of international co-operation. Why would it be targeted?

It had taken three days to travel back from the moon into orbit around the Earth. Three lonely days, surrounded by the emptiness of space with the guilt of failure to save his son gnawing away at his stomach. The crew of the orbital rocket guided Sim's weightless body through the docking area and strapped him into his seat for re-entry. He let them do everything, as if he were as lifeless as the doctor. Questions continued to tumble through Sim's mind even as the rocket plummeted back to earth. The violent shake barely registered on his senses. The rocket slowed, re-oriented itself and gently landed.

"OK Sim, lay still there, buddy. Earth gravity is gonna feel pretty rough for a while. The team will come to help you in a few minutes." The Commander patted Sim on the shoulder and headed for the exit door while Sim lay back under the mountain of pressure bearing down on him. He wanted answers. He wanted revenge. But that would have to wait for his body to recover.

"Wait. Take these," he said. Sim pulled the foil-wrapped seeds from his chest pouch. Seeds that might help combat a virus the terrorists wanted to spread across Europe's wheat fields. The effort of lifting the packet out and stretching his arm was exhausting. He tried to remember the name of the woman who had been leading the research into plants on the moon base, but it was too hard. He closed his eyes and slept.

Alan Wardle looked out from his office on the sixth floor of City Centre Tower, over Birmingham, wishing he was in a tent on the banks of the Dee, and that fishing for salmon was today's agenda. But he was Director of Overseas Division, OFWAT. The man to whom Sim Atkins and Freda Brightwell reported. Stress and pressure came with the job. Like a football manager, once you've sent your team out onto the pitch, there's not much you can do. Just hope they stick to the plan and adapt when adversity strikes.

Well, the Russian rescue had only been a partial success. Freda, Gopal and Rabten were still stuck deep in Russian territory and now Wardle was going to have to bring on his substitutes. And he still needed to do a full de-brief with Sim Atkins. Those were just two of the holos occupying his in-box. The right-hand side of his desk glowed with reports he needed to read, assess and prioritise. His wife had gone to stay with her sister for a break, giving up on the brief, sporadic evenings Wardle managed to spend with her. That, actually, had been a relief. Not that he didn't love his wife any more. Just that it was easier to be selfish and switch off when he had the chance, not having to worry about making polite conversation. Wardle looked up as the handle on his oak door turned. David Feinberg, his IT expert, barged into the room, clutching a roll tab. "Sir, I've done it."

"Done what?"

David's beam quickly vanished from his face. "The roll-tab we recovered from the Terror Formers. I managed to crack it open. Even logged in as one of them. We can start to monitor their messages."

"That thing? You've had it for two weeks. I thought you must have given up by now."

"Triple-layer of security. Encryption. Plus a sandbox."

Wardle tutted. "Fine, it was difficult. Have a gold star. Now tell me something useful."

"That virus they stole from Russia. They're planning to sell it to a rogue government."

Gopal and Rabten had boarded a Russian airship last month, one that had been hijacked by the Terror Formers. The agents had escaped with a sample of the virus, a stolen roll-tab and their lives, but only just. Despite all efforts to track it, the airship had simply vanished.

"If you can tell me when and where the exchange will take place, I might even give you another gold star."

David rolled his eyes and turned to leave. "You're welcome," he muttered as he strode out of the office.

Three days later, Sim was finally allowed to fly back home. He had been tested for diseases. Standard procedure but an extra test was carried out in case the Ebola virus had spread further than realised on the moon base. His physical condition had been thoroughly and painfully assessed. His muscles were beginning to recover their strength.

Some quack had asked him a bunch of inane questions about butterflies and beetles. Even used a Rorschach test on him. The blobs of ink had been nothing like the mottled skin of his son's chest as he had lain dying in Moon Lab One. But if the quack had been any good at her job, she would have noticed the twitch in Sim's left eye.

After that, NASA representatives had had more questions for him. This time about Yusuf, the man who had carried the virus to the base. The CIA had got involved. These questions Sim had not minded. He wanted answers too. And he wanted to be involved in the investigation. But he had been met with a stonewall defence. Every request to be included, to be assigned to the inquiry, had been deflected and ignored. Well, he wasn't going to take no for an answer. There had been a real-time holo with Rosie, his wife. She had seemed a bit distant even allowing for the time delay and the awkwardness of talking to an avatar instead of the real person.

She had appeared to be pleased to see him, but there had been something else. A coolness, something being held back.

Sim just hoped that Rosie had forgiven him for accepting the mission to the moon base. To see his son and the woman who had borne him, Elsa Greenwood. She had been left behind at Moon Lab One, amongst a handful of survivors. Physically OK, but mentally crushed from the loss of their son. James had not even reached his sixth birthday. Sim had got to know him for a few precious days. Until a couple of months ago, Sim had not even known James existed. But for Elsa, the boy had been her whole universe. And now there must be a black hole right where the sun used to be.

Sim knew how difficult these past three years had been for Rosie, trying for a baby. The months when she was late, and the disappointments when the test came back negative. Perhaps it would never happen. Perhaps James had been his only chance to experience fatherhood. And perhaps things would never be the same again between Sim and his wife. The plane touched down, jolting Sim out of his reflective mood. Rosie had been told his flight details and should be waiting for him in the arrivals lounge. Too short to look over other people's heads, Sim struggled to spot her at first. The group of students blocking his view dispersed. And there she was. His bonnie blonde lass. A smile for him, yes, but also a gaze half averted. A hint of shyness, maybe reluctance even? Public displays of affection had never been his strong point, but Sim could not help breaking into a run and gathering her into his arms.

"Oh, Rosie. My love."

She returned the hug. "You came back, then?"

"Course. Try keeping me away."

"How did it go?"

Sim unwrapped his arms and put his hands on her shoulders. "It was... bad. James is gone."

"What do you mean, gone? Where has that woman taken him?"

Sim shook his head and blinked hard. "He's dead."

Rosie's face creased. "But. What happened?"

"I can't say. The whole thing is still very delicate. Maybe one day I'll be able to explain. Explain it all. The mission. Me and that woman. She has a name, you know. Elsa."

Rosie opened her mouth to reply and then stopped. She grabbed his hand and pulled him towards the car park. They walked in silence for a while.

"So. What have I missed back home?" Sim rubbed Rosie's hand with his thumb as they walked along. "Have Callie managed to win a game yet this season?"

"Football? You've just been to the Moon and back and you want to talk about football?"

Sim shrugged. "I want to talk about life. Normal stuff. It's so weird up there. Artificial. Controlled. Would've done me head in if I'd stayed much longer."

Later that evening, back home in Dornoch, they snuggled on the sofa. Not saying much, just enjoying close physical contact. Remoulding their bodies to one another. A bowl of snacks on the table, which Rosie devoured. Something inane on the TV screen. A moving image that required no strain, no mental effort.

Sim leaned across and stroked Rosie's cheek, moving a stray hair away from her eyes. "I thought about you. Every day." His hand caressed her hips, then her ribs and continued moving upwards. "Whoa. Have you got a special bra on, or something? Because these puppies have definitely grown."

"Sim."

Before Rosie could say anything more, Sim was pressing his mouth to hers. And for a while at least, everything was back to normal. Afterwards, they slept.

It was still dark outside when Sim noticed Rosie get out of

bed. He rolled over and tried to make sense of the clock. 5am. And then he heard a retching noise from the bathroom. He sat up.

"Rosie? You alright?" He rubbed his eyes. They had not drunk last night, so it couldn't be a hangover. "You have a dodgy burger at the airport, or something?"

Rosie came back into the bedroom, her face flushed. Sim stared at her, in her underwear. Definitely more curves than a few weeks ago. Putting on weight? Comfort eating?

Lightbulb.

He looked at her belly and then up into her beautiful face. Rosie looked back and nodded.

Sim's eyes began to water. He tried to smile, despite his wobbling chin. "Oh Rosie. My sweetheart. Are you sure? When?"

Rosie just shrugged and blinked back her tears. "The doctor's confirmed it. Ten weeks gone. I've booked in our first scan for next week."

Sim jumped out of bed and hugged Rosie like she was the most precious thing in the world. "Oops, not too hard," he said, shifting away from her body fractionally.

Rosie shoved his shoulder. "Daft bugger. If we survived last night's pounding, I think we can survive... Oh, Sim. I'm sorry. I didn't mean it like that."

Sim's smiled had vanished. He looked at the ground and sniffed. "It's OK. Not your fault." He looked up and smiled again, taking a deep breath. He placed his hand on Rosie's belly. "You are amazing." He kissed her lips. Soft and slow.

3

———

The North Sea

Captain Euan Hamilton was on the bridge of The *Endeavour*, feeling hungry. He was roughly halfway between breakfast and lunch, while the boat was roughly halfway between The Orkney Islands and the Norwegian port of Bergen. Hamilton always ate five meals a day when on assignment. Had done while in the Royal Navy and kept it up now that he had become part of Overseas Division. A unique asset, Director Wardle had called his boat. Flattering Hamilton's pride and joy – the submersible vessel he had designed – was an easy way to win him over.

So far, Wardle's missions for The *Endeavour* had been boring surveillance work. Hamilton's appetite had stayed in check. But not this day. Today there was a chance of some proper action. Catching some terrorists. Or at least preventing an attack. That meant a full English breakfast. A second breakfast around mid-morning and onwards to lunch. The captain was not sure if it was nervous energy that used up all the calories. Or was it merely a sensible survival strategy? In battle, you never knew when you would be able to stop for your next meal. So, load up while you can. Whatever the reason, Hamilton was making short work of the toast, fruit and coffee that had just been served.

The intel from the roll tab that David Feinberg had managed to crack suggested an imminent attack from the Terror Formers. The information was not perfect, but implied that some part of the Norwegian Carbon Capture and Storage facility was at risk. For over ten years now, European industry had been capturing its CO_2 emissions, compressing the gas and shipping it to the Mongstad industrial site, near Bergen. From there the gas was piped across the sea bed to a drill site where it was pumped into salt caverns deep below the North Sea.

The Norwegian government had been bold enough to invest billions into the project at the turn of the century and was now turning over a tidy profit, charging other European countries to deal with their emissions. Those countries were happy to pay because at a stroke it made their Paris Accord emissions' targets easy to meet. The shipping industry was happy to have a new stream of cargo now that the Chinese conveyor belt had dried up. Everyone, it seemed, was happy except for the Terror Formers. Hamilton scratched his chin, reviewing the evidence.

Attacking one of the ships that brought the compressed gas to Norway seemed like an obvious target but not exactly spectacular. Somali pirates had been doing that to oil tankers for decades. They barely even made the news these days. More often than not, the pirates would be repulsed by the ship's robotic defences. At least that's one good thing about progress with automation, thought Hamilton. Even if the terrorists did attack one of these boats, it would not achieve much. All that non-flammable gas in the middle of nowhere? Like farting in a farmyard, it hardly seemed worth the effort. No, the captain was convinced that the target had to be something else.

An assault on the coastal storage site? Certainly, that would represent a bigger target. There would be huge disruption to the whole chain of infrastructure if the site was destroyed. And undoubtedly a better candidate for media coverage. But still, Hamilton had read the briefing notes on the installation. It was guarded like a nuclear power plant. Round-the-clock armed guards. Razor-wire fencing, motion sensors, buzz drones. And a third-generation Kongsberg surface-to-air missile system. Even a suicide squad would have a hard time getting near the site.

No, for Hamilton's money, it had to be the entrance to the undersea caverns themselves. Where there was no protection, except for the 400 metres of sea sitting above it in the Norwegian Trench. Which is exactly the sort of place that The *Endeavour* could show her worth. If the intel was correct, the attack would occur this evening, which meant that they had a few hours to get into position and wait. Hamilton rested a hand on the stomach that was starting to bulge over his belt. A bulge that didn't used to be there.

Oh well, maybe just a small snack to keep me going until lunchtime.

At a depth of 200 metres, there was nothing to see in the Norwegian trench. Unlike some of the exploratory craft that operated at this depth, The *Endeavour* did not have any external lights. Inky blackness is a common phrase, but really has anyone ever put their head in a bucket of ink and tried opening their eyes? Hamilton shook his head, looking out through the graphene toughened windows and seeing precisely zip. About the only equivalent experience that the captain could think of was when he'd visited the dungeons at Norwich Castle and the guide had switched off the lights. After a while, your mind begins to play tricks on you and ghostly images start to appear.

Even as a youth, Hamilton had loved gadgets. As soon as the lights had gone out, he'd slipped on a pair of night-vision goggles and smirked at the other tourists looking weird in the darkness of the dungeon.

This time, he was relying on sonar buoys. They were deployed and programmed to spread out, encircling the site of the valve arrangement at the entrance to the undersea caverns. There's a limit to how fast a craft can travel underwater, but even so, Hamilton wanted all the forewarning he could get. About the same time as supper was being polished off, the Sound Room alarm went off. Passive sonar had detected multiple contacts closing from the west.

"What have we got, Hansen?"

"At least ten bogies, Captain. They all have very small signatures, so I can't get an accurate count yet. Range five kilometres, depth 50 metres, speed 20 knots."

"Must be droids, travelling at that speed. OK, launch the counter measures. And, Hansen, keep working on that total. We can't afford to let any slip through."

The klaxon sounded for action stations and a dozen pairs of shoes drummed the beat of Hamilton's favourite tune. Four times, the Warfare Officer pressed the button on her console that launched The *Endeavour*'s own deep-see drones. Greatly out-numbered by the incoming drones, but these were built for combat, not speed.

"Sound Room, make sure we stick to passive sonar for as long as possible. We don't want to give away our position until the last possible moment."

"Aye, aye, sir."

All of the crew were now in position and the waiting game began. Range had closed to 3000 metres and the drones had dropped to a depth of 200 metres.

"Damn, they are diving fast. Helm take us down to 300

metres." The captain stabbed a button on the arm of his chair. "Hansen, when are you going to confirm the number of targets?"

"They're spreading out now, sir. Right. We have twelve, no thirteen, fourteen. Hang on. Damn. They keep crossing in front of each other. As if they know we're looking for them. Range 1000 metres. Fifteen of them, all told, sir."

"Shit. That's too many. Can we use torpedoes?"

The Warfare Officer replied. "Drones are probably too fast. And we'd risk damaging the Carbon facility if the explosions were too close to the valve."

"Let's hope our own robots are up to it. And get word up to Mongstad, tell them to seal off the pipes at their end for now. Don't want this to get any worse than it has to."

"Surface link deployed," said the Comms Officer.

"OK, target and destroy. Sounds Room, bring in the active sonar. All hands, full battle stations."

The lights on the bridge dimmed and turned red. The screens of the four drone controllers flashed up multiple contacts as the officers twitched their glove readers and manipulated the 3D screens in front of them. The drones received their instructions and tried to ward off the unwanted visitors. Several hits were registered and the Sounds Room counted down the targets from fifteen to eleven. But then one of the drone controllers cursed.

"We've lost number three, sir."

"What?"

There was silence on the bridge. Then: "And number two." Captain Hamilton stood up and looked out of the windows, catching a faint glimpse of something. An explosion? An acetylene torch? "What the hell kind of weapons are they packing?"

Sounds Room interrupted. "We've got three of theirs, sir. But that still leaves eight heading to the seabed and the main valve structure."

The Chief Engineer came up on deck. "It's just occurred to me, sir. What they might be up to."

"I know what they're up to, for Christ's sake."

"I meant when they get to the valve. These drones seem pretty powerful. What if they're not going to destroy the valve, but open it up and reverse the gas flow?"

The captain sat down heavily. "But... why? That would be environmental suicide. All those greenhouse gases rushing to the surface. Surely even the TF aren't that stupid."

"Yeah well, maybe we can ask them after we've stopped this attack. If we can."

Hamilton bowed his head. "It's too late. Unless..." He grasped the arms of his chair. "Spin up the EMP."

The Warfare Officer turned around in her seat. "At this depth, sir?"

"No, deeper. Need to make sure we're close enough to get the little shits."

"Aye aye, sir."

"And Comms, tell Norway what's about to happen. They might get a diving bell to us in time. And they'll need to collect up the drones in case they can reboot themselves."

The bridge fell silent while preparations were made. Captain Hamilton watched as each of his crew went about their duties, proud that none of them had challenged his order. Just accepted their part in the chain of command. The Electro-Magnetic Pulse would knock out all of the drones but also incapacitate the submarine's own controls.

The Sound Room broke the silence. "Drones have reached the valve, sir."

"Fire."

As the EMP detonated on board The *Endeavour*, the screens

on the bridge went blank. The lights went out, and for once, the back-up lighting failed too. A wave of blue energy radiated out from the ship in all directions. Within a few seconds it had reached the seabed and the drones attacking the Norwegian Carbon Storage facility fell inert. The boat creaked and continued to sink towards the sea bed.

A chain of voices from down below relayed a message. Finally, somebody at the bottom of the stairs shouted up to the bridge. "Leak in the torpedo room."

"Get everyone out. Seal all bulkheads."

The loudest ever game of Chinese whispers was repeated back down the chain and the captain heard through the darkness the clang of metal doors closing and pressure clamps being spun into place.

"Chief, did you get a look at the O2 reading before it went dark?"

"We've got about twenty hours left. Should be able to reboot systems. If we don't suffer any more damage."

Hamilton's vessel was unique in being equally at home on the surface and underwater. But some compromises had been required, and one of those was a much shorter reserve of oxygen than a normal submarine. The ship continued to glide deeper into the Norwegian Trench, creaking as she went, before finally settling on the seabed with a jolt. Amidst the carcasses of sea creatures and drones. The captain shifted in his chair. The temperature was already beginning to drop.

At least I won't grow hungry, he thought, patting his stomach.

The first four hours passed quietly, as most people just sat around trying to conserve oxygen. A few whispered conversations between friends. The next four hours were more restless. With communication links severed there was no way to know when the rescue team would reach them, assuming there was one on its way. The temperature had become bitingly cold. It was impossible to sit still anymore. But moving about used the oxygen more quickly. In the following four hours, signs of panic were starting to emerge. The crew began to vocalise their morbid thoughts, the darkness allowing them some anonymity.

"Why is it taking them so long?"

"There's gratitude for you. We come down here to save their precious facility and they can't be bothered to come and rescue us."

"Stop hogging the blanket, you've got more than enough insulation on you."

"Fuck you and your skinny ass."

The captain stumbled his way through the ship, talking to his crew, telling them how well they had performed during the attack and reassuring them that everything would be fine.

And he was right. The Norwegian response was first-rate. No doubt fine-tuned after decades of deep-sea operations, their rescue team was able to drop a diving bell to The *Endeavour* in just under twelve hours, pulling out those who were suffering most from the cold and the claustrophobia. A skeleton crew remained on board with the captain, reinvigorated by some warm food and drinks. There was even some Akvavit, a spiced schnapps, that was handed round as thanks for saving the Norwegian facility. The boat's O2 tank was topped up and the emergency lighting kicked back into life.

Six hours later, all systems were back online. The boat slowly rose back towards the surface while the captain composed his report for Wardle. There was a knock on his door.

"Come."

The Comms Officer entered. "Sir, when we were under attack, I managed to trace some of the signals being sent out by their drones. And intercepted an incoming message. I've triangulated its source. Middle of the Norwegian Sea, near the Jan Mayen Islands."

"Good show, Martel. Give the co-ordinates to the bosun and tell him to set course straight away."

It took them nearly two days of continual sailing to arrive at the destination suggested by the Comms Officer. The *Endeavour* was far from peak performance even though the worst effects of the EMP had been repaired.

"The co-ordinates don't indicate a land mass. Those drones must have been controlled by a ship," said the captain, surveying the sea ahead. The neck strap on his binoculars was made of dark brown leather, frayed and thinning after years of use. There were other, better, sets of binoculars onboard but the last person who suggested that the captain try them had been quickly sent below decks. He rubbed the soft leather between finger and thumb. "Chances of the vessel still being around seem rather slim."

"Overseas Division has sent us satellite imaging of the area at the time of the attack. No ships in the vicinity," said Martel.

"A submarine, then?" asked the captain, looking at a copy of the photo.

The Comms Officer shook his head. "Too far away to communicate underwater."

Hamilton pointed at something on the picture. "Is that an iceberg?"

"Yes, sir."

"Distinctive shape." The captain looked through his binoculars again. "How come that lump of ice hasn't drifted at all in the past 48 hours?" He pointed at an iceberg that was starting to show itself between the swells of grey, foam-flecked sea. "On these currents, it should be leagues away by now. Let's take a closer look."

The boat stopped a few hundred metres from the icy behemoth. It had a curious, flat top on the right half of its body and a bulbous, curved hillock on the other half.

"Instruments suggest it is hollow, sir. Nasty, dangerous sort. They can topple over with just a shift of the wind. We ought to keep our distance."

"What's sonar say about its profile?"

"Hmm, that is unusual, sir. Almost the same underwater as above the surface.

The captain shook his head. The *Endeavour* was still damaged. It had a skeleton crew. But an iceberg that didn't drift and didn't sit seven-eighths below water? This needed investigating. "Scramble a message to HQ. I think we've found us some damned Terror Formers."

$$4$$

Frontera, El Hierro.

Mattias Larsson paced the small apartment while dictating notes. His close and very personal assistant, Precious Osundare, made sure that the voice recognition app was transcribing accurately and added thoughts of her own. It had been easy to find an apartment to rent on the smallest of the Canary Islands. Harder to find a block of six contiguous apartments. Three to house security, one for Mattias and herself, and two just to act as a buffer zone from the general public. Precious was used to these sorts of requirements. They were by no means the strangest thing she did for Mattias.

"So. Rendezvous point is the Faro de Orchilla. Is the lighthouse operational still?"

"Yes," replied Precious. "But automated. No maintenance visits scheduled for another week. Basically, some tourists stop by most days."

"Let's get a closed-for-maintenance sign put up then to keep them away."

"On it." Precious made an extra note in her roll-tab.

"And the local beach, the Embarcadero de Orchilla. Is that where they'll be landing?"

"Seems that way. It's about a klick from the lighthouse. A steep dirt track between the two spots."

Mattias shook his head. "I don't like this set up. Seems too cramped. No easy way out if the devils get in the machines."

Precious paused for a moment. Mattias's English was excellent but literal translations of Swedish idioms were sometimes confusing. "Relax Matty. We have somebody on the books in local law enforcement. Basically, I can get the beach, the whole approach, barred. We'll say there's been a rockslide or something." Mattias nodded. He looked out of the window, down at the tourists and the local residents. He smiled in a way that reminded Precious of a scientist watching rats run through a maze, glad that she was his confidante and not one of his experiments.

"I thought we needed this virus for population control?"

Her boss shook his head. "Better to sell it while we can. Besides, I have a better plan. And if I can get approval from the Arabs they'll fund the whole project while we get to keep the golden share."

Business school had been full of smart students but none could hold a candle to Mattias' razor-sharp commercial mind. Barely out of teenage years, his superiority had been obvious even at that early age. And like a midnight moth, Precious had been drawn to the flame of his intellect. She jolted out of her memories and looked at her notes again.

"The usual fireteam accompaniment?" she asked.

"Of course. Better include some SAMs in case we get buzzed by helicopters. And fix up a drone dome on top of the lighthouse. Exclusion zone at least a klick."

Precious looked up at her boss. His brow was creased and his pacing across the room had intensified. She rose from her seat and took hold of his hands. "Let us finish off the details later. You need therapy, big time." Mattias nodded and let her lead him into the bedroom.

Two days later, a procession of 4x4 vehicles rumbled along the Calle Lomo Perejil. It was a rough track even for these capable transports. A barren, steep slope down to the sea on the right. And an impressive view to the left, along the crescent-shaped ridge that formed the spine of the island. The crates of weapons, ammunition, and special equipment in the back of the vehicles scraped together as the cars tilted sideways on the rough terrain. Normally, even the small risk of being stopped by a police spot check would have made Precious nervous. But with local law enforcement in the terrorists' pocket, there was little danger of that. The vehicles ignored the Spanish signs that said, 'Rock slide, track closed.' The grey granite tower and smartly painted white buildings around the base of the lighthouse sat proudly amidst the plateau of pumice stones.

An hour before their rendezvous with the Africans, the team had set up look-out posts and broken into the locked tower. At the top, they had set up the equipment that would establish an invisible electronic shield to render lifeless all drones within a thousand metres.

The phials of pre-historic virus, stolen from Russia weeks ago, were packed in a temperature-controlled, double-skinned crate. The package was unloaded and deposited in the small courtyard formed by the old lighthouse keepers' cottages. A larger crate was laid out near the base of the tower.

Quite what the buyer had in mind for the virus was not entirely clear. A virus that had the potential to devastate the wheat fields of the buyer's enemies. Precious assumed that he was the dictator of one of the smaller African states, or perhaps a local warlord. Maybe they wanted the disease simply as a deterrent. Nuclear proliferation, in theory, had ended after North Korea had joined the list. So, if you couldn't threaten your neighbours with nukes, maybe biological destruction was the next best thing. As long as they paid up, who cared? Not Precious. Mattias had a vision for achieving a better world and the ends would always justify the means in her eyes.

Within half an hour, the approaching speed boats were spotted. Three ribs loaded with men in sunglasses, Kevlar jackets and bearing guns. Radar showed up a larger vessel out to sea, presumably where the ribs had launched from. The African coast was at least 250 miles away, too far for a journey in small craft.

Precious looked across at Mattias and he nodded. "Send the guide down to show them the way. And when they get here, you do the talking."

Precious tutted.

"What?" said Mattias. "No harm in using your heritage to break down barriers. Practically neighbours, aren't you?" He slipped on a bio-mask and handed one to Precious. The disguise moulded itself to Precious' face, changing her contours. Just in case the buyers tried to record the transaction through hidden cameras.

She flexed her jaw and arched her eyebrows, getting used to the second skin. "As long as they're not from Ghana."

The meeting was, despite Precious' efforts, a very tense affair. Armed body guards on both sides bristled with muscles and weapons. An initial handshake. Digital palms exchanged encrypted codes, ensuring both parties were who they claimed to be. The diamonds that would form the payment were checked for quality. A laborious and slow affair. One random phial was removed from the ice box and examined by one of the Africans under a microscope.

"You figured what your boss plans to do with this virus, yet?" asked Mattias.

"You figured what you plan to do with all those diamonds?" came the reply.

Mattias shrugged. "Sell them. The security business is very expensive these days."

"You make joke? Funny guy, yes. Ha hah ha."

"No reason we can't be civil. I have some cold beers in the pick-up. Anybody fancy one?"

The sun was beating down from a cloudless sky. The temperature was nudging 40 degrees. A couple of the African body guards licked their lips, but held their ground. The man who seemed to be in charge shook his head. "I'd rather be back in international waters as soon—"

"Sir, we have incoming aircraft. Too big for drones, too slow for jets. Must be choppers."

Mattias looked at the African party. "Not yours, then?" The scared look on their faces gave him his answer. He pulled the tiny microphone from the end of his sleeve. "Code red." He caught Precious' eye and ran towards the unmarked crate while his body guards took up defensive positions around the low buildings at the base of the lighthouse.

The Africans started running back down the path towards the tiny beach. One of them lunged towards the bag of diamonds first, but was met with the butt of a rifle in his face. Four helicopter gunships swept into view, hugging the side of the island, nearly low enough to skim the water. One peeled off. A stream of bullets spat out towards the rib boats waiting on the beach. There was a series of explosions as fuel tanks ignited. The Africans stopped running down the hill.

The other three helicopters slowed to a hover in v-formation, facing the lighthouse, guns bristling. A megaphone burst into life, above the wocka-wocka-wocka of their blades. "This is the Club of Rome. Put down your weapons. You are under arrest."

One of Mattias' soldiers popped up from behind the lantern room at the top of the lighthouse. He squeezed the trigger on a tube that rested over one shoulder and a surface-to-air missile streaked towards the middle helicopter. All three choppers tried to take evasive action. Bright phosphorescent flares filled the sky. But there was not enough time. The missile accelerated unerringly toward the lead helicopter, which plummeted down into the sea even as the fireball of the explosion soared upwards.

The remaining helicopters opened fire with chain guns, saturating the side of the island with a lethal stream of bullets. The glass at the top of the lighthouse shattered and the man holding the missile launcher screamed as he was showered in deadly shards. The brickwork of the tower and the walls of the cottages began to fragment as they were pummelled by ammo. Two more soldiers fell. Another guard ran towards one of the 4x4s but stopped when he saw an armoured truck appear over the horizon on the only track away from the lighthouse. The African party had thrown away their weapons and were lying flat on their bellies, arms covering their heads.

Inside the unmarked crate, Mattias and Precious were shuffling into position, feeling their way in the darkness. They could hear bullets clunk into the armour-plated sides of the box.

"You ready?" said Mattias. He tucked the bag of diamonds inside his flak jacket and pressed a button without waiting for a reply. Outside their box, the other crate exploded, killing one of their own guards and two of the Africans who had been sheltering next to the cargo they had come to buy.

Mattias and Precious slid into their respective coffin-like tubes and closed the lids. There was a whine as ram-jet engines span into life and small stubby wings folded down from each of the tubes that they occupied. The sides of the crate fell outwards, clanging onto the ground.

There were no windows in these fat missiles. Precious simply stared at the inside of the lid and hoped the auto-pilot that Mattias had programmed earlier would work. She did not have long to wait. A surge of acceleration pressed her back and down.

The helicopter pilots swung their craft around to give chase, but it was soon clear that their pace was no match for the fleeing vessels. They turned back to help mop up the remaining terrorists. It was only later, after the head count and IDs had been finalised that the Club Of Rome agents came to realise that the two main targets had escaped. Hydras had been adapted to carry humans. This was a first.

At least it seemed like the virus that had threatened to wipe out this year's wheat harvest had been vaporised. The captured Africans, even after intense interrogation, failed to identify the masked leaders. The black men said that they had paid with diamonds, but there were no signs of these. Divers had even been sent down to search the sea below the lighthouse, but the only thing that glittered down there were the fish.

5

———

Russia

Freda threw away the clump of moss in her hands and hoisted up her blue boiler suit. "How come James Bond never had to do that?"

Gopal and Rabten stared at her.

"You must have heard of double-oh seven. Never mind. C'mon guys, we can't wait for Wardle to send another rescue team. Need to find some different clothes. And that means finding some people."

"Which way?" said Gopal.

Freda shrugged. There was dense pine forest on all sides, pot-marked with occasional ponds and fractured by faint tracks. Whether the latter had been made by humans or animals it was hard to tell. "We move parallel to the road. It has to lead to a settlement eventually."

Rabten whispered something to Gopal in a language Freda did not understand.

"Rabten isn't used to women leaders. The monastery always had a man in charge."

Freda turned towards the ex-monk. "Welcome to the twenty-first century."

They approached the road that passed the prison, staying just close enough to keep it in sight but far enough away to stay invisible to any traffic. The prison break had been several hours ago and daylight was starting to fade. There had already been several near-misses with the local police who were trying to round up the escapees. Under the canopy of trees, the ground was dark enough to make travel very difficult. But they had no torches. Rabten asked a question of Gopal. The Gurkha interpreted.

"Shouldn't we stop and make camp?"

"Can't risk a fire this close to the prison." Freda looked up at the sky just visible through the thick canopy. There was no cloud-cover. "The Moon should be up soon enough. We'll rest now and carry on when we can see where we're going." She sat down on a log and rubbed her calves.

Rabten moved off into the woods, saying something to Gopal as he left. Freda turned towards the Gurkha and jerked her head.

"He said he's going to find some food."

"Good luck in the dark, with no hunting equipment," she called out.

Rabten returned just after the Moon had started to cast faint beams throughout the trees. He fetched inside his prison suit and brought out some nuts, berries and a few tubers covered in soil. He said something to Gopal with a grin.

"Err, he says they don't teach this in the twenty-first century."

"Touché." Freda smiled and pressed her hands together, bowing her head.

After the simple feast, they set off again. A stream crossed their path, its waters flowing fast and clear, glinting in the pale moonbeams. They all drank deeply. As moonlight gave way to the dusty pink hint of dawn, and as forest gave way to scrubland, their steps slowed with fatigue and caution. An occasional hut became a steady trickle of houses and eventually the outskirts of a town. It was still only around 5am, but light enough for the agents to be spotted out in the open if they were careless.

"Well, either we wait in cover all day, or we try to break into somewhere before people wake up."

Gopal and Rabten conferred before the Gurkha replied. "He spouted some nonsense about a patient heron catching fish but I say we crack on. They might be tracking us with dogs or drones for all we know. Got to keep moving."

Freda agreed and they continued their scuttle between hedges and huts until they spotted a place that seemed to be a clothes store. The back of the building was not overlooked. Ignoring the fire exit they pulled a large bin on wheels over towards a high window. Rabten's elbow made short work of the glass. They paused for a moment, waiting to see if an alarm had been triggered but the only other noise was the chorus of birds welcoming the new day. The smell of fresh bread wafted towards them from some unseen baker already at work. It reminded Freda just how hungry she was.

Inside the store they rushed around trying to find clothes that would fit. Freda stripped down to her underwear and noticed Rabten staring at her as she got changed. "Djeez, wherever you go, there's always one..."

She grabbed a messenger bag, stuffed a spare top into it and found a waterproof jacket in her size. Gopal located the office at the back of the store and after several attempts with a pair of scissors, broke open a box that had some American dollars. He kissed the banknotes. "In your face, crypto currencies."

They climbed back out of the shop and let their noses guide them towards the bakery. Freda left the other two outside and through a smattering of Russian words and lots of pointing, managed to obtain a loaf and some things that resembled a Cornish pasty. The foreign money no doubt helped with the hapless-tourist routine. The baker did not bat an eyelid at making a sale so early to a foreign woman using US dollars. Freda noticed that he gave her the change in Russian currency, but shrugged it off.

The three escaped prisoners nibbled on their breakfast as they walked the still-quiet streets, looking for something to drink. A garage provided a drinks dispenser that used their Russian change and gave Freda an idea. Naturally enough for a country still rich with oil reserves, and a government that put climate change bottom of the priority list, most cars in Russia continued to run on petrol. This particular garage had petrol pumps and a few used cars for sale on the forecourt.

Freda was sizing up their options when a vehicle came around the corner. It slowed as it passed the garage. Freda's heart began to race and she prayed that the others would not do anything stupid like dive for cover. She just smiled and waved her cup of coffee at the driver, not daring to shout a warning to the others. The vehicle seemed to be a normal, civilian car; its driver a normal, rotund Russian. His rosy cheeks broke into a smile and the man waved at Freda, then quickly disappeared from view.

"Dammit. He's not going to forget seeing us this early in the day."

"But maybe he doesn't know there's been a breakout?" said Gopal.

"Even with a news blackout, the local gossip will reach the town soon enough. They can't hide that hole in the prison wall from prying eyes. Besides, some of the other prisoners that escaped are bound to have been re-captured by now." Freda threw away her empty cup. "No. Sooner or later, there'll be an appeal for help and that man will say he saw three strangers. We need to get far away from here. Fast."

Gopal pulled out a penknife from his pocket. The plastic label from the clothes store still dangled from its keyring. He pointed at the cars lined up for sale. "Let's check to see if any have been left open."

The oldest, cheapest car at the far end of the row of vehicles was not locked. Frankly, Freda wasn't sure it was worth stealing but all the other cars were properly secured. Maybe that was no coincidence. The garage owner probably wanted this one stolen so they could put in an exaggerated claim on the insurance. The three agents got into the rust-coloured car and Gopal prised off the ignition cover to fiddle with the exposed wires. The engine spluttered into life like an asthmatic chain smoker waking up.

"Fuel gauge is close to empty," said Gopal.

"Just drive. That way," she said pointing to her left. Freda scanned the road for other approaching cars. "Must be an open petrol station around here somewhere."

The automatic gearbox had a habit of changing up too soon and even managed to stall itself while crawling up a hill. Gopal gradually got used to its foibles and learned how to help the quirky gear selections with some deft feathering of the accelerator. They drove steadily through the centre of town. Freda told Rabten to lie down on the back seat, figuring that just a man and woman in the front seat looked more natural. And less like the three escaped OD agents being hunted by the authorities.

"Which way?" asked Gopal as they approached a roundabout.

The gearbox did its best to select the wrong gear.

Freda noticed the blue stripes of a police car approaching the junction from their right. "Just keep going straight on."

For a moment, Gopal was confused and panicked. He looked the wrong way at the roundabout and failed to slowdown for the police car that had right of way. At the last moment, he slammed on the brakes, the squeal from rusted pads drowning out his shouted expletive. The car stalled just to show its disapproval at such rash decision making. The police car circled the roundabout and passed in front of them again, while Gopal desperately tried to restart the wretched machine. A grin and a wagging finger from the police officer and then the vehicle proceeded onwards. Freda breathed out hard and turned her head to stare at the Gurkha.

They found a petrol station a few kilometres outside the town, filled up the tank, and bought a bag full of snacks and drinks with the rest of the cash they had stolen from the clothes shop. They all took the chance to use the restrooms with the luxury on offer of toilet paper, sinks and handtowels.

Ten kilometres further on, Gopal spotted another police car, in the rear-view mirror. He sped up a little, but the car stayed the same distance behind. He risked a burst of speed, as much as the rust bucket of a car would manage. But still the police car kept a steady distance. Finally, the blue flashing lights were switched on and the police car moved up alongside them, signalling them to pull over.

Freda's hands were clammy. She gestured to Rabten to stay down, out of sight. If they could distract the police for a moment, the monk might be able to surprise them. There was no time to co-ordinate and translate a plan.

One of the police officers approached their car and turned out to be a woman. Plans of action whirled around Freda's head. Even if she could subdue the woman, the policeman had stayed on the far side of the car and rested his hand on top of his sidearm. The woman signalled for Gopal and Freda to get out of the car. They did so, hands held high. The policewoman glanced down the road, in both directions and told the two agents to lower their hands. In English. Freda frowned. And then Rabten burst out of the car, launching himself at the policewoman. He used a judo-like throw and grappled her to the floor even as Freda shouted out "Stop."

The policeman drew his gun and slowly moved around to the front of the car. Gopal told Rabten to let the woman go. The monk looked up, bemused.

"We're on your side," said the woman, still pinned to the floor by Rabten. She gasped for air and the monk finally got up.

An hour later, they were proceeding towards the Kazakhstan border, having hidden the stolen car under a tarpaulin, in a remote barn. The woman explained that she was with the service and had been assigned the job of extracting the three agents for Wardle.

"The trouble is, you guys carried on moving through the night and then went through the centre of town. Difficult to find a secluded spot to pick you up."

"You've been tracking us?" said Freda. "I thought our implants were designed to go silent if we ever got captured."

The woman nodded. "The insect that visited you before the jail break. Left a homing device on you before it scarpered. We were worried you'd wash your hair and lose the connection."

Freda ran her hands through her greasy hair, trying to feel for a piece of grit. She wondered what the three of them smelt like to their rescuers. "What's the next stage of the plan?"

"We get you over the border into Kazakhstan tomorrow. And then across the Aral Sea to Uzbekistan. Less likely that Russian agents will be watching the ports there. New IDs and travel the Silk Road to somewhere safe."

Gopal translated the plan for Rabten, who nodded and pressed his hands together in prayer, saying something in Nepalese. "He says blessings of ten thousand sunrises on your home. And sorry for sitting on you."

45

6

———————

Qatar

Mattias Larsson was thinking about football. It was a blazing hot Sunday afternoon and he was heading for a business meeting. A normal day of business for the Middle East. Years ago, his dad had insisted on Sunday school every week for Mattias even though he knew it had clashed with football training. Mattias' chances of making the local youth team had been ruined by his father's idiotic devotion to the Catholic Church. Even Midsummer celebrations had been deemed too pagan and banned in his household. Mattias' memory of his teenage years was filled with images of his friends playing football or sneaking out with beers to celebrate solstice in the forest, while he seethed at home.

Even now, Sunday afternoons were filled with pangs of bitterness and thoughts of his favourite sport. A five-year old boy staying up late in his pyjamas to watch Sweden beat Romania on penalties. In a Stockholm bar, spilling beer over his fellow students, when Sweden thrashed England and Zlatan scored that bicycle kick. But also, that sick feeling in his stomach, when the Blågult's were knocked out of the group stages at the Qatar world cup. Not terribly surprising. The whole tournament had been corrupted by money. Every referee was in somebody's pocket. Besides, how was a team from Scandinavia supposed to cope in the heat of that tournament? Yes, the stadiums were air-conditioned. But the training grounds weren't. Just lounging around in this country was an effort.

Mattias and Precious were approaching one of those football stadiums, protected from the afternoon sun by their air-conditioned SUV. There were guards in the other vehicles, ready to protect them from anything worse than a case of heatstroke.

The building rose up out of the desert with no connection to the rest of the landscape, like it had fallen from the sky. The huge car park was now covered in a thin layer of sand. A few plants were clinging to life in the cracked concrete, surviving on the mist blown in from the Persian Gulf. All of the electronic posters were black and lifeless, except for one that kept showing the same five seconds of an advert for aftershave. Every time the model went to splash the product on his chiselled face, the grainy picture flickered back to the start of the film. The solar panels above this poster had somehow evaded the thieves and the grind of a thousand sand storms.

The vehicles pulled up outside the stadium entrance that players and VIPs had once used. Sand piled up against one set of doors. A pane of glass had cracked into a thousand shards years ago, but the pieces still clung to each other refracting the image beyond the door into a mosaic. Mattias's protection team spread out from the cars and two of them went through the doors that had been cleared of sand. They nodded to the main car and Mattias got out. He approached the doors, pausing briefly to let Precious catch up and then walked into the building. There was definitely no air conditioning left in the stadium. He wondered why his clients had chosen this site. Secrecy, sure. But sweating up a staircase? Mattias didn't mind, but he knew that heat and exercise were virtually intolerable to wealthy, middle-aged Arabs.

At the top of the stairs, he caught a glimpse of the once-verdant football pitch. Now just a rectangle of brown dirt. Even the white pigment of the lines had bleached into nothingness. What a waste of effort bringing the World Cup here. When was it? He counted back. Twelve years ago. So much for the legacy. A bit like this lot. The Organisation of the Petroleum Exporting Countries. Decades of wealth, when money literally gushed out of the ground. Some people had lined their pockets, sure. But when nuclear fusion and solar panels deliver all the energy the world needs? Who's going to buy oil then? What are these countries going to live on?

Mattias' foot slipped as he reached the top of the stairs. Precious grabbed his arm and smiled. He knew he couldn't hide his nerves from her.

They were both on edge after the near-miss in the Canary Islands. Still, the haul of diamonds was safely on its way to the Netherlands for conversion into hard cash. The investigation into why they had nearly been caught would have to wait. Compartmentalise. Focus on the here and now. He breathed deeply and walked into the conference room.

Around the table were some familiar faces. This was the committee that met away from the glare of the press, taking decisions in private that were definitely not for the world to see. But Mattias had met some of these men before, only three months earlier.

The attack on Moon Lab One had been an attempt to disrupt nuclear fusion. It had failed. The first time Mattias's firm ESCO had not delivered. He had a radical new plan. An even bolder attack. A place perhaps even more inaccessible than the Moon. Would the OPEC committee give him the chance to make amends? For the first time in a long while, Mattias was unsure of the outcome of this meeting and was afraid.

The Chairman of the inner council welcomed him to the gathering. Mattias nodded as he looked around the room, noting the position of the doors and where the guards were standing.

"Please report, Mr Larsson."

"Thank you, Chairman. As you know, three months ago, Operation Blue Cheese was instigated. A viral attack on Moon Lab One. It failed. The details are sketchy. From the reports and interviews we've managed to intercept, it seems that the infected host, Yusuf Abdel Misih, changed his mind at the last minute. Threw himself out of an airlock."

The men around the table shook their heads in disbelief. One of them spoke up, above the general murmur. "I thought he had been hand-picked by your people?"

Mattias wondered if any of these men were brave enough to even cross the street without a bodyguard, let alone volunteer for the task Yusuf had accepted. "Yes, that's right. But we had such a very limited choice in the time available. Getting a convert onto the moon base staff was not easy. And don't forget, nearly one-in-four suicide bombers fail to press the trigger at the last minute."

One of the ministers shook his head. "Shocking. Young people of today…"

"Err, we did have a back-up plan. A bomb had been smuggled up there. It seems that British Intelligence got wind of this somehow. An OFWAT agent stopped the attack."

"I trust you will be dealing with this interfering son of a whore?" said the Chairman.

"You have my word on that. Now. I believe we still need to find a way to boost your oil revenues, yes?"

Heads nodded vigorously.

"All this clean energy. It's a dirty trick to play on you all." Mattias smiled and waited, hoping that his audience's grasp of English was good enough to get the pun. "Electricity, especially from solar panels, has replaced a lot of the demand for oil in the past twenty years, has it not?"

"We don't need a lecture on the global supply-demand mix for energy, thank you."

Mattias recognised the heckler as the chief economist from their last meeting. Others joined in the show of displeasure. He waved his hands for quiet. "What if I told you I'd found a way to turn off all the solar panels?"

"You're no magician, Mr Larsson," said the Chairman. "An attack on that scale would be unprecedented."

"Unachievable," said the chief economist.

Mattias was beginning to dislike the economist. He reminded him of his dad, always sucking the energy out of a situation. "No magic involved. And no swarms of suicide bombers either. But I am going to need one very large bomb. This is going taking careful planning, meticulous execution and plenty of money." Mattias proceeded to explain his plan to the gathering. He watched their faces as the realisation dawned on them. It was feasible. Chaotic, yes. Some parts of the world would suffer catastrophic consequences. Other countries, especially those represented at this table – and this is where Mattias' plan really started getting approving nods – would benefit. Especially with the forewarning now being afforded them. Mattias could not help grinning as the vote was put to the committee and every single response was a 'yes'. Operation Ashes to Ashes was given the go-ahead.

Mattias slalomed through the German defence, played a one-two with Zlatan and buried the return pass into the far corner of the net. The crowd went wild.

7

Sim was hanging out the washing in the back garden. Light fluffy clouds gambolled across the early summer sky. Rosie was watching Sim through the open back door.

"I'm not an invalid, you know?"

"That bag of washing was heavy," said Sim coming back in. "Besides, you need your rest."

"Och, the doctor said I was fine. The morning sickness will pass soon. And the scan was A-OK. Stop your fretting."

Sim held up his hands in mock surrender. He started to prepare some lunch. As Rosie went to sit down, he pulled out the chair and plumped up the cushion before guiding her into the seat. A growl like that of an angry badger emitted from Rosie's mouth.

"If you don't get back to work soon, Mr Atkins, so help me, I am going to scream this house down."

Sim started to protest, but Rosie cut him off. "Strangers are not going to start bumping into me on the pavement just because my tummy is a bit rounder. I managed to feed myself perfectly well while you were away on the Moon. The only thing that's bad for my blood pressure right now is your molly-coddling."

Sim returned to Overseas Division headquarters, in Birmingham, at the end of the week. He had reluctantly agreed to get back to work. Part of his reluctance was because he knew that the lust for revenge still ran deep in his veins. Back in the field, with access to kit and information, he doubted he would be able to resist following the path to payback. And that meant leaving Rosie on her own again, for who knew how long? Maybe not even coming back this time. Two missions, two near misses. Would the third be so lucky?

Sim strode into Wardle's office. "So, all that stuff about being extremely grateful, when you persuaded me to go on the Moon mission, that was just bullshit was it? Sir."

Wardle looked up from his desk and swiped the glass top clear of virtual files. "Welcome back, Atkins. Not wanting to skulk around in the satellite department, any more, I trust?"

Sim's original job at OFWAT had been keeping tabs on the satellites that helped Overseas Division fulfil their monitoring role. A job that he had reverted to after the Himalayas mission six years earlier. The mission to the Moon two months ago had fallen to Sim because of Elsa Greenwood's specific request, but even so, it had been voluntary. Wardle had used all his oily charm and precious promises to get Sim to say yes. Now Sim wanted to be included in the follow-up investigation.

"The CIA have already said no to my involvement. I need you to reverse that decision. I deserve some answers. It was my son that got killed, sir."

"Along with ten other people, yes, I know. All the more reason not to get involved in the follow-up. Personal agendas and professional discipline don't mix well. I should know."

Wardle swirled ice cubes around the tumbler and stared at the frozen water.

Sim paused for a moment, processing that last statement. "Care for a drink, Atkins?"

"It's a bit early for whisky, isn't it, sir?"

"Oh, don't you start. Look, I know what happened at Moon Lab One was tragic. But you saved the base. If we'd lost that facility... the resources, the research. Well, who knows how big the indirect effects would have been? But you should be very proud of what you achieved. The CIA will deal with the investigation. And I will let you know, as soon as I get their findings. That I promise." Wardle put his glass down, swiped into a file and started reading its contents.

"Sir." Sim turned to leave, formulating a plan even by the time he had passed through the door. There was somebody else who owed him a favour.

The curve of the Earth, viewed from a passenger plane at extreme altitude, still caused a murmur from those lucky enough to have a window seat. And a grumble from those with cheaper seats in the centre aisle. Crossing the Atlantic only took three hours these days. And Sim had seen enough views to last a lifetime. He leant back and closed his eyes. He was already feeling guilty about the lie he had told Rosie. About needing to fly to America on another mission. Well, that was kind of true. A mission Sim had assigned to himself and one that Wardle knew nothing about, yet. Of course, the subcutaneous tracking device resting in Sim's arm would soon alert Wardle of his journey. Those reprisals Sim would deal with when he got back.

Diane Butler had been easier to persuade than his boss. She had headed up the equivalent department in the CIA when Sim and Freda had teamed up with the Americans back in '28. The American agents had been repatriated; both of them buried as heroes. But Sim knew that one had been a traitor. Chung had killed his compatriot and nearly killed Sim and Freda. Sworn to secrecy, the deception still caught in his throat every time Sim thought about that man. But the overall success of the mission, despite its tragedy, had led to Diane's promotion. And Sim was a major part of that success.

Wanting to make the call as personal as possible, Sim had got through on the real-time holo line. The brief call to Diane had been enough to refresh her memory of the salient facts. It was so much harder to say no when it seemed like the person was standing in front of you, in the same room. It hadn't got him onto the Company team in charge of investigating the incidents on Moon Lab One. Diane had not risen to her elevated rank by being a pushover. But Sim would be granted access to the team leader and time at the Johnson Space Centre to interview key personnel. Maybe that would be enough.

The George Bush Intercontinental Airport was the wrong side of Houston for the space centre. But Beltway Eight, on a quiet Tuesday afternoon, made short work of the final part of Sim's journey. The computer in charge of the taxi tried to make polite conversation with the British agent, but Sim soon stopped responding to the AI's inane questions. What was the point of replacing real drivers with robots, if the robots were just as annoying as the humans? Beltway Eight, Gulf Freeway and finally Nasa Road One. Sim liked to memorize routes, even sitting in the back of a driverless car. Without a visual sense of where he was on the map, he felt untethered. Unsafe.

Sim tapped on his wrist watch to pay for the journey and headed for the Space Centre's reception with a small rucksack over one shoulder. He had spent a week here only two months ago, training for the mission to the Moon. The various buildings that made up this hi-tech village, the cloudless skies and sweltering heat, all those memories came flooding back to Sim.

The man on the reception desk recognised him at once. Although space tourism was now big business, most of the time that involved low-Earth orbits in rockets that really were just glorified aircraft. Sim was one of only two people who had been allowed up to the Moon on a tourism pass, and that made him something of a celebrity. He smiled and shook hands with the man on reception even though he could not remember his name. But maybe Sim would need another favour. No harm in making friends. He suggested that they meet up for a drink later, promising to tell his new friend all about the Moon flight. Well, nearly everything.

The CIA had set up an incident room in one of the vast training buildings. The head of the team had clearly been instructed to share with Sim their findings so far, but maybe Diane had forgotten to say they should treat him with any respect. Jet-lagged and hungry, Sim was in no mood for verbal sparring. After waiting for twenty minutes outside the operations area, he was shown into a meeting room. The drinks machine in the corner was ignored and the plate of biscuit crumbs spoke of earlier visitors hosted with courtesy. Sim sat down at the conference table, opposite the big American agent, Steve Roberts.

"Tell me what you've got on Moon Lab One."

Roberts shrugged. "We interrogated the staff who flew back to Earth early. Instructions from Adams Holdings. Just obeying orders from their employer. Nothing to link them to the bomb."

"And Richard Taylor?" The boss of Adams Holdings, who had ordered the base to be blown up, had been captured by the British but taken to a secret base in Greenland.

"I woulda thought you knew all about that, Agent Atkins."

"You guys are the experts at enhanced interrogation, aren't you? Did he confirm the plot as an insurance scam?" The American nodded and looked at his watch. "What does he know about Yusuf?"

"Who?"

Sim slammed his hand on the table. "Stop pissing me about. You know who. The guy who walked onto a NASA rocket carrying the Ebola virus. The guy who would've spread the disease throughout the base if he hadn't changed his mind at the last minute. The guy who killed..." He couldn't finish the sentence.

"Rich Taylor knows nothing. We're pretty sure he's telling the truth about that." The corner of Roberts' lips turned up by a few degrees. "All of the NASA medical staff are being investigated. All the pre-flight records double-checked."

"Somebody must know something."

"Look. It's been a long day. Why don't you come back tomorrow morning? We're interviewing Yusuf 's handler at O-nine hundred hours. I'll let you watch, OK?"

Sim's shoulders slumped even as he rose from his seat. "Yeah, thanks," shaking Roberts' hand. Sim was shattered and wanted to get some sleep. But first, he had promised a beer with the guy on reception. He hoped that the bar sold stim drinks too.

Director Wardle was too busy to notice Sim's tracer was pinging on the other side of the Atlantic. After the debacle on the Canary Islands, the Joint Intelligence Committee was taking no risks with the iceberg that Hamilton had discovered. 42 Commando had been sent in, with *HMS Duncan* for back-up. The destroyer had an anti-air missile system capable of dealing with any attempts to escape via Hydras this time. Wardle watched the operation unfold from the communications centre in Overseas Division headquarters. As the commandoes approached in rib boats, concealed machine-gun turrets rose out of the snowy plateau on the right-hand side of the iceberg and opened fire on the craft. The boats swerved, slicing S-shaped curves across the grey sea as their motors screamed even harder. Two men fell. Lucky shots that found gaps between the bulletproof vests and helmets.

Rocket-propelled grenades from the commandoes arced towards the berg and exploded against the ice. The machine gun turrets kept firing. *HMS Duncan* trained its laser tower on the iceberg and a deadly ray lashed out, silencing the turrets. As the boats closed in, grappling hooks shot upwards and dug into the top of the ice. Even as the commandoes began climbing the ropes, several drones took off from hidden openings in the iceberg's bulbous left-hand peak. The little helicopters dropped tiny bombs around the grappling hooks, one of which came loose. There was a yell as a soldier fell backwards into the freezing cold ocean.

Again, the destroyer's death ray beamed across the sea and cut the drones from the sky. Eighteen commandoes approached the icy hillock at a stooping run. No more bullets or bombs. The only sound was the howl of the wind across the plateau. The soldiers approached the hillock and broke in with explosives. Beneath a carefully constructed outer shell, they discovered the airship that had been hijacked by the Terror Formers several weeks ago. The decomposing remains of many Russian aircrew were still on board, not even given the dignity of a burial at sea. It had cost three commandoes their lives and the British were still no closer to capturing the terrorists.

8

<hr>

Houston, Texas

Frank Herbert was a nervous guy. Nervous because he had something to hide or just because he was sitting in an interrogation room opposite a two-way mirror? Sim was watching from the darkened side of the glass, trying to interpret the NASA medic's body language. Roberts entered the brightly lit room and noted the time and date into a mic on the table. He shuffled an old-fashioned file of papers that Sim could see were blank, but that remained hidden from the interviewee.

"So, Frank, you like your work here at JSC?" asked Roberts. "Sure, I guess."

"I prefer it when you don't guess. Yes, no or don't know. Understood?"

Frank started to jig his legs up and down, underneath the desk. "Yes."

"Describe exactly what happened the day you prepped Yusuf for launch on Orion Twelve."

Frank looked puzzled for a minute as if the memory was translucent, ephemeral. "20th May, right? I didn't work that day."

Roberts shook his head. "Frank, don't lie to us. We have your security card swiping in to the JSC car park that morning. CCTV shows your car pulling into your usual space. And then you get out of the car and use your swipe card to enter the medical centre. Did you think we hadn't checked?"

"I wasn't there. I'm telling you. I was on vacation. Sailing, up on Lake Livingston. There was a competition on that weekend."

"You expect us to believe that? Your word against all this evidence?"

"Why don't you check the Cape Royale Boating Association's results site. Me and my crew came second. And while you're at it, see if CCTV picked up my car heading along the Eastex Freeway. Must be a tape of that somewhere, right? NSA archives everything, doesn't it?"

Roberts turned to look into the mirror, then terminated the interview. He left the room and came to see Sim.

"What do you think?"

Sim stared through the mirror again. The NASA medic's legs had stopped jigging. With a few glances at the watch, he looked more annoyed than nervous now. "I think he's telling the truth. Maybe somebody cloned his security pass. Bought some fake plates that matched his car. And came in that day to inject Yusuf with the virus."

"That would require a lot of planning and resources," said Roberts.

"Delivering a version of Ebola even more deadly than the usual strain? To Moon Lab One? Evading all the security checks here? Yeah, I think amateur hour finished long ago."

Frank Herbert's story checked out. He had been sailing, eighty miles away from the space centre on May 20th. Thorough analysis of the CCTV tapes had shown that the car driven to JSC on the day in question day was sprayed with a slightly different version of Toyota red paint. *Ruby Flare*, instead of *Ooh La La Rouge*. Honestly, who thinks up these names, thought Sim. And the man entering the building, trying to hide his face from the cameras, was at least three centimetres shorter and four kilos lighter than Frank. It took another day for the National Security Agency to come up with a match. The culprit had taken out a six-month lease on a property in Fairview Road, Alvin back in March.

"Chances of him still being there?" asked Sim.

"Yeah, well, maybe forensics will find something useful." Roberts grabbed his jacket and beckoned for Sim to follow. "He might have left a forwarding address." Sim didn't bother laughing. He was just grateful to be involved in the case still. He doubted it would last.

The culprit was still there, as it turned out. It seems he hadn't moved for several weeks, judging from the stench that greeted their nostrils as the front door crashed open. Agents swarmed into the house, as the flies tried to swarm out. The body, hidden inside a chimney cavity, had been an ideal hatchery for the larvae but difficult for the forensic team to extract. As if that hadn't been bad enough, the aircon had packed in long ago. Several weeks of a Texan summer can do awful things to a human body even without the help of the flies. Sim hurried outside and retched in one of the dried-up flower beds. As his vision cleared, he noticed something metallic sticking out of the soil. A key ring. Staying bent over, Sim placed his hand over the object and gently teased it out. There was a single silver key attached.

Roberts came out and patted him on the back. "Doubt he'll

tell us much now. We'll get everything bagged up. But I'm not hopeful. Like you said, we're dealing with professionals here."

Sim grunted something in reply and closed his fingers around the keyring, shifting it to his pocket as he stood. Maybe he'd be able to keep working on this case after all.

The most dangerous report that Wardle had seen in years was now hovering above his desk glass as innocent as a kite. Some budgetary committee in parliament was questioning the need for a separate Overseas Division. The World War for Water – hyperbole at the best of times – was a faded international crisis. Surely the UK government could revert back to its regular intelligence services? It seemed that Wardle's department could be shut down on the whim of the mandarins in Whitehall. The pen truly is mightier than the sword, he mused to himself.

Yes, it was true that water shortages were becoming less acute. A better understanding of the situation had helped to reduce consumption. And improved technology was bridging the gap to supply. But his department was still stretched to the limit, dealing with incidents across the globe. How many were directly related to conflict over water, and how many were the knock-on effects: economic poverty, displaced people, food shortages? It was always hard to tell. Wardle suspected that the accountants took a dim view of loose connections. And some of his team's successes were too sensitive to even appear on the audit trail.

Hmm, Overseas Division could do with a high-profile result, and soon.

Wardle took a bite from a BLT sandwich and walked across his office to the holo-globe sitting on its virtual plinth. The red dots showing the location of all his active agents still included one in Texas. Sim Atkins. There was no mission assignment that required him to be there. But the Director of Overseas Division had cut him some slack, it was the least Sim had deserved after the success of the lunar mission. But the sojourn had been going on too long. Atkins was needed back here, delivering results. Wardle sent a priority recall message.

A file pinged onto his desk glass, glowing orange. A field report. It was from Freda Brightwell, Sim's old partner. Wardle ignored the rest of his in-box and selected this one straight away. It must be good news. Surely the rescue from Russia had succeeded.

After making contact with the undercover agent, it had taken Freda, Gopal and Rabten another couple of days to cross the Russian border. They were now travelling by train and car from Uzbekistan towards Nepal along a branch of the resurrected Silk Road trading route. Afghanistan, Pakistan then India. Slow but sensible to be keeping a low profile. Wardle knew the checkpoints in that part of the world. They were more interested in checking for smuggled water than fake IDs. The Division's network of local helpers would see the three agents safely back to Kathmandu.

But Freda's report contained a worrying hypothesis. The nature of their arrest a couple of weeks ago at the Russian border was not bad luck. There was nothing wrong with their ID cards. Somebody must have had a tip-off about their presence. And that probably meant a security breach or, worse, a mole in Overseas Division. Wardle swiped the file closed immediately, as if somebody might be peeping over his shoulder. He buzzed the intercom.

"Feinberg, get in here now."

After a few minutes the Israeli appeared, a roll tab under his arm.

"Not letting the precious thing out of your sight?"

David shook his head. "I don't even want to risk another person touching it in case some internal alarm gets triggered. Like I said before, this was very tough to break into. It could be the best chance we've had in years of cracking open the TF network."

Wardle gestured for his colleague to sit down. "If this office had been bugged by some outside group, would we know about it?"

"There is a full sweep done of every room in the building once a week. If we were unlucky, maybe six days before the device was detected and removed. Assuming they could get it inside the building in the first place."

"Humour me, and get a sweep done of this room. Immediately." David wrinkled his nose. "OK, boss."

Two hours later, he rushed back into the office.

"You found something?" asked the Director, closing down the report he was reading.

"No... Yes."

"But nobody's even come into the office to check, yet."

Feinberg shook his head. "The nanobots have been crawling all over this place ever since I left you. They found nothing to report. Except that empty bottle of scotch in your drawer."

"It's not scotch. It's 18-year old Balvenie. Was. Anyway, it's none of your business."

"No, sir. But the roll tab has brought up some interesting results. Something about the TF using an artificial iceberg as a base. It's been abandoned now, but might be worth checking out."

Wardle looked like he had stepped in something unpleasant on the pavement. "Your timing is fucking impeccable. You know that, Feinberg?"

· · ·

Wardle climbed the stone steps as the low sun cast long shadows down Pall Mall. He nodded to the doorman, trying to ignore the ridiculous outfit the man was wearing. The head of Overseas Division fingered his collar. He had chosen his cheapest, gaudiest tie in the hope that it would pass the dress code but still offend the members of this absurd club. He knew he shouldn't let it get to him. Wrenshaw had set the venue for the meeting, almost certainly to emphasise his own membership and Wardle's status as an outsider.

"Ahh, good of you to trot down from Birmingham, old boy." The head of MI6 held a large brandy glass in his pudgy fingers. He swirled its contents around and took a sip, before motioning for Wardle to sit in the green leather chair opposite him.

The head of MI6. C. Wardle knew what the consonant stood for. Another man appeared at Wardle's side and took his order for a Balvenie. There was silence for a few moments after the waiter had disappeared. Wardle's chair squeaked as he tried to make himself comfortable.

"How can I help?" he asked.

"Made a bit of a mess of things, hmm?"

Wardle tried not to react. "I'm not sure what you mean."

"Oh come now, old chap. The iceberg assault? Three men dead, no terrorists caught. A very expensive operation. I'm sure you've seen the auditor's report on all of our budgets. Don't you think it's time to call it a day?"

"You think I should fall on my sword, just to protect your own precious budget?"

"Departments come and go. You remember MI9?" Wardle shook his head.

"Neither does anybody else. Your lot had its time when the world war for water was at its peak. You fulfilled your duty, just like department nine did, and now it's time to step back. What about your fishing? When did you last get up to Speyside?"

"Too long. Water's rather peaty at this time of year, puts the salmon off the take."

Wrenshaw took another sip of brandy and then patted Wardle on the knee. "Let us do our job properly. Without interference."

For a moment, Wardle's resolve had been crumbling. But that last sentence had stiffened his spine. "I'd rather use my own testicles for bait. If you'll excuse me, I have to get back to HQ and do some proper work."

9

Aktobe, Kazakhstan

A car, driven by the woman who had helped Freda and the others escape from Russia, pulled up outside a cheap-looking office. The headlights switched off as she killed the engine. The sparse street lights cast a watery yellow sheen across the road and up the sides of the buildings. A solitary figure walked past the car and disappeared from view. The driver looked again. There was nobody else around at this hour. She opened the car door and stood up. A hand gripped her throat, with enough power to hurt but just soft enough to let her keep breathing. A voice whispered in her ear.

"Don't do anything stupid."

She could feel something sharp in the palm that gripped her. It pressed against her skin.

"Tell me where you took them."

She managed to rasp a question of her own. "Who?"

The point of a needle pressed into her neck and punctured the skin. The pain was not as bad as the fear of what might come next. "Don't mess me about. I know you helped three people escape. Two men, one woman."

No reply.

"If you don't tell me, I squeeze. The needle in your neck releases a toxin. And you die. So, no sudden movements. Talk."

There was a noise off to their left. The woman's eyes darted towards the sound, hoping for a witness or a distraction. But the tall man's grip remained tight. He used his spare hand to pull a gun and pointed it towards the side alley. A black cat emerged from between two buildings. Unlucky for some.

A tear formed in the woman's eye. "You think you can make me talk? You can go to hell."

"Probably," he said. "But you will get there first, I think." He squeezed the capsule, releasing the toxin, and the woman's body began to convulse. A few moments later, he let the corpse fall to the ground. The man holstered his pistol and straightened the ski hat on his head. He got into the woman's car, shifting the driver's seat back for his long legs. The on-board computer asked for voice print identification. The man pulled a small device from his pocket and pressed some buttons on the screen. The machine analysed the few words of the woman's voice it had just recorded. It spoke to the car in a perfect match for her speech patterns and the engine started up. The tall man called up a log of the car's recent journey and set off.

Freda's turn at the wheel had just begun. Gopal was asleep on the back seat and Rabten was riding up front, next to Freda.

"So, you can understand English, right?" she asked. He nodded when she glanced across at him.

"Good. How about we try to get you talking some? Yes?"

"Yiz," he replied.

"Repeat after me. My name is."

"Namaste," said Rabten.

Freda shook her head. "No. Listen. My. Name. Is."

"My num iz."

What had Gopal called Rabten's language? A form of Tibetan that sounded like *Dbus*? She couldn't even pronounce the name properly. Freda looked at the road stretching up and over the hills ahead of them. It was going to be a long drive.

It took three days to cross Uzbekistan. From Nukus to Dushanbe, Rabten's English gradually improved. He had never learned to drive at the monastery, so Freda and Gopal had to share the driving between them. Three hours on, three hours off, half an hour for re-charging. The electricity stations were always busy. Car batteries had improved greatly through the years, with longer ranges, in part thanks to regenerative brakes. And better recharging technology allowed a battery to be topped up in a fraction of the time it had taken when they first were used on the roads. But still, the bigger batteries were thirsty. And there was only so much could be done to force juice into a car. Thirty minutes at rest every 500 kilometres was not so bad.

"How are you so thin?" Freda asked.

Rabten looked up from his second plate of food and shrugged. "If you ask me, he's got worms," said Gopal.

"Tajikistan should be a doddle," Freda said. "Whut is doddle?" asked Rabten.

"It means very easy," said Gopal, mopping up the last of his soup with a bread roll.

"Plane easier."

Freda shook her head. "We're staying away from the airports.

HQ says that our helper in Russia has been found dead. The Russians could still be trying to track us. C'mon. The battery should be full by now."

The monk's spoon scraped the bowl in double-time.

Gopal saw him looking at the food counter again. "I'll get you something for the road," he whispered.

Three hundred kilometres away the tall man with a ski hat plugged his device into a charging station. His software infiltrated the system controlling the charging points at the garage. It then burrowed through to the network of systems at each of the charging stations across Kazakhstan and cross-referenced vehicle identities to see which ones had traversed the country all the way from the Ural Sea to Tajikistan. Ten had made that journey in the last two days. An image of each vehicle flashed up on the screen of the man's device. Six were HGVs, one was a motorcycle and three were cars. He zoomed in on the images of the cars. One had a single occupant. He pulled up extra images of the remaining two. One of them had the same passenger each time but between charging stations the driver kept changing gender. The tall man thought for a moment. A woman and two men travelling together. He breathed deeply and sniffed at the air, grinning. He got back into his borrowed car and headed out onto the road.

Tajikistan blinked past with just one recharge required. The road took Freda and the others briefly into Kyrgyzstan. Each border crossed was a risk. But there was nothing remarkable about a car on a dusty road, over a thousand kilometres away from the scene of a prison break-out. And their high-quality

Overseas Divisions IDs were perfect forgeries. The border officials paid them little attention.

The three agents had a decision to make. Turn right for Kashmir and Himachal Pradesh, across the worst terrain in the most hostile regions of Pakistan and India. Or keep straight on and risk crossing into China, driving through Tibet and finally into Nepal. Neither seemed very appealing. Tibet was where the two men had first met Freda. They had helped to rescue her from a secret base built by the Chinese to steal the frozen water in the Himalayan glaciers. All three had lost a friend on that mission.

"I think we have to risk China," said Freda.

"No like that place," replied Rabten. "What they did to monastery..."

"I know. But Kashmir. The politicians could have closed the border. And even if it's open, this car might not cope with the roads."

"They won't expect us to try the China route," said Gopal. "And if they try to capture us, we go down swinging, OK, pal?" He smiled at the monk.

"I'll get in touch with HQ," said Freda. "Get them to fill in on-line paperwork for our permits. Pull in at the next station Gopal."

They crossed the Chinese border at first light. The road hugged the outside of a promontory whose peak was adorned with an ancient fort. As the sun rose above the far distant mountains, the stone walls of the stronghold briefly turned orange as if some siege engine had set them ablaze. A hairpin bend forced the road almost back on itself and the fort dropped out of sight. Up ahead, the hexagonal tower of a modern castle appeared where the Chinese custom officials lorded it over passing traffic. As they pulled in for their passes to be checked, Gopal kept checking the rear-view mirror.

"Something wrong?" asked Freda.

"Apart from the sense of impending doom, going back into China, you mean? If you must know there's a red truck been following us since we past Nur a while back."

"Plenty of cars along this road, headed towards Kashgar."

"Maybe. But it's been going exactly the same speed as us. Always about four hundred metres back."

Freda turned to look through the back window. "Let's get through this trial first before we start imagining other problems."

On the far side of border control, Freda was starting to get a sore neck. She kept turning around and sure enough, four hundred metres away was a big, chunky, red vehicle. It was still possible that it was merely going the same way as them. And a driver maybe who felt comfortable keeping another car in eyesight but not wanting to crowd them. Possible, but not likely. After another hour, the three OD agents pulled into a recharging station and plugged in their vehicle. They moved into the restaurant but chose a table next to the window so they could watch what the truck would do. Freda let out a deep breath when it sailed straight past them. Rabten ordered a huge bowl of rice and stir-fried vegetables and Gopal went for a pee.

An hour after they had set off again, Freda swore loudly. Rabten asked what the words meant, but she just pointed in the rear-view mirror. The red vehicle had re-appeared.

"I wish we had Lach with us," said Gopal. His friend had helped them on the Himalayan mission and was a crack shot with his sniper rifle.

"We got any weapons?" asked Freda.

"Only Rabten's hands. They're lethal enough."

"If we can get the driver out of his truck."

They continued to head East. The valley floor gradually widened as the mountains on either side shrank back. The fecund plain of Kashgar appeared as the shadows of a low sun started to stretch across the countryside. Hopes for a welcome night's sleep were ruined by the flash of red on the road behind them. Like the echo of an unwelcome flare on tired retinas.

"Does that vehicle ever need recharging?" asked Gopal in a raised voice.

"Does the driver?" said Freda. "I say we stop for the night, somewhere busy in the centre of Kashgar. Take it in turns to keep guard, yes?"

"I stand guard," said Rabten. "Just sat here all journey. Make useful, yes?"

Freda nodded. "OK, thanks."

They shared a large twin room. Even with a martial arts expert sitting up all night, Freda found it hard to sleep. Her muscles tried to relax into the bed but she could not switch off her brain. Gopal's snoring was not exactly helping. She had shared so much time, in close physical proximity to the other two agents, they were starting to feel like brothers. Privacy and embarrassment at bodily functions had been lost on the road many miles ago. But still. Listening to somebody sawing logs at 2am was excruciating. She threw a trainer at the other bed. The ex-Gurkha grunted and rolled over onto his side. The faint, comforting sounds of a hotel in a busy city filtered through the walls, until Rabten began to chant his quiet prayers. Freda screamed silently and pulled the pillow tight against her ears.

Freda was staring out of the window, grasping a mug of steaming coffee. She had given up trying to doze as soon as sunlight had crept across the hotel window. At 4am there had been few people around, but she had tracked down a pawn shop and banged on the door until the owner opened up. Inside, she had found an ancient revolver and tried to buy it. The contact from Russia had supplied each agent with a pair of gold sovereigns – untraceable and highly acceptable in every country in the world. The pawn shop keeper had wanted both sovereigns for the gun and when he had included a box of ammo, Freda had agreed. It was ridiculously over-priced but Freda just knew that their tail wouldn't keep his distance forever.

Gopal and Rabten joined her for breakfast, eating at the table just behind her perch at the window. The caffeine was starting to revive Freda, but the lack of sleep still left her confused. She was looking at their car across the parking lot. Well, she was almost certain it was theirs. She vaguely remembered choosing that spot in the car park the night before because it was highly visible. But there was definitely a man doing something to the vehicle, trying to get in. He jammed something into the lock on the driver's door. Freda frowned.

"Hey, guys, I think somebody is trying to steal—"

The man pulled open the door and slipped into the driver's seat. He reached down to do something with the bottom of the dashboard and then closed the door behind him. A fireball erupted from under the car, tossing the vehicle up into the air. All of the windows in the hotel breakfast bar shook. Freda saw the car enveloped by flames, and then as the fireball continued upwards, the vehicle arced back towards the ground, landing on its side. The metal frame had buckled and all of the glass in the windows had smashed. There were flames inside the car and a blackened torso with a stump, like a spent match.

Gopal ran outside even as Freda sat there staring, trying to process the carnage. That was their car. A car bomb set off prematurely by a thief. They'd had a very lucky escape. She blinked as the noise of approaching sirens snapped her out of the trance. The agents needed to make themselves scarce. And they needed to watch their backs. That ancient revolver might have been a bargain after all.

The three agents walked for a few hours, away from the scene of explosion. They knew the authorities would be keen to question any witnesses – they needed to be miles away before that happened. And whoever planted the bomb would find out soon enough that the intended victims had escaped. The panicked crowd near the explosion helped them flee without picking up a tail. It turned out to be surprisingly easy to hitch a lift. Bored, lonely truck drivers seeing a western woman with strawberry blonde hair tended to stop. The truck drivers were disappointed when Gopal and Rabten sprung out of nowhere to join Freda in the cab.

The journey towards Nepal was broken up into three separate lifts from truck drivers, who were happy to share their life stories with Freda via the Babel app. At least driverless vehicles were not yet the norm in this part of the world. Freda envied Gopal and Rabten, able to rest in the back of the cabin, while she played the part of interested passenger up front. At one of the many stops for drinks and toilet breaks, she managed to send off a field report to Wardle, while Rabten re-affirmed his infinite capacity for food.

As the road climbed towards the Tibetan plateau, the drivers gradually nudged up the heat controls in their vehicles and the journey developed a backing track from the whistle of wind through the trailer coupling. The agents had no choice but to keep hitch hiking. The wait between willing trucks became longer and more unpleasant as the temperature dropped along with the frequency of traffic. Freda did not need acting skills to look like a forlorn, vulnerable female as she hunkered down into her hooded coat by the side of the windswept road.

Their hurried escape from Russia and race along the silk road had left little time for the agents to re-equip themselves. AppCore payments were not accepted in this part of the world. The four remaining gold sovereigns were not enough to buy a vehicle and too flashy to spend on small items of expense. The little local currency they had was being saved for food and drink. The next truck driver who stopped was looking to drive all night. He was especially welcome as a source of free accommodation.

Within a couple of days, they were getting close to the border with Nepal. The road to Kathmandu was just showing on the edge of the driver's map that projected onto his screen. Gopal's mood was improving with every hour. But Rabten was becoming restless for another reason. At the next roadside station, he stopped eating halfway through his meal.

"What if I take some leave?"

"Yeah, think I might do the same, once we get back to Kathmandu," said Gopal.

"I mean, what about taking leave now."

"What?"

"I carry on hike-hitching along this road."

"Why would you want to do that?" asked Freda.

Gopal looked at his friend and put his cutlery down. "It's not a good idea, Rabten. They might still be looking for you."

Rabten shrugged. "I have to see it again."

"Can somebody explain, please," said Freda.

Gopal turned to her. "If you carry on along this road, and don't turn for right for Nepal, you eventually get to Lhasa."

Freda looked blank and Rabten played with his food.

"That's where he was born and raised. Where he became a monk. And it's where his master's shrine is." Gopal reached across the wooden table and gripped Rabten's upper arm. "Wangdue was a great man. Generous, strong and wise. He wouldn't want you to walk into a trap."

"They not still looking for me."

"You don't know that."

10

____

Inside the Arctic Circle

The *Endeavour* was crashing through high waves. The Arctic Ocean in summer meant constant sunlight, little ice and strong winds. They had found themselves caught in a particularly nasty storm. The boat lurched up into the slope of a seething slab of water that towered above the bridge. Captain Hamilton leant forwards to counteract the motion and wondered whether to submerge the vessel and sit out the storm. His crew were experienced sailors but even some of them were starting to look unwell.

The captain was searching for more evidence of Terror Former activity within the Arctic Circle. And he knew that diving below the waves would restrict the use of radar and surveillance equipment. Yesterday evening he had spoken to Director Wardle. A debrief about the mission to the iceberg and the stolen airship.

"How did they know we were coming?" Hamilton had asked.

"Maybe we were just unlucky," Wardle had said, not sounding

very convinced at his own answer. "Perhaps they had abandoned the base a while ago."

"Or, they were tipped off. Bloody bastards."

Wardle had just shrugged. The video conference had not lasted much longer. Hamilton had thought that his boss had seemed very distracted. His implicit agreement to the mission had been all the captain needed. He had gone to sleep that night thinking about the marines who had lost their lives on the mission. Soldiers he would have thought of as comrades when he had still been in the service. The authorities may have thrown him out of the Navy, but he was determined to see that the marines' sacrifice had not been in vain.

The mess was a mess. The chef was struggling to serve up food and keep crockery from sliding off the surfaces as the boat continued to pound through mountains of water. Captain Hamilton was almost alone in the dining room, tucking into a large plate of scrambled eggs and bacon. One of his crew ran into the room. He paused and bent over one of the tables. The captain wondered if the sailor was going to be sick and lifted his plate out of the way. The man stood up again, after he had caught his breath, looking a little green.

"Sir, the bosun thinks you should come and see this."

Hamilton grabbed two slices of bread, scooped the rest of his breakfast in between them, and followed the sailor back to the bridge. The sandwich had vanished by the time the captain walked onto the bridge.

"Report."

"Sir, radar has picked up something unusual. Just on the edge of the Franz Josef archipelago."

"Unusual, how?"

"It looks like a very large vessel. But it's so close in to the coastline. A ship that size must have a ten-metre draught at least. Our charts show only five metres of water where she is."

The captain looked at the radar screen. "OK, so she's run aground. Always a risk in weather like this. Any distress signal?"

"Radio silence," said the comms officer.

"Hah, maybe their captain is too embarrassed. What about other vessels coming to their aid?" asked Hamilton.

"Nothing at all," said the bosun.

"Well we better investigate, then." The captain sat in the chair on his dais in the middle of the bridge and stroked his chin. "Of course, this could be the result of a terror attack, instead of an accident. Or a trap. Helm, take us down to twenty metres. Half-speed. Let's approach nice and quiet."

Hamilton was observing coastline through the periscope. Just in front of the island Zemlya Aleksandry, he could see the stricken vessel. Too much hull above the waterline. The boat was listing at least 15 degrees from vertical. Definitely grounded. The captain zoomed in on the hull and snapped a picture. His onboard computer analysed the image and reported a few seconds later.

"*Arktika* is a nuclear-powered Russian vessel. Originally commissioned as an ice breaker, it is now registered as a cargo ship. Length, 173 metres long. Beam, 34 metres. Twin nuclear reactors, running on low-enriched Uranium 235."

The captain continued to watch the waves crash into the hull of the ship. The midnight sun cast a faint glow across the vessel. Hamilton smiled at the colours: a thin strip of red was visible at the bottom of the hull, blue above that, and a white superstructure. A perfect match for the Federation's flag. *Whatever you think about their policies, the Russians sure are a patriotic bunch.*

He continued to watch the vessel through the periscope, zooming in on the infrastructure. The image was fuzzy for a moment and then the stabilizing software kicked-in and Hamilton could see lights on the bridge, and a couple of crew members running about on the deck.

"Doesn't look like a terrorist attack. No obvious damage to the superstructure. Comms, hail them and see if they'd like some assistance."

"Aye, Captain." The comms officer relayed the message three times, but there was no reply.

"You sure the Babel app is working?" Hamilton asked. The comms officer nodded.

"Ask them for permission to come on board."

The response to this was almost instantaneous. "Negative, *Endeavour*. This vessel is under quarantine. Nobody is to come on board. Keep a minimum distance of 500 metres. We have a medical emergency. I repeat, nobody is to approach the *Arktika*."

"What's the Russian for bullshit?" the captain wondered out loud once the speaker had been turned off.

The radar operator looked up from her screens and turned to Hamilton. "I'm picking up quite a bit of radiation from that ship. Far more than should be coming from their reactor engines."

"Now we're getting somewhere," said the captain. "A leak? Probably some of the crew have radiation sickness. And with the engines out, they've been driven onto the rocks."

"Surely they'd welcome some help getting the rest of the crew off the vessel. And try to stop the boat breaking up, losing its cargo," the bosun said.

"What is their cargo?" asked Captain Hamilton.

"Hang on, searching now." There was a pause. "Nothing on the Lloyds of London list or the Marine Traffic site," said the comms officer.

"The radiation signal is odd, not the right mix for low U-235. Seems to match rich plutonium," said the radar operator.

"So, they swapped fuel sources?" suggested the captain.

"Not possible, sir. The radiation must be coming from their cargo."

"Well that's just great. We've got an environmental disaster waiting to happen and the Russians are too proud to admit it. Welcome or not, we're getting on board."

The Endeavour remained just below the surface and had closed half the distance to the stricken vessel when the radar screen lit up. "Incoming bogey, altitude 300 feet, speed Mach one point five. Range one click and closing fast."

The sonar operator shouted. "Screws in the water, acquiring, acquiring. Locked onto us. Impact in twenty seconds."

"Launch countermeasures," said the captain. "Sound collision alarm."

A claxon filled *the Endeavour* with its warning while more than a dozen micro drones were fired out of tubes at the prow of the ship. The drones immediately adopted a tight formation like a trio of hexagons and linked frail metallic arms. They swam straight towards the incoming torpedo. The impact triggered the torpedo's detonator, instantly wiping out the drones. On board *the Endeavour*, the explosion rocked the ship. Captain Hamilton was thrown out of his chair.

"Damage report!"

"Nothing sir, the explosion was too far away," said the bosun. "Bogey is changing course, coming around for another pass."

"Full speed ahead, helm. Get us right next to the *Arktika*. They'll never risk another torpedo there."

"But the depth sir."

"Blow the ballast tanks. Up planes, ten degrees. Get us on the surface."

The submarine immediately began to tilt upwards as orders were followed. The captain got back in his seat. "Sonar, anything?"

"Negative, sir."

"Bogey is heading back for the mainland," said the radar operator, as she wiped her sleeve across a glistening forehead.

The captain and the chief engineer boarded the *Arktika* along with two armed escorts. After a standoff with the Russian crew, Hamilton was finally able to convince them that he was here to help. The cargo hold was full of nuclear waste and one section had been damaged when the ship ran aground. One of the Russians was suffering from radiation sickness and was taken on board *the Endeavour* for medical treatment. The chief engineer was appalled at the state of the engine room. The loss of power seemed to be the result of excessive wear and tear. Multiple components were fatigued and most had been patched up several times already.

"It'll take me at least a couple of days to get anything out of these engines, even just to float it off the rocks," the engineer confided to Hamilton.

"She'll have broken in half by then, with this storm on us."

"Can't the Russians get the cargo airlifted off?"

"Can't use planes, and it would take thousands of helicopters to lift this lot. There won't be time."

The Russian captain asked after his sick crewman.

Hamilton put his hand on the man's shoulder. "We'll do everything we can to make him comfortable, but it doesn't look good. Where were you taking this cargo?"

The other captain just shrugged and the Babel app

translated. "We found big cavern on sea bed. Near the pole. Can bury lots there. No problem."

"No problem, or somebody else's problem?" replied Hamilton.

"Hang on. I've just had a thought. What we found a few days ago. That giant airship. It's Russian after all. That had a huge cargo hold. Could be here in a few hours. No runway needed." He turned to look at the chief engineer.

"If the winds die down a bit, aye, it might work."

"Spasiba, spasiba."

Hamilton did not need to wait for the translation. "You're welcome."

11

───────

Pasadena, Texas

Sim's hotel was near Strawberry Park in Pasadena, just a few miles from the Johnson Space Centre. Close enough to get there in a hurry if the investigation team made a break through, far enough away to avoid accusations of cramping their style. His cheap accommodation did at least include air conditioning that worked. As Sim walked into his room, the wet patch between his shoulder blades started to dry and his shirt unstuck from his clammy skin. He cracked open a can of some brand of sugary American drink he'd never heard of while his roll tab rendered a replica of the key he had found into its software. Once the key had been washed, Sim could see a set of numbers etched into its bow, just above the shoulder. And there had been some sort of emblem on the keyring, possibly scratched away with a file. He turned the key over, or rotated it, every time the machine beeped, showing a different aspect to the tiny camera lens built into the roll tab.

The computer finally finished running its programme and Sim could see a 3D image of the key and its keyring, twisting and

84

turning on the screen. He encrypted the file and sent it to OFWAT HQ for analysis. He ordered a T-bone steak with fries and rings from room service and flicked through endless channels of mind-numbing nonsense on the TV.

The results came through just as a spotty teenager delivered a slab of beef that could have fed a small village in Scotland. The key was of a type used throughout America in both domestic and commercial settings. The numbers on the key were too generic to pinpoint any specific location or owner. Sim's appetite for his steak was fading fast as he read the bad news. But the end of the report gave a glimmer of hope. The emblem had not been filed away completely. After some digital enhancement, a set of initials had become legible.

TCYC

Sim tucked into his steak while his mind tried to think of combinations of words that might make sense of those initials. Sleep came uneasily as his stomach tried to digest half a cow and his brain tried to process images of words fluttering around that keyring like butterflies with letters on their wings.

Sim returned to the investigation unit at the Space Centre to see if the CIA had made any progress with the dead man. Unlike the weather, the trail had gone cold. For the past eighteen hours, Roberts and his team had investigated the impostor from the NASA medical team. The rental agreement on the property had provided a financial route into the dead man's history. A legend, which had been well put-together, sufficient to get a credit rating that had passed the landlord's due diligence, but not one that led to a real person.

So, they were looking at a ghost in both senses of the word. The autopsy had shown death by strangulation, but nothing useful under the finger nails. No struggle, but there had been needle marks on his arm. Dental records drew a blank. Even Border Control had no match for the fingerprints. If this person were foreign, they had sneaked into the country through unofficial channels.

The vague amount of professional camaraderie that Sim had built up with Roberts was ebbing fast. The CIA man was increasingly frustrated at the lack of progress.

"What about toxicology? Those needle marks might indicate something," said Sim.

"We've already tried that. Haul your ass back to Britain and let us do our job." Roberts turned to his secretary. "Get me Diane Butler on the phone. I need to tell her we've drawn a blank."

"What about the contents of the house? Anything unusual in that?" Sim would not be fobbed off that easily.

Roberts sighed. He slid over a print-out that listed the contents by room.

Sim scanned the list and halted over two items. "Don't call it off yet."

"What you seen? Holding out on us, kid?"

"More of a hunch. Just give me 24 hours." Sim handed back the report and headed out of the office. Deck shoes and a waterproof grab-bag were on the list. Maybe YC stood for Yacht Club. He wanted to know for sure before he confessed to Roberts about the keyring.

The Texas Corinthian Yacht Club was a very up-market place, not far from the Space Centre. The man at the gate wore a white uniform with creases sharp enough to cut paper. His expression suggested that the club took a dim view of non-members turning up un-announced or un-invited.

Sim needed to think fast. He changed his Scottish accent

into something that resembled Wardle's English hoping the American would not be able to tell how bad it was. "Good day, my man. Bit of a long shot, I know, but I'm staying here for a few weeks while I tie up a property deal in the area and I'm desperate to get out on the water. Everybody says this is the tip-top club so I was wondering if I might have a chat with the secretary about some sort of short-term arrangement."

The man on the gate stood for a moment, unable to decide how to proceed. Sim drew out a twenty-dollar bill and flashed him a smile. The security guard went to make a call in his booth and a few moments later, the gates rolled back and finally the guard's face cracked into a smile. "Welcome to the Corinthian, sir."

Sim was enjoying the view across the water from the secretary's office while sipping a mint julep. The secretary of the club, a black man with tight grey curls, was expanding on the virtues of membership.

"It'd be our pleasure to have you on board, as it were, Mr Watkinson."

Sim had adopted the surname he had used when he was undercover at the Moon base. "Jolly good."

"Minimum of six months' membership, I'm afraid."

"Not a problem. Though I will need to hire one of your lock-ups. I can get my people to bring over some of my kit if I have somewhere to store it."

The secretary pulled a face. "You're plum out of luck on that one. 'Fraid all our garages are already taken."

"Ahh." Sim tried not to smile. His whole plan had relied on this. "Perhaps there's one that isn't being used actively. Maybe we could share it, temporarily? Would an extra six months' membership cover the inconvenience?"

There was no moon to reflect across the dark waters when Sim returned to the club. The roads were deserted and he could see a different guard sat inside a little cabin by the gates to the Corinthian. Sim did not need his night-vision goggles. The cabin was illuminated from within and the big windows afforded a perfect sight of the bored woman inside, paying scant attention to anything going on around. This was going to be easy.

Sim was about to scale the fence when he noticed a faint hum coming from the barrier. He switched his goggles to infra-red mode and the whole fence lit-up like a Christmas tree. Motion sensors. The club took its security more seriously than the guard did, it seemed. A high-end system like this could be defeated, but not with the equipment Sim had with him. It was time for plan B. Sim's black outfit was perfect camouflage in the sea but had none of the thermal protection of a wetsuit. Fortunately, the waters in the bay were a pleasant temperature. He was relieved not to be doing this in one of the lochs near his home back in Scotland. The yacht club's defences continued out into the harbour on top of and below the jetties that defined its part of the marina. Even the gap between the jetties, where during the day boats would sail out into the bay, was blocked by a stout aluminium chain and a laser beam.

Sim took a deep breath and dove below the surface. He flicked a switch on his goggles and a beam of light illuminated the waters as he swam below the chain barrier. It extended down to a depth of at least two metres. Sim could feel the pressure building in his ears as he swam lower and then he was past the barrier, swimming back to the surface. He gasped as he broke the surface, turning off the beam from his goggles. The club's marina was silent except for the gentle creaking of hulls against rubber fenders and the chiming of sail wires against masts.

Sim swam between two yachts and used a ladder to climb onto a jetty. He crept towards the lock-ups. The secretary had explained that number 13 had not been used for a couple of months. The foreign gentleman who had taken up membership back in March had not been seen since. Sim plugged his wrist tab into the key pad and soon heard a click as the software cracked the code. He pushed the door open and once inside switched on the beam from his goggles again. The thin beam immediately picked out the jackpot. A Toyota in Ooh La La Rouge with plates that matched Frank Herbert's car.

It was all going a little too well. Sim was relishing the look on Roberts' face when he told him in the morning about the find at the yacht club. But as Sim arrived back at his hotel, a message from HQ pinged. Wardle was on the warpath. Sim was needed urgently back in the UK for some 'real work'. Pleading for just another week cut no mustard with his boss. There was a flight leaving in a few hours. Sim's ticket had already been purchased and failure to get on the plane would be a sackable offence.

Terminal B of the George Bush Intercontinental Airport was blessedly cool as Sim walked towards the check-in desk. He smiled at the person on duty and started thinking about Rosie's little bump. He patched through at the terminal and told his wife he was coming home. He was pleased to hear that the morning sickness had passed. And the bump was definitely starting to show by now. Sim needed to be there. Vid calls were just not the same. All the way through security, duty free and at the departure gate. Rosie, Rosie, Rosie. He was definitely not thinking about the need for revenge. That would be pointless. All he could do was go home, look after his wife and wait. Do some boring assignment for Wardle. Pretend that everything had returned to normal when the truth was, it never could.

12

————

At least Roberts and his team had something to go on. Sim had called from the airport and explained where to find the missing car. The CIA man had been furious at first. A shouted list of misdemeanours: withholding evidence, lack of procedure, entering without a warrant. This was the last time he was liaising with any foreign agencies. But he was glad to be rid of the bothersome Brit.

CCTV footage of the roads near the boathouse were trawled through, just before and just after the likely time of death of the NASA impostor. Red Toyotas were surprisingly popular, but finally the right one had been spotted. The driver was wearing a baseball cap pulled down low, but at one junction he had carelessly looked up to read one of the road signs. The car itself had been clean of fingerprints but there had been some hair strands that did not match the DNA of the dead impostor. Not for definite from the killer, but a possible match. The final piece of the jigsaw had been the opioid found in the glove box of the car. Not the usual pure cut from the Golden Crescent or Golden Triangle but a new synthetic, not yet found on the streets of America. It was taking market share all over Europe and it was being produced in Turkey.

Roberts had needed to work hard to get his boss to approve his plan.

"Just because the drugs were from Turkey, that doesn't mean the killer was too," Diane Butler had said.

"But the killer didn't show up on the face recognition algo at NSA."

"So?"

"So, he's almost certainly foreign too. Maybe even worked in the same terror cell as the infiltrator. That would explain why there had been no signs of a struggle. No break-in. I would say the two knew each other," Roberts had replied.

They had a photo, a DNA sample and an approximate date of entry. It was just enough for Diane to agree to a mission in Turkey. Roberts leant back in the seat of the private jet and smiled as the runway disappeared below the clouds.

Now we're getting somewhere.

Nazim Oktar, the Turkish killer, was good enough at his job to know that he had picked up a tail. The CIA agent was good enough at tailing not to lose his mark, even through the busy streets of a chaotic town like Manavgat. It was hot and the town was not quite close enough to the Mediterranean to get the benefit of any cooling breeze. Monday meant market day, usually full of tourists at this time of year. But it was also RTE day – the annual celebration of the glorious Turkish leader. Eighty years old and still going strong. And that meant the locals were out-numbering the tourists for once. Live musicians were giving the crowd an excuse to sway and sing in the sun. Cheap, strong booze was being poured from unmarked bottles into little shot glasses at numerous tables covered in plastic sheets. Everybody who went past such a table was being offered a drink. The Turkish killer pushed away the glass. A firecracker went off in a side alley and he ducked, turning fast. The tail was still watching him. Hair cut so short it was almost not there. American silvered shades. Hi-tech wrist communicator. No gun drawn, not yet.

Oktar jumped onto an electric bus heading west across the river, just before its doors closed. The tail broke into a run and slammed his hand on the back of the vehicle as it pulled out into traffic. Oktar leant back into the hot plastic of his seat and smiled, not realising that the bus now had a magnetic homing device clinging to its rear battery cover. A small drone took off from a nearby roof top and started following.

The Turkish man rested while the bus wound its way through heavy traffic towards the D400. He dozed lightly, letting the chatter of old women and the leaking music of head-phoned youths wash over him. At Gundogdu he got off the bus and checked the passing traffic to make sure the bus had not been followed. Nothing. During a lull in the traffic, he ducked behind a hedge and started walking towards the abandoned village of Kisalar. Only a couple of kilometres across the fields. A walk that most people around here dared not take any more. The fields were baked-hard and barren. Abandoned by the farmers after the spread of rumours about the cursed hamlet.

Well, let them think that for a while longer, he thought. The plants were trying to reclaim the village, but it was a perfect spot for a hide-out. Only one other person used these huts now and they were more interested in people smuggling than his line of business. Oktar pushed open the warped door of his humble abode and sat down to encrypt a report for HQ.

· · ·

The preparations of the CIA team were not ideal. After tracking the assassin to his hide-out, they had put together a hasty plan for the bagging operation. Taking the Turk alive would be crucial. The runway was a good hour's drive away, but that could not be helped. Chances of being spotted in this remote village were slim but afterwards they would have to run the gauntlet of any possible spot checks by local police. Even if it came to that, there were expensive options still available. One was financially dear, the other would cost lives. But they would get their target to the waiting plane one way or another.

As stars emerged, the CIA team moved into position and closed in on the village from all sides. Roberts heard voices from the path that led down to the coast. Little pin-pricks of light bobbed up and down. Ten, maybe twenty, people were approaching the village, wearing head-mounted torches. The language was nothing he had encountered before and he didn't have time to fiddle with his translator module. This was going to complicate the mission, but Roberts was too stubborn to abort now.

"Shit. Team, we've got witnesses headed our way. Keep your heads down and make sure they don't distract you from the mark." Roberts ducked behind a bush and watched as sixteen Africans walked past. They were chatting loudly, white teeth grinning in the darkness. Back-slapping each other, and a bottle was being passed down the line with each person taking a swig. A chant began. "Dee, Dee, Dee." The man at the front turned and held his hands out for quiet.

"That can't be," thought Roberts. "Fuck me." The face of one of the CIA's most wanted terrorists had flashed past him in the middle of a deserted Turkish village, in the middle of an unrelated mission. Which one needed priority? For once, Roberts was not sure. As he stood up and drew his gun, his foot crunched on a fallen branch. The group of Africans fell silent and a dozen tiny light beams swung around to partially blind the American agent. He ducked down again and whispered into his mic. "Prusak, we've got a new primary target. Leader of this African gang. Take him out while they're distracted by me. Non-lethal force, do you hear me?"

"Understood. Moving in now."

"Johnson, Fielding. Get Oktar, he's going to break cover."

The pop of a firearm being discharged was all the answer he got to that order. A muffled yelp, and then a cry of "Man down, man down," in his ear piece. The Africans heard the gunshot and scattered off the path in all directions, headlamps now switched off. Roberts pulled his torch and shone it along the barrel of his automatic pistol to where he had last seen the African leader. An empty space. The operation was unravelling fast. He needed to decide whether to pull the plug.

"Prusak. Give me some good news."

"Target acquired."

"Fielding?"

"Johnson took a round to the shoulder. He'll live. Unlike the Turk."

By the time the plane took off from the unlit runway, Johnson's wound had already been cleaned and dressed. The African prisoner's head was sheathed in a thick cloth bag and his wrists were tied behind his back. The dead assassin had been left behind after his clothes and house had been searched. With one wounded agent and a prisoner to handle, Roberts had decided to ditch the body. No big loss compared with the incredible bonus of stumbling across a person who had evaded the CIA for so long.

Prusak gave the prisoner's foot a kick. "So, Skipper, you gonna tell us why you risked the whole op for this piece of shit?"

"This, my friends," said Roberts as he whipped off the head bag, "is the guy who broke George Washington's nose. The man who brought down the French government in '26 and defeated the Terracotta Army the following year. Meet Jember Abdi.1"

The plane touched down on an island in the middle of an ocean. An island not officially recognised by most of the world, but which for CIA purposes counted as US mainland. A well-paid lawyer might have disputed that point, but the nearest one was 200 kilometres too far away to raise the issue. Roberts entered the interview room with a big grin on his face.

"You'll be pleased to hear that my agent's gonna be fine. Don't want to add a murder charge to your long list of misdemeanours, do we?"

Jember Abdi shrugged and looked away.

"Care to tell us why you were hanging around with Nazim Oktar?"

No reply.

"Or what you were planning with all those other Africans, sneaking into Turkey?"

Jember raised his eyes. "They just want a better life."

"At the expense of other people's lives?" asked Roberts.

"I never kill nobody. George Washington. Carved rock. Big deal. French government. Politicians lose their jobs. Boohoo. Terracotta Army. Toy soldiers die. So what?"

"Oktar killed somebody in Texas."

"I have nothing to do with him. He have nothing to do with me. We both use deserted village. Not ask each other why."

"I'm asking you. Why were you using that deserted village?"

Jember shook his head and rattled the handcuff links against his chair. "Because it is deserted. I told you. I smuggle people into Europe, from Africa. Nice quiet spot to land."

"You expect me to believe that's all there is to it? You are one of the most wanted men in three continents." Roberts took a slurp of tepid coffee from a plastic cup, watching Abdi's face.

"You haven't asked me why it is deserted."

Roberts looked in the two-way mirror and raised his eyebrows briefly. "I'm all ears."

"What in it for me?" asked Abdi.

Roberts laughed. "This is not a negotiation. This interview is not even happening, officially. If you talk now, you avoid all the unpleasant methods my colleagues have devised for forcing the truth from an unwilling prisoner. If you don't talk now, you'll talk later."

"And they say I the terrorist." Abdi shook his head. "At least gives me a smoke."

Roberts reached for a packet, took out a cigarette. As Abdi held it between his lips, the CIA man lit it and waited while the African took a deep drag. Roberts took the cigarette and rested it on the edge of an ashtray.

"I had been looking for a quiet base to use for smuggling people on Turkish coast. Towards end of last year, I heard rumour of a village that had been cursed, abandoned. I thought the Lord had answered my prayers. So, I went to investigate. People in the nearby villages, they not want to say anything at first. But finally, I found somebody who would talk." He paused while Roberts gave him another drag on his cigarette.

"Nine months ago, a pharmaceutical company had visited. They wanted to try out new drug on the whole village. They offered so much money, so much. Everybody suspicious. One condition. Nobody was allowed to leave the village once treatment started. No-one in. No-one out. Quarantine for a month. Most people said yes in the end. Money is money. Village was poor. Crops not grow in this heat."

"Go on," said Roberts.

"At end of month, the village was empty. No sign of villagers, no pharmaceutical company. But somebody did find a newly ploughed field. In it, big, big trench. That person dug up a body, but they not survive long enough to find any more bodies. Some people said it was a plague village. Others said it was cursed. Everybody stayed away after that."

"Everybody except you."

"Whatever happened there, not last forever. I started using it to deliver people to the promised land. Maybe the Lord sent a plague to help me. Like he sent to Egyptians in holy book. But one day I found one of the missing villagers, washed up on shore. In a raft he must have built to try escape. He had been dead long time. But his body still had a suit and breathing mask on. What you call in English? Haz-Mat? It had some markings on it." Abdi looked up at his captor.

"And?"

"You want to know what really happened in that village, you go check out ESCO."

PART II

He took his vorpal sword in hand
    Long time the manxome foe he sought

13

Arctic Circle, Norwegian-Swedish border

Captain Hamilton and three of the crew from *The Endeavour* were given diplomatic immunity passing through the border into Sweden. The guard had looked up and frowned when he saw the group wearing biking leathers. An unusual choice for visiting dignitaries but the clearance checked out. The E10 ran from the port of Narvik in Norway right through to Kiruna in Sweden. A route that had been used for over a hundred years, bringing iron ore out of the ground and onto the sea. The diplomatic cover that was extended to Hamilton had been the Norwegian government's way of saying thank you for saving the Carbon Capture and Storage facility. Now the captain had another assignment: to investigate ESCO.

Jember Abdi's testament had been confirmed. The CIA had shared the information with the British in accordance with the UKUSA *Five Eyes* agreement. The Brits had bio-chem experts who were closer to Turkey and able to go in there at once. As well as a dead assassin, a mass grave had been uncovered. Three dozen corpses. Men and women. Young and old. Some with soil beneath their fingernails. All had traces of a new strain of Ebola. The same variety that had been used up on Moon Lab One. So, the testing ground for this foul weapon had been found. Would the possible link to ESCO hold true as well?

ESCO was a well-respected Swedish company. Operations all over the world. And unusual operations at that. But everything seemed to be above board. Financial accounts were logged, taxes paid. Even the occasional interview on the global news channels from its owner, Mattias Larsson.

Sim Atkins had been desperate to head straight to Sweden and beat the truth out of Larsson. Wardle was having none of it. Not least because first, they needed some proof of a link to the Ebola incident. Second, because if it really was ESCO that was behind the attempt to kill off the Moon base, they in turn probably knew all about Sim helping to thwart that plan. Turning up at their headquarters in Kiruna would be like tattooing a target on your backside during the hunting season.

Captain Hamilton had chosen a Swedish member of his crew to bring along as well as petty officer Simpson and his medical officer. The Swede, Jansson, looked up at the brown mountain peaks on either side of the road. "I remember when you could cross-country ski up there, even in summer. Now. Even at this altitude, no snow." He shook his head slowly. The four electric motorbikes accelerated away in silence. The long, thin Torneträsk lake kept them company for over fifty kilometres along the left-hand side of the E10. A glorious sight with the mountains reflected in its still waters. Hamilton did not allow himself to dwell on the pleasures of such frivolous things. He had a serious task ahead.

Kiruna is one of the newest towns on the planet. When it was realised twenty years ago that the huge iron ore mine had caused irreversible subsidence in the old town, the difficult decision to start again had been made. As Captain Hamilton drove into the centre of the new settlement, every building except three were sparkling examples of modern architecture. The bikes passed the old red church and its distinctive wooden bell tower in their new location as the team drove towards the town centre.

Hamilton and his crew parked their bikes outside a large hotel, opposite the other building that had been saved from the old town: the Stadshus. The captain looked up at the square metal tower sticking out of the top of the city hall, like a giant robot pointing a finger skywards. On each side of the tower, a golden clock face halfway up, resembling a signet ring on the giant's knuckle.

The brand-new hotel exuded an air of luxury as soon as the team walked in through the grand glass doors. First, there was the heavy weave of the carpet beneath their feet. Second, the opulent crystal lights that hung from a high ceiling. Third, the disapproving look of the receptionist as soon as she saw the biker clothes and heavy paniers.

"May I help you, sir?" The receptionist's English accent was perfect. She smiled without seeming to use any of the muscles on her face.

"My friends and I need your best suite, for the week."

The woman started using her face muscles. "Why of course, sir. We'd be delighted to have you stay. The Queen Charlotte is on the top floor, with fine views across the countryside. May I take a swipe of your watch?"

The captain pressed his wrist band against the device and started filling in a form. He hesitated, trying to remember the details that Overseas Division had come up with as his cover. He let the rest of the team carry the kit bags as they were escorted to the suite. After they had been shown the spacious suite and left alone, Simpson turned to the captain.

"This must cost an arm and leg."

"Have to create the right impression, Simpson. If I'm going to pretend to need ESCO's services, they must think I'm a high roller."

"Probably best to ditch the leathers then, sir."

"Only the truly wealthy can get away with wearing what they like. It helps round out my legend. Eccentric businessman."

Jansson was looking out of the window. "Hey, look guys. You can see the spaceport from here." Out beyond the edge of town, a giant clamshell building sat at one end of a runway that stretched beyond their field of vision. Virgin Galactic's first spaceport in New Mexico had been such a success that a second one had been commissioned. Built quite recently, according to Jansson. Ticket prices had come down but were still way out of most people's league. New Kiruna was a base for visiting the Ice Hotel ('Open 365 days of the year!' as the pamphlet in the lobby had said), for going on Northern Light safaris and now for visiting space. No wonder the town could support a five-star hotel.

"This IRF, the Institute for Space Physics, that's near here isn't it?" asked Hamilton.

Jansson nodded.

"And it checks out? Nothing suspicious? No links to ESCO?"

The doctor spoke up. "Government run. They mostly study the ionosphere and magnetosphere. A lot of the early analysis of the Great Flux was done here. Highly respected."

"Yeah, well so is ESCO. If you believe their shiny brochure," said Simpson.

ESCO offered bespoke security arrangements, covering clients wherever they go in the world against all threats, be they kidnapping, terrorism, theft or cyber-attacks. The company's fees made their services viable only for ultra-high net-worth individuals or corporations. And there seemed to be plenty of paying customers if the rumours of Mattias Larsson's wealth were to be believed.

"I think you might have to seriously bling yourself up, sir, for this one."

The phone call was made, the story was fabricated and the appointment was scheduled for the next day. The captain spent the evening wandering around the new town, visiting bars with the rest of team, keeping ears open for any gossip about ESCO and eyes peeled for any possible staff that might want a drink bought and lips loosened.

"Course, when I was a student up here, it was all Carlsberg and juniper schnapps," said Jansson as he finished a bottle of very expensive Nigerian beer. They were seated around a carved wooden table, with three plates of tapas interspersed between the drinks.

"If you're going to keep on moaning about how everything used to be so much better, you can piss off back to *The Endeavour*, right now. It's getting on my tits," said the captain. He stared at Jansson for a moment and then looked across at Simpson. "No offence, course."

Simpson did not respond. She was intently watching a young blonde man weave through the crowded bar to a table near the back wall. He sat down on his own and tapped something into his bracelet.

"Not sure he's your type," said Hamilton.

Simpson's gaze shifted back to the people around her table, and she blushed slightly. "Shut up. I think he's ESCO. Sure I saw him tuck away a lanyard as he came in the front entrance. Thought I caught their logo on it. Could've been mistaken."

"Worth checking out." The captain handed her a €100 note.

"In case your womanly charms aren't enough on their own." He winked.

She rolled her eyes and grabbed the money.

"In my day," started Jansson. And then stopped as he saw the captain stare at him. "My turn to buy a round, yes?"

The alcohol kept flowing and the volume for the music cranking out of the bar's sound system kept rising. Simpson finally squeezed back through the crowd to join their table and flopped into her chair.

"Jeez that was hard work." She looked at Jansson. "Not natural talkers, you Vikings, are you?" Turning to the captain, she said "He finally admitted to working at ESCO. But whenever I asked him about what he did there, he clammed up and started looking around the room. 'We're not supposed to discuss anything' was all he would say."

"Shame. OK. We stick to the plan. Jansson and Simpson you look after Bill tomorrow, while me and the doc take the appointment." He finished his beer and slammed the glass down. "Let's get some sleep."

Simpson paused. "Think I might stick around for a bit longer," she said looking over at her new blonde friend.

Captain Hamilton and the doctor took a taxi to ESCO headquarters. Eccentricity was one thing, but biking leathers were more likely to get searched. The captain's business suit conveyed an aura of respectability. The taxi took them back along the E10 road and pulled off opposite the Kiirunavaara peak that signified the hub of the iron ore mine. A peak that had gradually been shaved lower as the mining operation followed the seam down into one side of the mountain. Hamilton had read up about it earlier. The mine was still producing millions of tonnes every year and had reserves that would easily last into the next century. Clouds of steam billowed out from the processing plant near the top of the hill, until the arctic wind tugged, fractured and finally dispersed them to invisibility.

The taxi drove between crumbling houses in the deserted old town. Some buildings had merely lost roof tiles and layers of paint to the weather of a dozen winters. Others had succumbed to the subsidence, dented and askew on their plots like bouncy castles that had lost their air. As the car approached the centre of town, the way was blocked by a fortified gateway. Two armed guards and heavy barriers were the obvious deterrents to anybody wanting to crash the party. But the captain could see additional posts that would rise out of the ground at the touch of a button and a rolled-up stinger ready to deploy. A tall metal fence stretched off to either side of the gateway, following the path of an old street.

The man on the gate checked the captain's details and waved the car through to the main reception inside the complex. Once past the fence, the captain could see some people making use of a firing range, letting off rounds from automatic pistols, scrambling through ruined houses. The reception building had clearly not been part of the old town. Highly polished silver metal beams melded with wooden panels and smoky glass to create a shape that resembled the Kiirunavaara.

"May I ask what your needs are, Professor?" asked Precious Osundare. She had greeted Hamilton and his colleague in reception and explained the services offered by ESCO once they were sat around a conference table. Somebody had already come to take their order for drinks as glowing testaments from previous clients played on the wall behind Precious.

Hamilton wished that Overseas Division had not given him such an honorific. He preferred appearing more stupid than he really was, not the other way around. That kept people off guard.

"You don't seem very well protected for somebody concerned about their safety," continued Precious. She clicked a button on the desk in front of her and an image of Captain Hamilton appeared on the wall. The image was like an X-ray in colour, showing a skeleton, the metal of the Captain's belt buckle, his wrist bracelet and the rims of the fake glasses he was wearing.

"How dare you!" he said.

"Sorry Professor, but we have to check all our visitors for guns. And it does at least demonstrate some of the technology at our disposal."

The captain shifted uncomfortably in his seat. "I'm not in danger yet. But soon. When my invention is revealed to the world. Then I'll make many enemies."

"I see. And may I enquire about this invention?" asked Precious.

Hamilton shook his head. "Strictly confidential for another five weeks."

"Anything that might affect our security brief?"

"I'll need cover for all regions of the world. But before we go into those details, can I ask to see the facilities here?"

As they were escorted down some stairs into a huge open plan hall, it became clear that the majority of the headquarters was underground.

"We had to dig out a lot of unstable sub-soil. Pin it, prop it. Seemed easier to build down than up after all that work. Except for the practice grounds, of course."

"Seems like you could train an army here," said Hamilton, watching Precious's face carefully.

"Or members of a secret service," she replied.

Hamilton's smile froze for a moment as Precious showed them into a large room filled with screens and desks. The largest screens on the far wall showed a series of news channels and scrolling tab feeds from around the world. A map tracked the split between day and night across the planet. Seated at desks, staff were watching smaller screens that seemed to have live video feeds. Glimpses of people in business meetings, at home eating, in the back of limousines. With a client name, time and location superimposed on each scene.

"This is our hub for monitoring each of our client's welfare. If a story breaks, our systems analyse the news and alert the guards protecting any of our clients affected. We also inform our corporate clients in case they need to adjust their operations or alert their staff."

"Impressive," said Hamilton. As they left the room, his wrist bracelet beeped. A message scrolled across. *'They've killed Bill.'* He stopped walking. The hawk-like drone the captain had designed was called Bill. It had been used on many previous missions. "Shit."

"Sorry?" Precious turned and waited for the captain to catch up. "Oh, just some bad news about one of the experiments that my team were trying out this morning."

"So disappointing when you can't validate your hypothesis, isn't it?" said Precious with a smile that seemed more playful than sympathetic. "Shall we?" She beckoned them down another set of stairs and led them through to a viewing gallery. On the other side of a long window several people, wearing goggles and white coats, tinkered with test tubes and microscopes. Others were controlling little robots inside a sealed chamber as chemicals were mixed and compounds created.

Hamilton stared through the glass, watching the people work without really paying attention. He was trying to process the message from Simpson and Jansson. The attempt to use Bill and its nano-bots to infiltrate the headquarters had failed. And Precious's last statement... If she knew who they were already, why hadn't they been imprisoned? Or worse. Would they be allowed to leave at the end of this tour?

The doctor asked about the work that was going on in the lab. "Trialling improved antidotes for every known toxin and developing anti-biotics that can still defeat the super bugs. Like I said earlier, we protect our clients against all possible attacks."

Hamilton made a mental note of where this facility was, within the overall complex. Having descended two levels, turned corners along a series of corridors, it was quite hard to visualize. He wondered if that was deliberate.

There was another room filled with designs for gadgets. One technician was working on a miniature re-breather that Captain Hamilton was especially keen to see. He used his engineering background to ask some detailed questions. But the worker just apologized and said that she was not allowed to answer any technical queries.

They returned to the conference room via a lift. By now, Hamilton was sweating, wondering when the snake sitting opposite him would strike. But Precious just smiled and asked what he thought of their facilities.

"Rather impressive. You and the team seem very knowledgeable, ready for anything."

"Most protection work is about preventing an attack in the first place. And for that we spend a lot of time getting to know our clients – their friends and their enemies."

Hamilton stood up. "Well, this has been great. My assistant here will be in touch to sort out the paper work. Will I ever get to meet Mr Larsson?"

"I can't promise anything. He's such a private person."

Precious shook her head. "He'll go to any lengths to stay out of the spotlight."

As they walked back to the reception desk, Hamilton fiddled with his cufflinks. He kept scanning the corridor ahead to see if some guards would appear to take him away. At least he had one gadget of his own that might enhance a bid for freedom. The doctor caught his eye, looking down at the cufflinks and nodded by the tiniest tilt of his head. Every muscle in Hamilton's body felt tight as they left the building. Two armed guards patrolled the area in front of the entrance, but were looking away from the captain. A car pulled up and Precious opened the door for the captain.

"A pleasure meeting you, Ms Osundare."

"The pleasure was all mine, Professor." She closed the door after him.

14

Kathmandu, Nepal

The pang of homesickness that had struck Freda in the Russian prison was gnawing at her stomach again. As she, Gopal and Rabten approached Kathmandu she could sense the eagerness, she could see the joy in her companions. Effervescing, like freshly poured champagne. Fingers being pointed, names being shared. She could not even tell if the men were talking about people or places.

The sprawling mass of the capital of Nepal, with its converging rivers, was laid out before them as they approached from the East, along the Araniko Highway. The truck dropped them off near the centre of the city when it stopped to deliver its consignment. They thanked the driver and walked the last couple of miles.

It had been six years since Freda had spent time in Kathmandu. Back then she had stayed for a month while Sim's punctured lung had mended. So, she knew the roads they were walking along. The noises were louder than she remembered. Drivers were still shouting 'jam, jam' in the midst of traffic chaos. There were more stray dogs lolloping through the gutters, nosing through the bowls that locals put out to feed them. Freda wasn't sure which smelt worse, the disease-ridden dogs or the gutters.

The tourist season was in full swing, judging from the broad mix of Caucasian and Asian people, along with the meandering stroll of groups whose attention was anywhere but the pavement in front of them. They were impossible to overtake, not without risking life and limb on the roads or wading through the effluence of the gutters.

Rabten offered to stop at the market for some food while Gopal led Freda back to his house. They passed a large group of men who were weaving across the road, singing as they went. Freda thought that they looked a bit different from the locals, perhaps Chinese. One of them bumped into a local on the far side of the road. There was a brief scuffle and then the Nepali man broke free and ran off. One of the drunks picked up a bowl of dog food from outside a house and hurled it after the retreating local. Other people in the street glanced up briefly and then carried on with their daily routine.

"What's going on?" said Freda.

Gopal grunted. "Started a couple of years ago. When the Chinese factories were busy sacking all their workers, replacing them with robots. Nothing much for the labourers to do. Too many lack the education to re-train. So, they come here to drink cheap alcohol."

"Don't the authorities do anything?"

"Yeah, they turn a blind eye. Been in bed with the Chinese since '25. Can't even ban them travelling here."

"That's terrible," said Freda.

The Gurkha shrugged. "Brings in some yuan. Better than being paid in crypto-crap."

· · ·

Gopal shoved the front door open. It had swollen slightly since the spring. Fortunately, the key had been in its usual hiding place, taped to the underside of the mail box. Freda smiled, wondering how long a house in London would remain un-burgled if the owners ever tried that trick. As they moved into the house, Gopal went around raising the blinds and throwing open windows. Freda watched him look in the fridge. Something that may have once resembled food was hastily discarded.

She remained in the main room, her eyes drawn down to the rug where she had saved Sim's life. Well, really, where he had saved her life by flinging himself at that traitor, Chung. The knife wound had almost been fatal, but Freda had managed to keep Sim alive long enough for the ambulance to get here. She wondered how he was getting on now.

Gopal came back into the room. He was about to say something to Freda, but there was a noise from upstairs. Freda's heart started pounding. She slapped her hand over her own mouth to muffle the panicked cry that wanted to escape. This was exactly how Chung's attack had begun. She looked around the room and, once again, found herself picking up the poker from the fireplace.

There was definitely somebody coming down the stairs. A young Nepali man charged into the room. He was brandishing a curved blade above his head, shouting something that Freda could not understand because her Babel app was switched off.

The man continued to shout, standing in the middle of the room and gesturing towards the front door.

"Hey, that's my knife," said Gopal in English.

The young man hesitated for a moment and Gopal used it as an opportunity to dive at him, pinning the man to the ground. Gopal knocked the knife out of the man's hand. Freda advanced towards the wrestling pair, ready to use the poker if the man wriggled free. A woman launched herself at Freda from just behind the doorway while Freda was focused on the two men. Freda's ankle twisted awkwardly. She tried to beat the woman off with the tool but could not swing it properly. The woman backed away from Freda. As she did so, her foot touched the dropped knife. She bent down to pick it up. Freda was hobbling, unable to put weight on the sprained ankle. She swung the poker, but the woman dodged out of the way and grinned as she slashed the knife in front of her. For a moment everyone was still. The quiet sound of panting breaths was interrupted by a baby's cry from upstairs. The woman's eyebrows creased and she glanced back towards the stairs. The young man's face went bright red as he forced himself out from under Gopal's grasp.

"What is going on here?" asked Freda.

Gopal said something that Freda could not understand to the man and woman. They replied in the same language and then the three of them conversed a little more. The woman dropped the knife. Gopal turned to look at Freda. "That's their child upstairs. They thought we'd come to take away their daughter. They've been squatting here for a few weeks."

By the time Rabten had returned with some food, the couple had explained their situation. A relationship that neither family had welcomed. An unexpected pregnancy. And a job that barely paid enough to feed and clothe them. The man had walked home from work many times past Gopal's house and had noticed it was unoccupied. After the baby had been born, they had run away from their families and had been squatting here ever since.

"What do you think?" asked Gopal to Rabten. They were speaking English so they could discuss the couple's future openly in front of them.

"They seem nice. Sleeping rough with young baby, not nice," replied Rabten.

"This isn't a hotel. We don't have a spare room."

"I sleep on couch, it's OK." The ex-monk bent down and patted the sofa.

"Maybe they could look after the house when you're away on missions," suggested Freda. Rabten nodded.

Gopal's shoulders sagged. "OK, OK, you win. They get to stay." He held out his hand to the young man who shook it vigorously. The young woman smiled and wiped away a tear.

For the next couple of days, Gopal, Rabten and the young Nepali couple fussed around the house, tidying and stocking up on essential supplies. The couple had been trying to keep their presence a secret when they were squatting here, so had never dared light a fire, open curtains or even use the lights. There was quite a collection of dirt and rubbish to expunge. Freda spent that time resting. During the brief wrestle with the young woman Freda had sprained her ankle badly.

Although Rabten seemed happy sleeping on the couch, Freda could sense that Gopal was starting to regret letting the couple stay. He had given his own bedroom to Freda, so he was sharing the sitting room with Rabten. On the third morning, Gopal had gone upstairs to wash but returned straight away, muttering under his breath.

"Why don't you and Rabten go for a hike in the hills? Get some space. Enjoy the weather, savour your homeland," said Freda.

"What'll you do?" he replied.

"Stay here and keep an eye on things. Besides, my ankle's still sore. I can check in with Wardle. See what they need us for next." Gopal had not needed much persuading. His hiking gear was packed within half an hour. He left some local currency for Freda and the couple to use while they were gone. Freda warned him to keep a low profile, in case the Russians or the Terror Formers were still searching for them.

Gopal had managed to coax Joanna, his old 4x4, into life and dragged it west to the Annapurna conservation area. The snow on the slopes was surprisingly deep for this time of year. The peaks of the mountains here were white all year round, but there must have been some freak storms while they'd been away to get thick snow at such low altitude.

The pair of OD agents set off from a local village, leaving Joanna behind, to climb the white slopes. As Gopal turned to admire the view down the valley, he noticed an unusual movement. One of the pylons carrying electricity to the village fell, landing almost on top of a building in the centre of the settlement. Rabten turned to watch too as the crashing noise reverberated up the mountainside. There was a blue spark and then flashes of yellow. Gopal and Rabten had already started to run back down the slope when the flames began to lick around the building next to the fallen pylon.

By the time they had returned to the village, most of the residents were crowding around the fire. Women were wailing, tearing at their hair, some having to be held back from the flames by the men. The only entrance to the building had been blocked by the pylon and the fire had taken hold all around the wooden building. Barely audible above the crackle of the flames and the anguished yells of the women, there were more voices crying out. High-pitched, hysterical shrieks. Children were stuck inside, soon to be burnt alive.

Rabten tried to get close enough to smash a window, but the heat from the fire drove him back. Gopal stood there, almost transfixed by the pitiful sight. There were no emergency services that could get here in time. He looked around, desperately hoping for an idea. Something. His face creased and he took a deep breath, nodding to himself.

"Tell the villagers to clear the square. I'm going to bring down the mountain," he shouted to Rabten, running towards his jeep. He jumped in and revved the engine. "Don't let me down now, Joanna."

Gopal drove the 4x4 up the mountainside, skittering along a snowy path that snaked back and forth. He kept glancing back at the village, checking on the progress of the flames and Rabten's efforts to clear people away. As the path crossed above a large area of virgin snow, Gopal stopped the vehicle. He stroked the dashboard and kissed the steering wheel. Getting out, he tore a strip of cloth from his shirt and wrapped it around a stick. He opened up the petrol cap and poked the stick inside. Once it had soaked up some fuel, Gopal twisted the cloth around the stick once more, angling it to form a long wick. He jammed it into the petrol tank. Lighting the end, he ran for cover.

Before he could get a safe distance, the jeep exploded. Gopal was lifted off his feet and sailed through the air. He landed in a pile of snow, scraping his hands and knees on the stone beneath. He sat up and knocked the side of his head with his hand, trying to get rid of the ringing sound in his ears. Looking up he smiled as he saw the snowfield accelerating down the hill, heading straight for the middle of the village. His view quickly disappeared as fine powdery snow filled the air.

The sound in his ears stopped, and he realised that the noise of the avalanche had stopped too. The air began to clear. Between puffy clouds of white powder, he could see the roof of the wooden building and the end of the pylon sticking out of a new heap of snow. The flames were out. Gopal got to his feet and started to run down the hill. The villagers had re-appeared and were already digging the snow away, desperate to get to their children.

By the time they had cleared an entrance to the building, the emergency services had arrived. And then came the press. The villagers were quick to praise Gopal's heroic efforts. His hands were scraped raw and there was a trickle of blood coming from his left ear as he stood in front of the cameras, explaining how he'd got the avalanche started. The cameras were there as the children were pulled free of the buried village hall. The men in the village lifted Gopal onto their shoulders and marched him around, cheering their saviour. The short film even made the national TV that evening. Hardly the low profile that Freda had suggested.

A computer on the far side of the world analysed the footage, among the thousands of news clips it examined throughout the world, all day and every day. Its facial recognition software found a match and an alert was pinged to its operator.

15

———

North Korea

A convoy of vehicles drove out of a vast underground cavern, through a heavily guarded entrance, into the darkness of night. The Milky Way spread its brilliance across a sky unspoiled by any light pollution. One of the guards at the gate looked up briefly and was shocked when he glanced back down to look through the big glass windows of the truck's cabin. It was empty. The drivers of the armoured vehicles in front and behind the truck were human, but unable to acknowledge the guard from the slits in their thick-skinned cars. And their passengers were locked inside windowless steel boxes, too busy checking weapons to worry about lonely sentries or the astronomical delights above them.

The driver of the armoured vehicle at the front of the convoy was following the route given to him at the last minute in a sealed envelope. The roads were clear, of course. It had been a long time since non-military vehicles had been given a fuel allowance. UN sanctions still counted for something these days. There had been a brief surge in traffic when sanctions were temporarily lifted in 2020. But then the North Koreans had re-started their nuclear research and the world had noticed.

Rumbling through the countryside, the driver was concentrating on the map and his restricted view of the road. It would have been much easier to drive with the turret fully open, but the orders from on high were typically paranoid. 'Remain buttoned-up for the whole journey.' Such paranoia back-fired on this occasion because the lead vehicle simply never noticed when the huge covered truck behind slipped off the designated route.

The computer controlling the truck did not notice the deviation either. The Chinese equivalent of the GPS network, the Beidou-3, had been hastily re-assembled after the Great Flux had destroyed all of the satellites in the `20s. Now the robot driver was using the system to ensure it stuck to the precise route programmed into its software. What the computer did not realise was that the real signals from satellites overhead were being overwhelmed by a powerful nearby transmission. The false positioning data forced the truck to veer off course without even realising anything was wrong.

The plan to hijack this truck had one weakness. The armoured car tailing the truck had not been given route instructions. The driver had been told simply to follow the truck in front. But there was a chance that, as the truck turned off the main road, this driver might notice that the first armoured car had driven straight on. A slim chance, given the limited peripheral vision afforded by the driving slits, and on this occasion a chance that went begging. The driverless truck continued on its way to a destination that seemed correct, but was by now miles off course. The computer onboard did not care that the armoured vehicle in front had gone. These were not part of its instructions. Finally, it stopped in a deserted lay-by. The tailing armoured car tried to radio to its companion vehicle. But the signal that was over-whelming Beidou-3 on board the truck was also blocking radio communications. The source of all this interference was a black van that had been tailing the convoy for the past 25 kilometres. The van driver's night-vision goggles ensured there was no need for headlights and without any roadside lights, the dark vehicle was almost invisible under the moonless sky.

The leader in the black van was called Ivan 'Shagger' Jenkins and he was used to working deep inside hostile territory. Long-range reconnaissance with the Australian Special Air Service Regiment had been a job once, one with transferrable skills as it turned out. He clicked a button on his wrist tab and a timer began to glow with accumulated seconds. "Right team. Eight minutes, maximum."

Doors to the black van opened, and the five occupants dropped to the ground in silence. They hurried over to the armoured vehicle and one of them threw a gas canister in through the driver's slit. Another one of the team welded the rear doors shut. As the top hatch of the turret popped open, two arms reached up and dropped grenades into the vehicle. The dull crump of explosions and a slight shift of the armoured car on its wheels were the only external signs of lives cut short.

The now defenceless truck surrendered its cargo in silence. Ivan hissed orders to the rest of the team. Two of the thieves unclipped the cables and threw back the tarpaulin, uncovering a pair of aluminium crates. A third person ran a Geiger counter over the two boxes. A spike registered for one of them; nothing worse than the equivalent of a full CT scan. Dosimeter badges on the robbers' clothes showed that they would be keeping a careful watch on their exposure. A fourth member of the team had, by now, strapped on an exo-skeleton and made short work of lifting the crates into the black van. Ivan looked at his watch. Seven and a half minutes. He surveyed the scene and nodded.

The combination locks on the crates could be dealt with later. Right now, the entire country's armed forces would be mounting a search for a missing nuclear warhead.

Ivan slammed the rear doors closed and ran to the passenger door. "It is time to disappear, people. Let's rock and roll."

16

Birmingham

Wardle read Captain Hamilton's report on ESCO. The medical research facilities certainly seemed capable of producing a new strain of the Ebola virus. But proving any link would be nigh on impossible. Their headquarters were well protected. Hamilton's cover had been blown and his drone destroyed. Another mission heading for failure. Wardle's counterpart in MI6 would, no doubt, take great delight in pointing this out to the bureaucrats. He could see Wrenshaw's smug face even now, that caterpillar he called a moustache curled into a grin. The desk creaked as Wardle's fist crashed onto the surface.

But then the rage subsided. Hamilton had been lucky to get out alive from the sounds of it. Maybe letting him go had revealed a weakness. Perhaps the head of ESCO, Mattias Larsson, was so supremely confident in his own safety that he felt he could toy with members of the British secret service. In hubris there was still hope. Wardle opened up another report.

Feinberg knocked on the door and entered, holding that infernal roll tab again.

"Sir, there's a lot of chatter on the Terror Formers' wapp about some big new mission."

"I thought those conversations were encrypted. That's why all the terrorists use them, isn't it?"

"Impossible to crack, yes. But my roll tab is a member of the wapp group."

"Anything more concrete to go on this time?"

"Even in their encrypted messages they're being cautious. But given where the messages are most frequent and references to local time, I would say it's probably close to China or Japan."

"Not again." The Director opened the drawer in his desk, looked at the new whisky bottle but resisted the temptation. He saw that Feinberg had noticed, closed the drawer and looked away, refusing to make eye contact. "Wait. One of the reports I was just reading... where is it? Ah yes. Sat Division is picking up an enormous amount of activity in North Korea right now. Seems like the whole army is on manoeuvres. The South Koreans are pulling their hair out, demanding an explanation. The Japanese have put their missile defence system on full alert. And the Chinese have even issued a denial that anything's going on."

"Can't be a coincidence. But why have the Terror Formers gone and kicked that hornets' nest?"

"I don't know, Feinberg. But keep monitoring. This is your only priority for the time being. Got it?"

Sim and Rosie were at home, playing 3D scrabble. The long daylight hours were preventing Rosie from going to bed early. But she was too tired to go out. So, a board game for the third time this week. Sim tried to teach her how to play a strategy game called *Where's My Oil Drum*, but she had never been into complicated rules. At school, Rosie had excelled at the arts, and languages in particular. Which meant – much to Sim's annoyance – that she usually beat him at word games.

Rosie put down cubes that spelt out BUMP.

"Triple letter for the B, and a double word score. That makes, nine plus seven, times two, 32."

"Alright, clever clogs." Sim stacked cubes for CRI on top of the

B. "Eight points."

NAP and Y were added by Rosie around the P. "Twelve points, oh and the Y was on a double letter, so that's 16." She took a sip of cranberry juice.

Sim rotated the board through 90 degrees and put S in front of NAPPY. Three more cubes magnetised themselves to the S to form SCAN. "Thirteen plus six and a single rotation makes 29. I'm in the lead for once."

It didn't last.

Sim and Rosie strode around the centre of Dornoch in the morning sun, hand-in-hand. Rosie beamed at a few people whose names Sim couldn't quite remember. They went into a clothes shop and Rosie tried on some maternity trousers.

"Can you see my tummy in these?"

Sim shook his head. Add a pair of oversized shoes and Rosie would look more like a clown in the circus than a proudly pregnant woman. But he kept the thought to himself.

"Hmm, no good." Rosie went to choose a different pair.

Afterwards, they went for lunch in their favourite café. Rosie had double helpings of smashed avocado, while Sim had his usual fisherman's pie and a side order of neeps.

"Dya think we need a bigger house?" he asked.

Rosie wrinkled her nose. "What for? The bairn can start in a Moses basket in our room. And we'll clear out the junk room, paint it up when the little one's ready for a cot."

"What about when our parents come to visit?"

Rosie shrugged and looked out of the window. "There's always the Castle Hotel for your mum and dad. They can afford it. Mine live close enough – they probably won't stay the night." They finished their meal in silence, exchanging an occasional smile.

A smudge of grey above Struie hill was all that was left of the daylight as Sim rode his motorbike to the Sat Division monitoring station at Wilkhaven lighthouse. The new guard opened the barrier for him. Sim wondered when the guard would stop being thought of as new. After all, Rusty Jimmy had retired a couple of years ago. As he parked his bike, Sim looked up into the evening sky. Cyan was merging with sapphire and cobalt towards the east. There, to the right of the lighthouse tower, was the silver crescent moon. A sickle blade slicing away at his heart, reminding him of terrible events and the vow he'd made to his dead son.

Sim had barely got settled at his desk when an urgent order came through. Wardle needed him in Birmingham the next day, to act as handler for an undercover agent operating in Asia. Painting the nursery would have to wait.

Wardle was enjoying the effects of summer weather on the amount of flesh displayed in Cathedral Square. A welcome, if guilty, distraction from the chaos building up on his desk back at the office. Wardle's assistant came to join him on the park bench. It had been twenty-four hours since North Korea lit up.

"Unusual choice for a lunchtime meeting, isn't it, Tom? I thought you were busy preparing the report for the bureaucrats. You know, keeping the department from being closed down. Quite important, that assignment."

"Sorry, Sir, but I needed to get you out of the office. Away from unwelcome eyes and ears."

"Seems like there are plenty of those around us right now."

The young man looked around. "The couple over there exchanging saliva have been going out for three years now. They work a mile apart but meet up every lunchtime for that." He pointed at their horizontal embrace. "The ice cream seller is Lizzie Hind. She's been selling here for two years. The tramp asleep on that bench is Roger Smith. Unemployed for five years, homeless for most of that time. I've got a pair of eyes at the top of the bell tower checking out passing footfall. I think we're safe."

"Why all this caution? I had my office swept yesterday."

"Who's the mole?" Tom shrugged at his own question. "Until we know that, I say we take full precautions. About everything."

"OK, fine. So, what do we need to discuss in such privacy?"

"We need to be careful with the intel we're getting from Feinberg's roll tab."

"Why do you say that?"

"What if they know? The Terror Formers. Maybe they've realised a roll tab has gone missing, been hacked into. Maybe they're spreading wild rumours about some mission in North Korea to put us off the scent."

"Possible, yes. But Sat Division has confirmed all that activity."

"Doesn't have to be anything to do with the Terror Formers, though. Perfect timing for some *legerdemain*."

"Well yes, I agree. Which is why I've already assigned an agent to check out what's happening on the ground."

Tom's eyes opened a little wider for a moment and then his face went back into poker mode. "That's great. Who's the lucky person? Wait, don't tell me. It's Jung Li, isn't it?"

Wardle took a slurp from his coffee cup.

"That figures. Good choice, sir. Of course, we need to be cautious about the roll tab for another reason."

Wardle screwed up his cup and started walking back to the office.

Tom caught up. "The mole, sir. It could be Feinberg. Recruited from overseas. Already been sacked by one agency, hasn't he?"

"That's was the Israelis' loss. And our gain."

"I'm sure you're right, sir. But if we're going to keep this department open, we can't afford another cock-up."

"You think I don't know that? I was catching Daesh agents when you were nothing more than a swipe right on your mum's Tinder app."

Tom grabbed his boss' arm, holding him back for a minute, before they reached the pedestrian crossing. "The snatch mission on the Canary Islands. Very high-level. Very well planned. But they still got away, didn't they? I reckon they must have been tipped off."

Wardle stared down at his assistant's hand until he was released. "Your concerns are duly noted." He threw his uneaten sandwich towards the bin. It hit the rim. The wrapping unfurled itself mid-air and the contents spilled over the ground. Wardle wondered whether the tramp would notice before the pigeons did. And then he crossed the road without even checking whether the traffic had stopped for him.

17

———————

Pyongyang, North Korea

Jung Li had been briefed by Wardle and Sim had been assigned as his handler. Jung Li realised it was a crappy job for an agent like Atkins, who had been such a star of the department. At his beck and call, any time of day or night, for the entire duration of the mission. Either Wardle was desperate or he was punishing Atkins for some misdemeanour that had not reached the gossip channels in Overseas Division.

Jung Li stepped down onto the platform after spending 36 hours on the train from Beijing. It should have been much quicker than that, but the power kept failing on the tracks once they had crossed the border into North Korea. Somebody had whispered something about electricity shortages but wouldn't be drawn further on the topic. Jung Li saw no solar farms or wind turbines as the train trundled through the countryside. Sights that were so commonplace in other parts of the world. Maybe it was not possible to build them with the ongoing sanctions squeezing imported materials.

Border officials had confiscated his roll tab, assuring him

that he would get it back when he left the country, and had let him rent a North Korean basic version that ran off the local network. That would be no use for keeping in touch with Atkins. The Overseas Division agent hefted a smart suit bag over his shoulder and made his way to the taxi rank. No sign of driverless cars here. Plenty of men and women clamouring for a fare.

The route to Ryugyong hotel went along Changgwang Street. Jung Li watched the masses of people cycling to work, heads bowed under bamboo hats that tried to protect them from the worst of the summer rain. His taxi was almost the only car on the road. Despite these signs of economic hardship, the hotel was still impressive. A modern tall building, like a three-sided arrow head sticking out of the ground. The approach across Potong Bridge made the most of the view of the splendid tower.

Despite the country's pariah state, there had been no trouble getting Jung Li's paperwork sorted to gain entry into Pyongyang and even to walk around the capital city taking photographs of the monuments. So that's what he did for the rest of the day, despite the hot, muggy weather and frequent showers. He visited the great slab of a building that was the Kumsusan Palace of the Sun. He went to the Arch of Triumph, opposite the old football stadium. The local people did not bat an eyelid at his presence. But when he tried to take a photograph of one of the government buildings, a guard came rushing over. He grabbed the camera off Jung Li and deleted the photo, shouting while he did so. The Babel app translated a warning not to take photographs of sensitive infrastructure.

Jung Li had seen all these sites before and knew the rules about what could and could not be photographed. But he also knew the local government would be tracking his borrowed phone, maybe even watching him via CCTV. He was trying to look like a businessman visiting the city for the first time.

Later that evening, he allowed the hotel to book him a table at a restaurant near the Juche Tower. This time he crossed over the Potong Bridge and then the bigger Okryu Bridge that spanned the mighty Taedong river. From the bridge, Jung Li could see the tall granite column lit up brightly against the dark clouds of the evening and at its pinnacle, the red torch flaming into the night. He wondered about the electricity shortages on the trains and about how much power this monument required to be illuminated.

The meal started with a cold-water noodle broth called Naengmyeon. Jung Li took a very small spoonful and quickly went back for another. He recognised one of the other customers; a female member of staff at the Ryugyong hotel. He doubted that was a coincidence. The next course was translated by his Babel app as Trout soup. Broth followed by soup? Still, the fish was delicious. Which was more than could be said for the wine. Another customer, a man in an olive boiler suit and long leather boots, arrived and sat on the far side of the dining room. Jung Li looked at the mostly empty tables between them and tried to raise a glass in the other man's direction, but he wasn't watching.

After broth and soup, Jung Li needed a toilet break and went off to find the gents. The other man was entering the rest room as Jung Li left. They brushed past each other and the agent felt a folded piece of paper thrust into his hand. He took it without looking at it, tucked it into a pocket and sat down to finish off his meal.

He wondered about offering his shadow from the hotel a lift back, but thought that might not go down too well. Back in his hotel room, he got ready for bed. He pulled the duvet up over his head and unfolded the paper, illuminating the message with a micro torch hidden under his nail. It gave the name of a guide who would be willing to show him around the rest of the country.

He was supposed to report back in to Atkins with an update, but with his roll tab confiscated and with little news to share, Jung Li decided to leave more risky methods of communication for later in the mission.

After a tasteless breakfast, Jung Li went to the front desk of the hotel and asked about getting a guide to take him to places outside of the capital.

"Of course, we can help you with that, sir. But you will need to get clearance for your route and destinations."

"That's fine," he said. "I have been recommended a particular guide. Would you see if they're available?" He handed the piece of paper over.

The receptionist frowned, looked at the name and then smiled. "Not a problem, let me see if she is free."

It took twenty-four hours to get approval for his travel plans. Back along the route taken by the railway line, towards the city of Anju and then veering right towards the mountainous interior of the country. Jung Li was posing as a film producer for a wildlife documentary company. Some remote parts of the North Korean mountains contained species and behaviour no longer seen anywhere else in the world. The authorities had not been keen at first but Jung Li, with the help of his guide, assured them that this was just a scouting mission to select some sites for filming. All of which could be vetted before he came back with camera crews, and of course, with the substantial hard currency fee they would pay for using these venues.

Jung Li's guide was called An Sun-Hi and she did not speak much on the drive to Anju and then onwards to the town of Kuwollim. Progress was slow. The jeep's ancient engine struggled on the hills. And the further they got away from the capital, the more the roads deteriorated. Some parts were almost impassable due to standing water. It was still raining. It didn't seem to have stopped since Jung Li had arrived in North Korea.

As they crossed over the bridge into the town, Jung Li could see that it was surrounded on three sides by the broad sweep of a river. Off to the right of the main area of the town there was a large railway station and a modern runway that seemed wholly inappropriate for such a small settlement.

An Sun-Hi pointed to the runway and station. "That area military. We get in big trouble if we go take a look."

"I thought that was the whole point of this trip."

"Hah ha ha, funny joke," she said, glancing up at the coupling around the rear-view mirror and pressing her lips together.

Later that night, they made love. Jung Li was pleasantly surprised when the guide sneaked into his bedroom and slipped under the covers, naked. But then he wondered if his request for a 'special' sort of guide had been misunderstood by his contact back in the capital.

"They find us together in the middle of the night, it is better we are fucking than discussing plans to spy on army," she said.

So, they whispered their plans in each other's ears, sweating in the dark, between the groans and thrusts. Nobody disturbed them, but at breakfast the next day, Jung Li could have sworn the waiter was smirking at them. Thin walls? Hidden cameras? Living in a country like this certainly made you paranoid, he thought.

The roads by now were little more than dirt tracks, heavy with mud, winding back and forth between the steep green hillsides that crinkled all of the countryside. Jung Li retrieved a pair of spectacles from his rucksack, and flicked on a micro switch hidden beneath the rubber nose bridge. He put on the glasses and waited for the connection to establish itself. While he was doing this, An Sun-Hi pulled off the track and parked the jeep behind some trees. Jung Li pulled some thin, strong rope from the lining of his rucksack and wrapped it around his torso. He took two fat pens out of the bag, putting them in one of his trouser pockets. And pulled something out of each of the heels in his boots, putting them in the other pocket. They started hiking over one of the hills. Near the top, a voice spoke in Jung Li's ear.

"J6, J6, this is SA. Do you copy?"

"Loud and clear, Sim," said Jung Li. A readout appeared on the lens of his glasses. Connection with Birmingham established.

"Nice view you have. Anything to report yet?"

"Negative. We're approaching the site now."

They descended the other side of the peak and were approaching a road when the guide signalled for them to stop. She dropped to the ground, crouching behind a tree trunk. Jung Li copied her. Three soldiers armed with automatic rifles were tramping through the forest. As they passed, a raccoon dog started clambering down the tree that Jung Li was hiding behind. It growled as it saw the agent blocking its path to the ground. One of the soldiers, a little apart from his comrades, turned to see what had made the noise and spotted Jung Li. He shouted to his comrades and raised his rifle.

A flash of metal left Jung Li's hand and the soldier dropped to the ground, a throwing star protruding from his throat. The silent attack confused the other soldiers who looked around for the attacker. The agent ran across to the corpse and grabbed the rifle before diving for cover behind a different tree. Bullets spat into its trunk and bits of wood splintered off. An Sun-Hi threw a rock that hit one of the soldiers on the side of the head. He turned to fire at her, giving Jung Li just enough time to poke the barrel of his rifle around the tree trunk and kill the second soldier. One left. Not as brave as the others. But more sensible. He started running down the hill, weaving between the trees. Jung Li raised his rifle and stared down the sights. There was a clearing in the distance that the soldier would have to cross. Jung Li took a deep breath and waited. A squeeze of the trigger, a smell of cordite and the body tumbled forwards to lie in a rare patch of sunlight.

"They'll soon be missed. In and out double speed, J6," Sim said, from the other side of the world.

"Already on it."

Back in Birmingham, Sim watched the live feed from Jung Li's glasses. Wardle and his assistant Tom were standing just behind Sim, watching the screen over his shoulder. The picture jogged up and down as the agent ran through the trees and approached a road. This one was properly tarmacked but on the far side there was a muddy lay-by. The picture stabilised and then swung rapidly up and down the road. Nothing.

"Is this the right spot, Sim?" Jung Li whispered.

"Yep. Dead centre on all the activity our satellites tracked on Tuesday."

"I thought it would be, you know, better guarded."

"Three guards not enough for a bit of dirt? Get on with it while it's quiet," said Sim.

The picture jogged across the road and focused on the churned-up ground of the lay-by. Thick with mud.

"We'll never get any tyre tracks from this," said Jung Li. There was a rustling while he got something out of his pocket and a pen appeared at the bottom of the frame. It started to crackle as he held the device near the ground in the centre of the lay-by. "Radioactive material here a few days ago, judging from the strength of this reading."

The picture scanned the ground for a while longer and then stopped. A hand bent down to pick something up from the mud. A ring of metal with a barb sticking out. And then the ground rushed up to meet the spectacles and the picture went black.

"J6? J6? Do you read me?" Sim's voice cracked a little.

No reply. Someone's face appeared between streaks of mud as the glasses were wiped clean. The face was the woman who had guided Jung Li here. An Sun-Hi wiped the glasses a little cleaner and smiled for the camera. "Hello, British people."

"Oh shit," muttered Sim.

The picture from the glasses swung round to show Jung Li lying on his side in the mud. His hands were tied behind his back. He was made to sit up and then the glasses were put back on his face. Back at headquarters, they could see the woman again and several armed soldiers standing behind her.

"Did you think you could fool our mighty leaders? Spy on our glorious country? Without us knowing about it all along." The woman pulled out a pistol. "You do know the penalty for espionage in this country, don't you?"

Wardle made a grab for the headphones Sim was using. "Wait.

I'm sure we can sort something out. A trade?"

"We don't negotiate, Mister Alan Wardle. But as gratitude for revealing the frequencies you use, we will give your man a painless end." She pointed the gun at the glasses and pulled the trigger. The picture turned to snow even as the noise of the shot rang out of the speakers in the Birmingham operations room.

Wardle sat down with a thud.

Sim broke the silence, trying the communicator again, even

though it seemed pointless. Nothing. He stared at the blank screen and wiped a hand across his face as memories of shared training with Jung Li bubbled to the surface. A ready smile, a great team player.

"Sir?" Tom approached. "Sir, we need to act right away."

"What can we do from here?"

"The mole. I told you. Feinberg has been sending encrypted messages all day."

"That's his job, isn't?" said Sim.

Tom turned to face Sim. "I didn't want to believe it either Sim. But I traced the messages. North Korea. He's been feeding them information all along."

Wardle looked up and frowned. "You sure?"

Tom showed him a roll tab, with rows of code and co-ordinates on it.

"Come on, then. Let's go nail the bastard."

They approached with caution, waiting for a security team to back them up. All exits covered. Feinberg looked up from a screen as Wardle and Tom walked into his lab.

"Not paying you enough, are we?"

"Sir?"

"You're nicked."

"For why?"

"For causing Jung Li's death, that's why. You're never going to see daylight again, if I've got anything to do with it," said Wardle.

Feinberg looked around the room. At Tom, just behind Wardle. At a security guard standing outside the other door. "I didn't do it, sir. I was trying to warn him."

"Save it for the interrogation room." Wardle nodded to the security guard who came in and put handcuffs on Feinberg. He did not resist.

"You've got it all wrong," he shouted as he was dragged out of the room.

Wardle turned to Tom and dabbed a handkerchief over his bald pate.

"You did the right thing, sir."

"Let's go over Jung Li's footage again," said Wardle.

They went back to the operations room and asked Sim to call up the video. They watched in grim silence, pausing just before the end of the recording.

"What's some fissile material doing in the middle of nowhere?

Even for North Korea, that's odd," said Tom.

Sim froze the screen as Jung Li picked up the metal object. "That sure looks like a safety pin."

"From an ET-MP American grenade, if I'm not mistaken," said Tom.

"Right. So, there's a shake down, in the middle of nowhere, involving some fissile material. And then the whole North Korean army goes mad, driving all over the country." Wardle chewed one end of his glasses. "I think the Terror Formers have gone and nicked one of their warheads."

Sim's eyelids pulled back. "Why would they do that, sir?"

Wardle shook his head. "I don't know. But if the North Koreans think the Western world is trying to steal its nukes... Shit, they'll be itching to get in the first strike."

18

———————

Kathmandu, Nepal

A message pinged on Freda's wrist tab. She scrolled through it and then checked to see if there was anybody sitting near the three agents in the dark cafe. "We're needed for a mission in North Korea. Terror Formers are up to something. Again."

After Rabten had finished his second breakfast, they made their way to the rental car park, looking around for signs of a tail. Still nobody, thank goodness. Maybe they had lost that guy in the truck for good. They checked the car, under and over for signs of interference but found nothing. Five kilometres outside the city, Freda was driving when a familiar red shape appeared in the mirror. The red SUV that had followed them across China had tracked them down to Kathmandu. How had that happened?

Freda tried accelerating, but the borrowed car had a feeble engine and the truck had no trouble keeping up. It did not try to overtake, even though Freda figured it had more than enough power to do so. It just remained a steady four hundred metres behind them. They could not even get a glimpse of the driver due to tinted windows in the vehicle.

As they approached the border with China, Freda noticed that the SUV slowed down and the distance between them quickly doubled. She breathed a sigh of relief.

"Maybe they don't have a visa for Chinese travel."

"Do we?" asked Gopal.

"Course. Wardle has sorted all that out. False IDs, the works."

"Last time, not work so good," said Rabten.

"That wasn't Wardle's fault, I'm sure," said Freda. But as they approached the border control, she found herself reaching to the pocket and feeling for the paperwork over and over again.

The border control was a breeze, even if Freda did have trouble keeping her breathing normal and controlling the quake in her voice. But fifty kilometres beyond the border, just after they had passed a service station, the red SUV had re-appeared in the rear-view mirror.

"It's bloody *Duel* all over again," Freda shouted.

"Huh?" said Gopal.

"Spielberg's first film. A salesman getting chased by an oil tanker."

"Ship?" asked Rabten.

"A truck." Freda shook her head. "Never mind. Although, actually. That does give me an idea. You might want to undo your seat belts."

"Umm, should we discuss this first?" Gopal asked.

Freda waited until there was nothing coming in the other direction. A relatively straight stretch of road, with grass verges on either side. She threw the steering wheel around until the car was facing the other way and accelerated towards the oncoming SUV. "Get ready to jump," she shouted, feeling for the door release. At the last moment, the three agents leapt from the car.

There was a screech of brakes as the SUV slewed to a halt. The agents' car smacked into the other vehicle. The bonnets concertinaed and the front of each car dipped. The SUV shunted the smaller car backwards, its back wheels rearing off the ground for a moment. The windscreen of both vehicles crazed into a thousand panes of tiny glass but stayed within their frames.

The three agents had hit the ground hard and fast, rolling over and over, trying to keep limbs tucked in. As they staggered to their feet, they saw the driver's door of the SUV swing open.

Freda got to her feet and winced as she put weight on her left ankle. She rubbed a hand against the back of her head and pulled out the old gun she'd bought a few days ago. Gopal had lost his service pistol when Joanna had exploded, so this was their only gun. She covered the SUV, waiting for somebody to get out of the truck. "Rabten? We might need those fists of yours."

A foot descended heavily to the floor, behind the open driver's door. Then a second foot and the door swung open a little further. The man stood up and rested his hand on the roof of the SUV as if to emphasise his height. A trickle of blood ran down his forehead from beneath a black beanie hat. He slammed the door shut and stretched his neck to one side.

"That hurt," he shouted, in English.

Shit, thought Freda. *He's twice the size of Rabten.* "Freeze."

The man lumbered towards her. Freda fired. Two shots found their mark in the middle of his chest and then the gun jammed. The man staggered and looked down but no blood emerged from the bullet holes. He wagged his finger at her and stepped forwards. Freda was trying to un-jam the gun, but an enormous swinging backhand smashed into her face. She went flying and the gun skidded under the wreckage.

Rabten jumped in between Freda and the man. He crouched

into the White Crane stance his beloved master had taught him a long time ago. A foot flashed out towards the tall man's legs. He blocked it. The monk tried another kick and this time the man caught Rabten's foot and twisted it, forcing him to fall over.

Gopal sprang from behind the wreckage and launched into a rugby tackle. The tall man turned at the last moment and brought his fists crashing down onto Gopal's back.

Shit, shit, shit, Freda repeated under her breath, hauling herself off the ground. She scanned the scene for another weapon. Nothing. She dashed around to the far side of the mangled vehicles and looked under the crumpled mess. She could not find her gun. Where the two vehicles had fused together half of a bumper had fallen off. She picked it up, disappointed that it did not weigh more. But it was long and the crash had left one end with a vicious hook. As she ran around to the side where the tall man stood, she saw Gopal still lying on the ground and Rabten trying to dart past his opponent's defences. Freda ran straight in and swung the metallic bar as hard as she could. The tall man, busy deflecting a punch from the monk, only just saw Freda approaching and ducked at the last moment. The bumper swished through the air and caught the top of the beanie hat. A clang resonated, like metal striking metal.

"What the hell?" Freda looked down at the metal bar in her hands as the tall man staggered, then rose up again. "You a fucking robot?"

He grinned at her and lunged for the bumper. As he did so, Gopal finally got back to his feet. He charged into the tall man's back, catching him slightly off balance. Gopal kept pumping his legs and drove the man, face first, against the side of the wrecked cars. There was a groan and a whoosh of air, like a giant balloon deflating. The three agents retreated slightly and took up fighting stances in a ring. The tall man turned to face them, pain creasing his forehead, eyes and mouth. Protruding from his stomach was a vicious shard of silvered glass. The remnants of a wing mirror. The man's hands, clutching at the glass, were already scarlet as blood oozed from the wound. He slumped to the ground and closed his eyes.

A giant truck zoomed past the wreckage and blasted its air horn. Freda jumped. She knelt next to the body and felt for a pulse. Nothing. She pulled at his hat and discovered a metal skull cap sewn into the underside. No terminators yet, thank goodness. Then she patted him down, uncovering the body armour that had stopped the bullets. The wing mirror had penetrated an inch below the vest. She found a wallet and a small electronic device that she did not recognise. Freda put both in her pocket. Gopal tried the SUV. Once he had finally forced open the glove compartment, he was rewarded with two guns and a silencer.

"Come on guys, we need to get away from here. I don't think the rental insurance covered this."

And then a thought struck her. She pulled the number plates from their mangled car and started walking back towards the service station.

19

Birmingham, UK

"I still can't believe it was Feinberg," said Sim. "Why not get Jung Li arrested at the border? Instead of waiting until he'd met his executioner?"

Wardle shrugged. "Maybe the Koreans wanted to see how much we knew. Maybe they just wanted to humiliate us."

"Hadn't he just got married?"

Wardle looked into the americano he had poured for himself and nodded.

Sim's chest tightened. He needed to get back to Rosie. "After I've written up my report, sir, I'd like to head back to Scotland. Resume my duties at the tracking station."

"The Division is under pressure."

"Aren't we all?"

"I don't need comebacks from you, Atkins. If the accountants have their way, the department is going to disappear."

"Cutbacks?" Sim's hopes of a promotion and a bigger mortgage were evaporating faster than the steam rising from Wardle's coffee mug.

"We need a result. A big one that proves our worth to the book-keepers in Whitehall. I can't have one of my best agents skulking around in satellite monitoring stations."

"If I remember, it was you called me back from America, where I was trying to help with the Moon Base investigation."

Wardle shook his head. "Even if you had managed to help, you think we'd get any credit? You saw what happened with the Himalayas. Diane Butler, rah, rah, rah."

An image of the round-faced CIA department leader popped into Sim's head. His first mission had ended with two dead American agents and all the plaudits going to the CIA. Death and glory for the USA. His reminiscences were cut short by an orange field report that popped onto Wardle's desk glass. Sim's boss opened it and began reading.

"It's from Brightwell. Follow-up to that death in Russia. She says that the three of them were tracked all the way through Kazakhstan, Uzbekistan. Even into China. Narrowly escaped a car bombing. And attacked again after they left Nepal."

"Is she ok?"

"She's as tough as they come."

"The attacks. Not that surprising, are they, sir? The Russians don't like people walking out of maximum security prisons."

"Freda's not convinced this was the FSB. The car bomb attempt was too amateur. The tail that they picked up in Kathmandu. Wrong sort of gun. Maybe Terror Formers again."

"Doesn't that mean we've still got a mole at large? Leaking information to the terrorists?"

Wardle stroked his chin for a moment and turned his chair to face the window. "Not necessarily. Could be that Feinberg fed this information to the TF before we locked him away. Could be that Brightwell is wrong. Maybe the Russians are leading us up the garden path."

"After we helped them sort out the *Arktika* mess?"

"I wouldn't put it past them," said Wardle.

Sim thought about David Feinberg, trapped inside a tiny cell somewhere in the depths of the building. They had not worked together much over the years. But he had seemed such a likeable guy.

Wardle's assistant came into the room. "You need to get going if you're going to make the afternoon meeting of the Select Committee."

Wardle waved a hand at Tom as if the assistant was a bothersome fly.

"This needs your full attention, sir, if we're to keep the department alive. Just stick to the answers I've prepared and you'll be fine."

Wardle sighed. He swiped shut the files on his desk glass and nodded to Sim. "Don't go anywhere. I need you here."

Sim thought of Rosie again. "How long for, sir?"

"Until I say so."

Sim was at his desk, dutifully waiting for Wardle to return, catching up with the news on his desk glass. Tensions were high in Asia. The international community was trying to rein in the North Koreans. The rapprochement of fifteen years ago all but forgotten. The scale of military activity was alarming, unnecessary. Nobody was threatening them. But the isolated country was not listening. They blasted out occasional proclamations. Foreign invaders would face the wrath of their glorious armed forces. Governments responsible would be wiped off the face of the Earth.

Sim took a gulp of tea and pulled a face, looking at the brown liquid. That drinks dispenser really couldn't make a decent cuppa. He clicked onto an article posted by the Tokyo Times but could not get his eyes to focus on the screen. He squeezed his eyelids together and squinted at the words. The screen started to tilt sideways and then he fell off his chair, hitting the deck hard. He didn't feel a thing.

Wardle came into the room and rushed over when he saw Sim's body on the floor. He looked up at the camera in the corner of the ceiling. The little red bulb beneath the cupola was not illuminated. He donned some latex gloves and twisted his head around to check the door was closed. Reaching inside his jacket, Wardle pulled out a syringe and needle, injecting Sim underneath the tongue. The head of Overseas Division stood up and calmly walked over to a control panel next to the door, while removing his gloves and hiding the needle and syringe. He pressed a button on the panel.

"This is Wardle. We need an ambulance and a crash team. Room L65. Urgent!"

When the medics finally arrived, sweat was dripping from Wardle's gaunt face. He stopped doing compressions on Sim's chest and unlaced his fingers. He tried to stand but his leg muscles were cramping, frozen into a kneeling position.

"We'll take it from here," one of the paramedics said. They ripped Sim's shirt off and placed defib pads on his chest. The machine buzzed and beeped, then Sim's back arched off the ground. The medics strapped an oxygen mask over Sim's face and lifted him onto a stretcher.

"I'm coming with you," said Wardle, standing up and rubbing life into his legs.

The paramedic shook his head. "Best you stay here."

"Like hell I am. I want to make sure..."

When Wardle returned to the office at 1am his assistant, Tom, was still working at his desk. He stopped typing and looked up.

"How is he?"

Wardle just shook his head and walked straight past. Tom got up to follow him. "Can I get you something?" The office door slammed in his face.

An hour later, Wardle re-appeared.

"Sir, let me do the paperwork for you. Go home and get some rest."

Wardle looked up, already half asleep. "Hmm? No, it's fine. Done already. Tell the team, will you? I won't be back until the afternoon."

"OK, sir." Tom reached out to touch his boss' shoulder as Wardle walked past.

Wardle's hands trembled as he grasped the steering wheel of his car down in the basement of City Centre Tower. His mouth gaped open as hours of tiredness tried to expel themselves from his lungs. He rummaged around in his pockets and pulled out a strip of foil packed pills. He squeezed one from its packet and threw it into his mouth. It started to fizz slightly on his tongue. He kept it there as if he were having second thoughts, then swallowed and pressed the starter button on the dashboard.

The electronic engine hummed into life. Wardle turned off some settings for his on-board computer and drove up to the security gates. He waited as the bollards dropped into the ground, closing his eyes for a moment. His wedding ring tapped against the steering wheel in time with the rhythmical clunk of machinery within the gates. He opened his eyes and drove off into the suburbs of Birmingham, not east towards his house but west.

20

———

Chinese-Nepal border

"How the hell are we going to get to Korea now?" asked Gopal. The service station had not been far. There had been a short detour while Freda had sunk the number plates from their hire car in a stagnant ditch away from the road. Rabten was eating again while they assessed their options.

"We could fess up why we're here. Ask for help from the Chinese... but they might not take kindly to our interference with a neighbour," said Freda.

"Especially an unstable one. Chinese administration is probably crawling with NK operatives anyway. So, we keep a low profile. What about returning to Kathmandu and catching a train from there?" said Gopal.

Freda shook her head. "Take too long. We need to be on the Korean border ay-sap, ready to go in."

"Internal flight across China?"

"If the Terror Formers could track our escape from Russia, they'll know we're in China. I think they'll be monitoring flights. We mustn't let them know we're closing in on their master plan."

Rabten gently splashed his spoon in the stew in front of him. "Master Wangdue helped us defeat silver serpent."

"I know pal, I know," said Gopal, rubbing Rabten's shoulder.

"Wait," said Freda. "The silver serpent. Of course."

The other two looked up with blank expressions.

"After we'd destroyed the water plants, the Chinese kept the pipes they had built. Put them to a different use." Freda sighed. "They built a hyper loop. Runs from Tibet all the way to Beijing. We could be there in a few hours."

"They sell tickets for this train?" asked Gopal.

"Government use only. We'll have to find a way to persuade them."

"Where is nearest station?" said Rabten.

Freda tapped a few keys on her wrist tab. "Hmm, not far. But off the beaten track. We might have to borrow a jeep."

Gopal stood up and tapped Rabten on the shoulder. "Eat up. Work to do."

The pipes that were going to carry freshwater from the Himalayas all the way to Beijing in the east had been re-purposed by now. A hyper-loop – like the train service set up in western America – only longer. And no commuters. The Chinese government had needed a cover-up after Freda, Gopal, Rabten and Sim had helped destroy their efforts to commandeer the Tibetan glaciers. Super-fast trains that could carry troops, officials, equipment from one side of the country to the other. They had not managed to steal the designs for a hyper drone yet. But a hyper-train, yes.

The various staging posts for this network were heavily guarded, even the one Freda was watching through her night-glass on a remote part of the Tibetan plateau. There was some sort of research facility out here and a small garrison of soldiers, judging from the buildings and foot traffic she could see. The front gate was heavily guarded, of course, thought there were large stretches of the perimeter fence in shadow and un-protected.

"We've had plenty of practice at getting inside places like this. But we need to get onboard one of the pipe trains. That's the hard bit," said Freda while continuing to squint through her scope. "How's your mandarin, guys?"

"Can't we just speak Tibetan?" asked Gopal.

"Not if you want to sound like a government official."

"Rabten can speak it OK. Mine is bad, but I bet yours is worse..." Freda turned to face the ex-Gurkha. "You're not wrong." She assessed their meagre equipment. The guns taken from the tall man. A night-vision scope, with laser signalling device and telescopic stand. Rubber-handled wire cutters. Three micro-sticks of plastic explosives, disguised as chewing gum. A wrist tab each. And a multi-purpose penknife that Gopal had stolen in Russia.

"We'll have to risk something a bit crazy."

They improvised some camo-face paint from the muddy terrain. The perimeter fence took longer to defeat than Freda had anticipated. Motion sensors had to be disabled before they could cut a slit through the wire mesh. Once inside the base, they headed for one of the buildings furthest away from the barracks. An armed guard was patrolling the outer fence. As she watched him walk past, from the shadow of a pile of crates, Freda prayed that he wouldn't notice the damage to the wire. They had tried to bend it back into place but had not had time to do a perfect job. The guard paused for a moment, scratched his arse, then kept walking.

Freda had observed people without guns and in different uniform to the soldiers. They were coming in and out of the building next to the agents' hiding place. She wanted more firepower but a silenced pistol would have to do. "Remember, we don't need to kill anybody. Just get their uniforms and passes. Without them sounding the alarm."

Gopal raised an eyebrow. He clicked the safety off the automatic pistol and signalled for Rabten to cover the other exit.

"My fists not fast enough last time," whispered Rabten.

"What did you do when you lost to Wangdue in training?" said Gopal.

"Tried harder."

The ex-Gurkha nodded and ran up to the main door, with Freda close behind. He counted to ten and burst through the door, gun raised straight in front of him. A Chinese man and woman looked up from their desks, their eyes widening.

Gopal shouted something in Tibetan and gestured for them to get down. Freda didn't want him to shoot. They needed the uniforms without bullet holes. Besides, silencers are not that effective on automatic pistols. But if they tried to set off the alarm... she hoped that the Chinese officials would be too scared to find out.

As Gopal advanced into the room, the man got down onto his knees and the woman started to lie face down. The man waited for Gopal to get a little closer and then dived at the agent's legs, toppling him backwards. The ex-Gurkha smashed the grip of the pistol down onto the Chinese man's back. The breath left his lungs in a rush that turned into a cry. Gopal tried to regain his feet, while Freda tried to wrap her hand over the Chinese man's mouth.

The woman sprang to her feet and ran to the far side of the room. She grabbed the door handle and fumbled with her ID card, trying to press it against a control panel. Freda let go of the Chinese man and ran after her. The woman sprinted through the door, which started to close. Freda reached the handle just in time to stop it clicking shut. She pushed the door open and saw a straight corridor ahead of her. Another door at the far end was swinging shut. She'd never reach that one in time.

"Shit." She turned around and saw Gopal knock out the Chinese man with the grip of his pistol. "Get that uniform on," she said. She wedged the door open with a stash of papers and jogged to the door that the other woman had disappeared through. It began to open. Slowly. Freda pressed herself against the wall, prolonging the moment before the person coming through would see her. She pulled out the stand from her night scope and raised it above her head like a cosh.

Rabten staggered through the door, carrying the Chinese woman over her shoulder. "Think I broke her nose, but she be alright."

Freda looked at the blood dripping onto the floor from the woman's face. "What about the uniform?"

The nosebleed had missed the uniform, but they still had a problem. Two sets of passes and uniforms, but only one was for a man.

"Hide me in the crate, and you use the woman's ID," suggested Gopal.

"Never going to work. I don't have my Babel app with me. And besides, nobody is going to believe I'm Chinese," said Freda. She picked her bottom lip. "Stick to the original plan. One of you is going to have be the dame."

Gopal and Freda turned to look at Rabten. "What a dame?" he asked.

Fortunately, Rabten's facial hair was almost non-existent. Freda had to remove the woman's bra because its clasp was beyond the skill of the monk's trembling fingers. He put that on, Freda stuffed the bra with a pair of socks and then the uniform was donned. At least Chinese female officials wore trousers, the same as men.

Freda stood back to admire the transvestite monk. "It'll have to do. Now remember, this is a top priority request from Beijing. You two need to accompany the crate, for immediate delivery. Got it?" The two men nodded and went to select the most suitable box, while Freda looked for a trolley to use. The two men came back and lifted the lid on a crate that was roughly a cubic metre in size. Freda looked at the space inside and tried to figure out how long the hyper loop took to get to Beijing from here. She found a half-drunk bottle of water on the desk where one of the Chinese officials had been working and took it with her as she clambered into the box. She folded her limbs and tried to get comfortable as Gopal lowered the lid into place. It was a dark, tight squeeze. It reminded her of a cargo hold she had once shared with Sim in the back of a plane. She tried to force herself to breathe slowly. But the urge to burst out of the box was almost uncontrollable. Freda wished Sim was with her.

The other two agents wheeled the crate towards the hyper loop and showed their passes to the guard. It was still night and the lighting outside, in the grounds of the base, was patchy. Rabten did his best not to look up at the guard too much. He breathed out when the guard waved them through into the terminal.

There was a small carriage awaiting them. It looked like a huge shell – the sort that train-mounted artillery guns used to fire in World War I. But this one had two doors in its side. There was seating for eight people in the front section and space for several boxes in the rear compartment. The crate was wheeled on and the two agents were relieved to see that nobody else was boarding here. They clambered into the seats and strapped themselves in, while a technician closed up the hatches.

"Safe trip," he said in mandarin. Gopal just gave the man a thumbs-up sign.

The train accelerated, pressing the two men into their seats and catching their breath. The acceleration kept coming. Far more than when a plane zoomed down the runway before take-off. Their rib cages began to feel heavy. There was nothing to see – the carriage was a sealed unit. A bullet flying down the barrel of a gun. Finally, they could start to breathe more easily again. While the carriage was in motion, there was no access to the rear section that contained Freda's crate which meant they could not check on her. They just sat and waited for their destination.

After an hour, the train started to slow. Gopal grabbed Rabten's arm. "Too soon. It ought to take us at least two hours to get to Beijing."

"They onto us?" asked Rabten. "I don't know. Get ready."

There was a clunk from the hatchway once the train had stopped and the two agents stood as the door swung up and out. There was a faint smell of hot metal that Gopal could almost taste. Four more people were waiting to get on. One man wore several stripes on his lower sleeve and an over-sized military hat, with a bright red band below its peak. He got on first. "No need to stand, let's keep it informal on board," he said. "Now, is there's anything to drink on board these flying tin-cans?"

Rabten sat down again quickly, trying to avert his face. But the Major insisted on sitting opposite the cross-dressing monk and started up a conversation. He rocked back when he finally got Rabten to look up at him.

The Major looked at his colleagues. "Phew. They breed them... tough in Tibet, don't they? I'm definitely going to need a drink for this trip."

The train accelerated away. The Major, sitting with his back to the direction of travel, swayed forwards and put his hand on Rabten's knee to steady himself. He winked at the monk as he settled back into his seat. Even at hyper-speed, it was going to be a long journey to Beijing.

By the time the train began to slow again, the Major had given up trying to chat up the monk. He had produced a flask of spirits from an inside pocket and consumed it steadily throughout the journey. At least the alcohol had taken the edge off his bad breath. The door swung up and out again and the Major pushed himself off first, burping as he stood. His colleagues followed him, leaving Gopal and Rabten the last to leave. Once off the train, they went to collect Freda's crate from the rear section. The door to this compartment had already been opened and some crates were being wheeled off. Inside the train there were no crates left. Freda had gone.

They stepped out again and Gopal looked across the busy terminal as the panic began to rise from his gut, constricting his throat. The pile of boxes that had been wheeled off their train was already almost out of sight. They had to catch up before Freda was lost forever.

21

______

Birmingham

Sim opened his eyes and groaned. It was dark, or his eyes were not working properly. He tried to sit up but that hurt. There was a huge bruise running across his chest. His throat felt raw and dry. Rolling over onto his side, Sim groaned. There was a glass of water on the table next to his bed. He sipped it urgently, spilling some onto the bedcovers.

A door opened and his boss entered the room. "Where am I?"

"Somewhere safe. For now."

"I don't remember. What happened?"

Wardle pulled up a chair and sat next to Sim's bed. The legs squeaked as they dragged over the plastic floor. "Somebody tried to poison you, Sim."

"Who?"

"I've been expecting an attack. I thought it better if it happened at City Centre, rather than your home."

Sim tried to sit up again. "Is Rosie alright?"

Wardle held his hands out for calm. "She's fine. I have

somebody watching your home, but I'm sure she's not a target." Sim sighed and slumped back into his pillow.

"I had to make it look as though the poison had worked. Gave you something to counteract the poison, but also to suppress your heart-rate."

"I don't understand."

"The ambulance crew will swear blind you died on the way to hospital. They're the only ones who know where you are now. We need to flush out the person who poisoned you. The real mole."

"What about Feinberg?"

"Misdirection. But he'll have to stay locked up for a while longer." Sim pulled a face. "Pretty harsh. How long's he been in already?"

"That's not the worst of it." He stared into Sim's eyes.

Sim looked back while the cogs turned. "But. You can't mean?" Wardle nodded. "She's strong, Sim. Stronger than you realise. She'll get through this. You both will."

"No, no, that's not on. She's pregnant. If she thinks I'm dead, the stress will... She might..." Sim was shaking his head, trying to prop himself up again. He winced as his sternum took the strain of his arms.

"Atkins, we have to do it like this. Everybody has to think you're dead. Everyone." Wardle stood up and paced the room. Then stopped to lean both hands on the end of Sim's bed. "I need you to go undercover in Sweden. Expose that monster for what he is. You want to find out who killed your son, don't you?"

Sim squeezed his eyes shut and clenched his jaw. Damnit. Yes, of course he did. But making Rosie think he's dead? The cruellest of tricks. "Won't Larsson recognise me?"

"We have a procedure to help with that. Besides, if his mole reports back that you're dead, well he won't exactly be keeping an eye out for a corpse, will he?"

"What sort of procedure?"

"Oh, it's doesn't hurt much. And it does wear off. Eventually." Wardle turned to leave. "Rest up, Atkins. I'll be back for your answer later."

~

Back at headquarters, Wardle popped another pill. When he got into the lift from the basement car park, he ignored the usual 6th floor button and pressed for the sub-basement level. He signed in to the detention centre. The guard stood up to sweep him with a hand-held metal detector.

Wardle tilted his head forward slightly and stared at the man. "Jones? I've been on the go for nearly twenty hours now. One of my best agents has just died. I have to go and compose a letter to his pregnant wife."

"Sorry, sir. Rules—"

"You want to sweep the director. Right here, right now?"

Jones averted his gaze and sat back down, mumbling an apology. Wardle continued along the corridor, past the room where Feinberg was being held and went to the toilet. Then he returned, a few pounds lighter, and went to see the disgraced IT expert.

David looked up from behind the bars keeping him in the far end of the room. His dark hair looked even blacker than usual against the pale skin of his face. "Sir, please."

"Save it," said Wardle. "We need to use your precious roll tab.

The one that talks the Terror Formers' language."

"I can help, sir. But the encryption. It's coded to my biometrics now. These systems only allow one re-reset. I don't think it'll work for anybody else."

"That's convenient for you, isn't it?" Wardle approached the bars, presenting his back to the camera filming them from above the doorway. He held up a finger for silence, that only David could see. "We really need to find out what's happening with the North Korean situation. If only you would help."

"Why would I do that?" said the IT expert in a raised voice. "Because if you don't, I'm going to dump so much shit on your lawn, you'll never dig yourself free."

"I'll think about it," replied David.

Wardle turned to leave. "I'll be back for your answer very soon." The director left the detention centre, returning to the sixth floor, while David Feinberg asked to be allowed to use the toilets. Taped to the underside of the cistern lid, in the second cubicle he tried, David found his roll tab. He used an alias to connect to the Overseas Division servers, then logged in as a TF member and started reading. The guard banged on the door. David groaned, farted and said he'd be a couple more minutes.

22

———

Beijing

Gopal was jogging across the wide, bright atrium. He saw no windows – this was all artificial light. Underground, presumably. No shadows, no hiding places. There was no time for subtlety anyway. Gopal knew that running across this busy hall would look odd. Drawing attention to himself and Rabten. But what choice did they have? If they lost sight of Freda's crate they might never find it again. And she might never get out.

The crates were on a trailer being towed by a low, wide vehicle that was too small for a human driver. A machine following a pre-set course. There was no human walking alongside either. That was good. The machine turned a corner and as the two disguised agents ran around the same bend a few seconds later, Rabten clattered into a Chinese official with an armful of papers. The documents flew into the air and fluttered to the ground in all directions. Rabten bowed and apologised in mandarin, then caught up with Gopal.

They were approaching a gateway to another part of this subterranean base. An armed guard stood by a body scanner.

162

Next to this was a low archway that the vehicle drove through and halted for a moment. Inside the archway a mobile scanner slid up and down the length of the tractor and trailer. It beeped and the light above the archway flashed green. The vehicle trundled away. Rabten turned to look at Gopal, who just nodded and charged.

The guard looked confused and started to unsling his machine gun, but Gopal was too fast. He pushed him into the wall and ran through the gate. The guard steadied himself and turned, raising his gun towards Gopal, but Rabten followed up with a punch to the side of the head. The guard fell, unconscious.

On the other side of the gate a second guard turned to see the commotion. He pressed a button on the desk next to him. Two things happened at once. Alarms filled the corridor with noise and flashing lights. And a screen dropped down, blocking the doorway with the scanner. Gopal had got through already, but Rabten was stuck on the other side.

The guard turned to face the ex-Gurkha and raised his gun. Gopal looked around the gateway for anything he could use as distraction. The pistol tucked into the back of his trousers would take too long to draw. He slowly raised his hands.

There was a noise to Gopal's left, like an object being dragged along the floor. The guard looked down to see Rabten slide out the end of the low arch that the vehicle had used only moments before. That was the second Gopal needed. He drew his gun and shot the guard. The man toppled backwards, clutching his chest. He put a bloodied hand on the floor and tried to get up, but Gopal shot him again. This time, the guard stayed down.

The tractor and trailer had already turned the next corner, oblivious to the chaos going on behind. The two agents gave chase. A guard burst out of a door in the right-hand wall of the corridor. Gopal shoulder-barged the door into the guard's face and kneed the man in the stomach as the guard clutched his bleeding nose. Grabbing the soldier's machine gun, Gopal sprinted to catch up with Rabten and the tractor.

The monk banged on top of the automated truck, but nothing happened. He ran ahead and then stopped directly in the path of the vehicle. It came to a halt with a squeak of rubber. The machine said in mandarin: 'Please keep clear. Delivery in progress.' And then repeated it. Gopal pressed the barrel of his machine gun against the tractor and emptied the clip into the tractor's brain. The message stopped and the lights on the front of the vehicle went out.

The crates were secured to the trailer by four arms, two on each side. The agents found the mechanism for unlocking the arms and twisted the handle. The arms expanded outwards and the men began banging on the sides of the crates.

"Are you there, Freda?" No response.

"Shit," said Gopal. "Just get them open."

"Which one?" asked Rabten.

Gopal called out. "Freda?" There was no reply. Unconscious? Or worse? "Get them all open, quick."

Using the stock of the machine gun, they pried the lid off the first one. It was full of polystyrene boxes and the smell of new plastic. The second one contained some medical equipment. Footsteps. From the sound of it at least a dozen guards were closing on their position. Gopal toppled the third crate and its lid burst open. Grenades spilt out onto the floor amongst the packing straw. He bent down and pulled the pins out of two of them and rolled them down the corridor towards the approaching feet.

Rabten prised open the lid of the last crate. A Chinese man, lay curled up at the bottom, his hands bound. He opened his eyes and tried to shout something past the gag in his mouth.

The grenades exploded just as soldiers appeared from around the corner. Three bodies were flung up and back. A part of the ceiling caved in and the lights went out in that section of the corridor. The two agents looked at each other and at the crates.

"Where the hell is she?"

The doors to the hyper train closed automatically and it began to roll forwards, slowly, heading for a branch in the track. Freda's arms and legs were screaming in agony, jamming her to the ceiling of the cargo compartment by pressing against the walls. As soon as the door closed, her limbs eased off and she fell to the floor with a bang. The British agent lay there for a moment in the dark, breathing deeply as her muscles unwound.

She knew that Gopal and Rabten would be worried, but she'd had little choice when that inspector had opened her crate. Fortunately, he was an administrator and not an armed guard. Without her to worry about, she hoped it would be easier for Gopal and Rabten to get out of this base. Freda did not want to cause them additional difficulties. She knew that she was endangering this mission. The wrong skin, the wrong hair to blend into the crowds here. Her colleagues were perfect for this mission. She was a liability. Why hadn't Wardle realised this?

Still, she could make herself useful in other ways. She needed to get to the British embassy. But first she needed to get out of this train compartment. Freda switched on her torch. The handle on the inside of the door would not budge. No windows to smash. There was a partition between the section where the passengers sat and the cargo hold. It was thin but metal. She lay on her back and tried kicking it with the soles of her shoes. After several attempts, her feet and calves were beginning to hurt but there was no discernible effect on the partition. The train came to a gentle stop. She crouched in the corner of the carriage and listened for signs of somebody coming to open the door. Nothing.

Freda got to her knees and started to scan the floor, torch held in teeth, feeling the surface for any cracks. Yes, there. Her fingers found a line in the rubberised mat. She followed it around in a complete square. In the middle of one side, Freda could see that the thin gap widened just for a few centimetres. She pulled from her pocket a thin set of tools that she had picked up in Kathmandu. The implements were tiny, all set into a slim rectangle like an old-fashioned credit card. Freda used the flat-headed screwdriver to lever up the mat and uncovered a circular handle recessed into the floor. She twisted and pulled. Through the opening, she could make out the track beneath the hyper train.

The screwdriver flew out of her hand, downwards, and slammed into a block underneath the train, sticking there. Freda could feel the set of other tools tugging, trying to free themselves of her fingers. Powerful magnets in the track below hummed, holding the train in a hover position. She put the tools back into her pocket and clambered through the hole in the floor, squeezing into the gap between the train and the ground. As she rolled sideways the humming stopped. The train wobbled slightly and descended, clunking onto the track. Freda was stuck in the gap between the sloped side of the train and the wall. She crawled along in the dirt. A pungent aroma – stale urine – arose from the grime. A brown and white rat in front of her squeaked and ran off.

When she was clear of the train, Freda heaved herself onto the narrow platform. No passengers here. It looked like a simple walkway for engineers or maintenance crew. She crouched down and stared in each direction, checking for movement. Nothing.

Freda set off in the opposite direction to the main platform. The walkway ended in a ladder stretching upwards into darkness. She climbed. At the top there was a white, bright corridor that led to a doorway with a control panel next to it. But there was another door, just next to the top of the ladder in the side wall. It had a green picture of a man running through a doorway and some Chinese characters that Freda did not need to translate. She pushed on the bar and the door swung outwards, letting in a welcome ray of sunshine. Freda blinked and stepped out into the city, smiling.

The British agent hurried through the streets of the vast capital, trying to orientate herself. She was reluctant to use her wrist tab, presuming it would be picked up by Chinese monitoring stations. Freda vaguely recalled where the British embassy was. She knew the un-manned taxis were all bugged by the Chinese government so was hoping to avoid using one of those. She began to perspire as the sun beat down from a hazy sky. She didn't mind that so much but the smell invading her nostrils was deeply unpleasant. A mix of body odour from the crowds jostling past her, the sweet sticky aroma of street food frying, and an acrid tang at the back of her mouth, like a bonfire of wet leaves.

Freda traced the banks of a river eastwards for a while and then turned left following a sign that pointed, in English, to the World Financial Centre. That definitely rang a bell. She saw some Western people approaching her and heard them speaking in French. She asked them if they knew where the embassy was, but they just shook their heads.

After a few more blocks, Freda's steps were shortening. Every few hundred yards, she stumbled as if the pavement was buckling beneath her feet. Her stomach was making noises and her tongue was sticking to the roof of her mouth. Another pair of white people, speaking English, approached. When she asked them, struggling to get the words out, they smiled back at her.

"You OK, honey?" Freda just nodded.

"The embassy's not far away. Quite close to ours, actually. Keep straight on for two more blocks, take a left and then second right. You'll find yourself in a circular park. The British embassy overlooks the park."

She smiled and tried to straighten her hair. "Thank you."

Standing in the middle of the park, Freda could see the embassy just as the American couple had promised. But she had one final hurdle. The front entrance was ringed with cameras. Not British ones, but Chinese cameras, monitoring people who came in and out of the little patch of foreign soil. And if the rumours were true, secret service agents were permanently stationed outside, ready to grab somebody before they made it to sanctuary, thousands of miles from blighty. Freda Brightwell had form in China. A known Overseas Division agent walking in the front door? Not advisable.

She sat and waited. Watching the people come and go in front of the embassy while hunger gnawed away at her insides. What did Rabten say about the patient heron? Catching fish? The memory just made her hungrier and guilty. She knew her companions would think she had abandoned them or worse, been captured. She prayed she had not led them into danger.

Once she was sure she knew which individuals were the Chinese agents, Freda started to concentrate on the people entering and leaving the building. She picked a black man in his thirties, wearing a smart suit and small glasses. Neither Chinese spy paid him any attention as he left the embassy, so Freda approached as he walked off towards the end of the afternoon.

Freda caught up and walked a couple of paces behind him. She said the phrase that signified an undercover agent in need of assistance, just loud enough for him to hear, without looking up.

The man stopped.

"Don't turn around," she said. "Just keep walking."

He did so, then looked sideways and down. "Can I know your name?"

"B17. That's all you need for now. I have to get inside the embassy. Without using the front door."

"OK. My flat's five minutes away, with my car parked outside. We can drive back in, using the basement entrance. Follow me."

They left the park and soon the man was unlocking his car, climbing into the front seat. As Freda got in, the man turned quickly to point a gun in her face.

"Don't move."

Freda rolled her eyes.

"I'm going to need more than a three-digit code before I sneak you into the embassy. Car, scan her."

There was a beep from the console next to the man's head. *'No gun. Some sharp metal objects in her left hip pocket.'*

"Pull them out slowly," the man said.

Freda extracted the tool kit. "Can we hurry up please, this is kind of urgent."

"Not until I'm sure. Car, run her code and face through the software."

Another beep and then. *'Freda Brightwell, Overseas Division. Active service. Chinese Ministry of State Security has her on their most-wanted list.'*

The man put his gun away. "Aren't you a naughty girl? Well, you better squish down in the footwell back there and put that blanket over you. Let's hope we don't get stopped."

23

Birmingham

Sim was channel-hopping. Trying to take his mind off the impending decision. Click. The news headlines. Another famine in Africa. Click. A game show: win a dream ticket on Virgin Galactic. Click. A London soap opera: the bartender is really an android! Click. A morning chat show: is it morally justified to send astronauts on a one-way ticket to Mars? The host of the chat show tells the audience that one of the crew has got his wife pregnant, but he still wants to go on the mission. An intake of breath, collective gasps and cut to an advert. Sim told the screen to shut down.

He closed his eyes and pictured himself in the TV studio. The door to his room opened.

Wardle entered and sat down opposite Sim. "So?"

"You ask too much, sir. I can't put Rosie through that pain."

"You think I enjoy doing this?" asked Wardle.

"I need more time to think."

Wardle shook his head. "Can't risk it. You not being dead won't stay a secret forever. Besides, this new Ebola strain. We don't when the bastards who made it intend to use it again. What if next time they unleash it in Washington? Beijing? Or London?"

Sim stared at the ground.

"If ESCO is behind this, we have to stop them," said Wardle. "Can't the egg heads in Colindale come up with a cure or a vaccine?"

"Working on it, sure. Ready in time? Certainly not in enough quantities if this thing goes pandemic."

Sim walked over to the window and stared at the people strolling past the safe-house. A mother holding hands with a child in school uniform. A jogger listening to something in their Personal Acoustic Field. A long-limbed dog taking a man for a walk. Ordinary people doing ordinary things.

"Can't somebody else try? Another agent from the division?"

"Hamilton already did. They saw straight through his false ID. Couldn't get close even with his drone surveillance. You're being removed from our database. If they think you're dead, it's our best chance."

"You mentioned a procedure," said Sim.

"Silicon implants for your eyebrows, cheeks, chin. Change the shape of your face. Crowns for your front teeth. Dyed hair. Contact lens to change your iris pattern. All reversible."

"What about retinal scanners?"

"Ahh, yes. That's the tricky bit. We can give you a new pair of retinas. Retinae, whatever. There's a small chance they won't take. Could lose your sight..."

"You ever had any of this done, sir?"

"Atkins. This is not about me. It's not about you or your unborn child. It's not even about avenging James."

"Fine," said Sim quietly.

"It's the millions of children who could get killed if this virus gets out. It's about bringing bastards like this—"

"I said, fine. I'll do it."

Sim woke up the next day with bandages over his eyes and the rest of his face. His eyelids itched. He felt like there was grit rubbing against his cornea. And worst of all, he couldn't tell yet if the operation had worked. Somebody came into the room.

"Sir?"

"No, it's just me," said the woman who had done the operation on him. "Sit up for me, please. Now, when I take off these bandages, I need you to keep your eyes closed. OK?"

Sim shuffled into an upright position. "Yes." He felt someone tugging at the bandages and winced as the skin along his forehead pulled from the dressing.

"Hold still, you baby."

The room seemed to get brighter. Sim gripped the sides of the bed with both hands as he resisted the urge to rub and scratch. Then the room darkened again. Worse than before. "Err, what just happened?"

"I've closed the curtains and turned the lights out. Just going to wash your eyelids, put some drops in. Lie back for me."

Sim tried not to wince again. He could feel his eyelids being pulled open fractionally. But nothing registered. The darkness of the room? Or a sign of failure? Retinal rejection? He tried to think of something else. *Give it time. Give it time.*

"Right. I've re-bandaged the eyes. The rest of the face seems to be healing nicely. I'll be back tomorrow, for the grand unveiling. Make sure you take your pills, OK?"

～

Wardle's assistant, Tom, stepped into the lift and descended to the sub-basement level. At the reception desk, the guard looked up at the approaching steps.

"Ah, Llewellyn. There you are. Needed up in the comms room.

Urgent message."

"I can't leave my desk. You know that."

"Don't worry. I'll cover for you."

The guard thought for a moment. "Thanks." He headed for the lift.

Tom sat down at the guard's desk and looked at the monitors showing pictures of each of the cells and the interview rooms. Only two cells occupied, no interviews going on. Tom tapped some instructions into the desk glass. The screen showing David Feinberg went blank. Tom got up and walked down the corridor to Feinberg's cell.

"You really are despicable. Eh?"

David Feinberg looked up, puzzled. "Why are you here?"

"Some of us have a job to do," said Tom.

"In case you weren't listening last time, I didn't do it."

"Show some fucking balls, at least. It's going to be your last chance." Tom pulled out a length of cord and a taser.

David's eyes went wide as he pulled away from the cell bars. "What the?" He looked up at the camera in the corner of the ceiling.

Tom shook his head. "You can stop pretending now. It's just you, me and the toys."

"You're mad."

"What did you do?"

"Nothing!"

Tom approached the cell bars and put a key into the lock. David watched the key turn and then his eyes darted around his cell.

As soon as Tom came into his cell, David launched himself at the other man. Tom's back smacked into the bars. His breath escaped in a hurry. Then his hand jabbed the taser into David's ribs and the fight was over. David collapsed on the floor, limbs juddering, teeth chattering.

Tom wrapped the cord around David's neck and pulled the ends through the bars, on the highest rung. It was hard work, dragging a body and lifting it. Tom grunted and heaved until David was more or less upright. The accused had stopped shaking but his muscles were not yet working properly. Occasionally his head flopped forward and he began to choke on the cord. With one hand holding the ends of the cord, Tom closed the cell door again and locked it, tucking the key into a pocket. Then he heaved some more and lifted David off the ground. A faint groan escaped as if David's soul was already departing his body. Feet shuffled a desperate dance, trying to stretch to a floor just out of reach.

Tom tied the cord off and left the room. Just as he sat down once again at the reception desk, the lift doors pinged and the guard stepped out. Tom flicked a switch to turn the camera back on and placed the key on its hook before the guard was close enough to see.

"Not sure what that was all about. Could easily have waited until I was off duty."

"Oh? My bad. I thought they said it was urgent," said Tom. "No harm done. You can sign me in, I'm going to see David Feinberg, OK?"

The form was filled and the guard waved him through. Tom walked back down the corridor, around the corner and reached out to the door handle, ready to shout in surprise at his colleague's suicide. He opened the door and was so surprised he forgot to shout out.

Wardle was standing in the middle of the room, hands on

hips. Behind him, David was sitting up on his bed, the door to the cell wide open.

"We've caught the real mole, finally," said Wardle.

"What are you doing, sir? You can't let this scumbag out."

"Knock it off, Tom. I saw the whole thing."

Tom's eyes darted up to the camera.

"You didn't think I would leave Feinberg here with just one camera for company, did you?

Tom edged backwards and spun through the door. A guard outside in the corridor brought a baton crashing down onto his head and the double agent went sprawling to the ground.

Wardle turned around to look at David. "You sure you're OK?"

He nodded and rubbed his throat. "Might have to give choir practice a miss."

"Just get me eyes and ears on the Terror Formers. When they find out they've lost their mole, who knows how they'll react. We need to be ready."

24

———————

S im was ready to open his new eyes. He'd struggled to sleep, lying in bed wondering whether this day would bring daylight or eternal darkness. Either way, for Rosie, he knew this day would bring pain. A black day. A day for tears and mourning. A coffin containing an unknown body had been taken up to Scotland and would soon be turned to ash. Wardle had promised to attend the funeral and offer his support to Sim's wife. Widow.

The surgeon had returned and was fussing with Sim's bandages. She prodded his eyebrows and cheek bones. They were still a bit tender. The room had gone dark again. Sim could tell even through eyelids still closed.

"That's a good sign, right?" he asked the doctor. "If I can tell you've dimmed the lights, must mean I can see something. Doesn't it?"

"I haven't dimmed the lights yet."

"Oh."

"Hang on a moment." She wiped a cloth across his eyelids. "OK. Now you can open your eyes."

Sim took a deep breath and looked. A dark grey fuzz. He

blinked a few times as his eyes watered. The dark grey became light grey in patches. A fuzzy image began to form.

"Errmm. Well, I can see something."

"Good. The next few hours will be key. If the new retinae are taking, your vision will sharpen. By tomorrow, should be back to normal."

"And if not?" asked Sim. He heard the doctor stand up. A grey blob moved away from him.

"We'll cross that bridge, if we have to." The door to his room clicked shut.

By the time lunch arrived, Sim could tell there was a plate in front of him. And some sort of food. Curry, from the smell of it. There was a screen in the corner of the room. Somebody else had come in and turned it on, typing in some commands.

"This is a live feed from Director Wardle, Mr Atkins. Hidden camera."

Sim shuffled closer to the screen. Rows of seats in a large, modern building. Lots of people in black clothes. Two people at the front, comforting one another. His mum and dad, presumably. Sim watched his own funeral in grim silence, letting his food go cold. As the coffin disappeared into the chamber behind the curtains, a figure next to his parents began to sob. Shoulders convulsed, head bowed. Sim couldn't see the face, and even the body was blurred thanks to his new eyes, but he could just tell it was Rosie. What had he done? What sort of a man does that to his pregnant wife? He looked down at the half-full plate in front of him and pushed it away.

David Feinberg was sucking on a strepsil, his throat still sore from his run-in with a noose. He had made his peace with God, thinking he was going to die, not knowing about Wardle's subterfuge. But David was glad not to be meeting his maker just yet. The precious roll tab had been retrieved, still linked into the Terror Formers' network. He had important work to do. The traffic on the terrorist's network was building in volume. The tone of the messages was approaching excitement. Still nothing explicit about the big mission – its objective and method of delivery. But it was imminent. He was sure of that.

A message pinged on David's desk glass. Another request for a progress report from Director Wardle. The third today. And it was only just gone lunchtime. Well, it would be just gone lunch if David had actually stopped to eat anything. He set a routine running to search for any financial details in the message boards and files being sent across the network. His stomach complained about the missing meal and the IT expert pushed back his chair in search of some kosher food.

Nothing decent in the staff canteen, but plenty of choice in the streets around the centre of Birmingham. David strolled in the sun, a gentle breeze tugging at his jacket. His feet were on auto-pilot as he walked to his favourite sandwich bar, still turning over the problem in his mind. How to find out what exactly the Terror Formers were up to? He hoped that his search algorithm would turn up something helpful while he was out eating.

David was disappointed in the corned beef sandwich, but not with his search engine. Sitting back down at his desk, he discovered that his routine had linked a number of odd transactions spanning the last two or three years. All of them involved pay-outs from a casino. Regular winnings across a number of Terror Former operatives. Too regular, too large to be a coincidence. David knew, from bitter experience, how fiercely casinos protect their profit margins. In his youth, he had tried to use his programming skills to defeat the odds in a Tel Aviv casino. He'd been lucky to escape with his balls intact. Why was this casino not being more careful? It had to be a front for something. The Golden Antlers, in Kiruna, Sweden. That place rang a bell. He looked it up on his desk glass.

Ahh, yes, the newest spaceport for Virgin Galactic. But look at that. The headquarters for ESCO are also located there. Shalom.

David put in a request for information to the Swedish authorities and leant back in his chair, slurping a sugary drink to try to take away the taste from that sandwich.

One fizzy can – and several sneaky games of *Angry Martians* on his wrist tab – later, the material from the Swedish employment agency came through. He cross-referenced the known employees of ESCO with the Terror Former operatives receiving pay-outs from the casino. Seven of the eight matched. Good enough for him. David sent an update report to Director Wardle.

His phone rang almost as soon as the message had been sent. "Feinberg? Wardle, here. This is good work. Not good enough, but helpful."

David felt his smile disappear as he listened to his boss.

"We already suspected the link to ESCO. In fact, we have an agent heading to Sweden right now. But this casino information may provide a useful entry point."

"Thank you, sir."

"What we really need is more information about the North Korean situation. I have agents on standby, of course. But they can't just barge in again like Jung Li did. We need to know if the Terror Formers really stole that nuke. And what they intend to do with it."

"Understood, sir."

"Do you? Because the South Koreans and Japanese are

already doing their nut about all the military activity in the area. Even the Chinese are on tenterhooks. If the Terror Formers blow up a warhead in Pyongyang, the North Koreans will assume the rest of the world is out to get them. They'll lash out with anything and everything."

There was silence on the phone for a moment.

Wardle continued. "But I don't know. Something doesn't smell right with that plan. Not quite their style."

David pulled a face, grateful this was not a vid call. "Style, sir?"

"All-out war in Asia. What does that achieve for the TF? I mean, it's not a climate change thing. Nothing about the environment or Mother Gaia. Could be wrong, of course. Maybe they are the sort of bastards who just like causing death and destruction."

"Understood. I'll keep monitoring and look for further clues."

Sim was getting ready to go to the airport. The cosmetic treatments – the dyed hair and coloured contact lenses – had been sorted. His eyesight was becoming sharper. Not quite 20:20 yet, but good enough for now. He bent over the sink to wet his face, ready for a shave. When he looked up, the face staring back at him was not his own. The razor blade ran over contours that were not there before. His skin felt dull – he could see the blade sweeping across his cheek, but shaving had become a visual task, not a tactile one.

The blade was unsteady in his trembling fingers. A line of red showed on his top lip as the razor slipped. He saw blood but felt no pain. It was strange and bewildering. Worse somehow than facing down an armed opponent in the field. This way, he had become a nobody. He waited until the bleeding had stopped, towelled his face dry and got dressed.

He was already dead, his loved ones thought. There was no turning back now. So, let that be his armour. Nothing worse could happen to them. The pain of losing a loved one had already happened. If he failed in this mission, they would never know. If he was going down, he was going down swinging. He grabbed his bag and walked out to the waiting car. Next stop Kiruna.

Director Wardle was missing his wife, almost as much as he missed his fishing. It was a surprise when he admitted that to himself as he browsed through the latest copy of Angling Times. Her cheerful presence at home, the gossip from friends that Anthea had used to distract her husband from the daily pressures of work.

A message from Anthea had popped up on his wrist tab. She, apparently, was having a great time at her sister's house in the Cotswolds and did not seem to be missing him much. He closed the message without replying and swiped the electronic copy of the fishing magazine into the trash. He checked on his calendar. Another appearance in front of the Joint Committee on Security later that day. Damn, he'd not read his briefing notes yet. He pressed one of the mic buttons on his desk.

"Tom! Why didn't you..." And then he stopped. Tom was not helping with JCS anymore because he was locked in a prison cell a long way from here. Maybe never to emerge again. Wardle still felt an unpleasant grip across his chest whenever he thought of his ex-assistant. Not spotting him as a mole sooner. How many lives had been jeopardised – agents and civilians – by his incompetence?

Wardle knew that he needed a new assistant, but did not trust himself to pick the right one, not yet.

Well, he would have to cram the briefing papers on the train down to London. He knew what most of the questions would be about anyway. Value for money, departmental budgets, results, blah, blah, blah.

The video conference line started flashing at him. The British Embassy in Beijing was calling. *Hmm, not used that channel in a long time.* He swiped it open. A subtitle appeared which said 'line secure'. Freda Brightwell was staring into the camera.

"Director Wardle, I'm glad I caught you."

"Brightwell. Everything alright?"

"I lost touch with GR8. We were heading to the North Korean border but things got messy. I think I'm jeopardising the mission, sir."

"Nonsense, still my best field agent."

"Right skills, wrong skin for this one, sir. Gopal and Rabten, they can blend in. Close enough at least to look Chinese. I stick out like a sore thumb."

"True. But do you trust that pair? We're still not sure what the Terror Formers are up to, or what you'll need to stop them."

"I've been stuck in a Russian prison with them, trekked halfway across Asia with an assassin on our tail. I trust them, sir."

"Well, you're probably right. The best hope for the Korean mission is secrecy, not numbers. OK, come back to the UK straight away. Don't worry about covering your tracks. If the Terror Formers are still monitoring flight details, that may help them think we're abandoning the investigation. Besides, I have some bad news. You ought to know, Atkins is dead. Terror Formers got to him."

At first, Wardle thought that the transmission had been lost.

Freda's image just froze on the screen. She was looking down. A faint nod of her head and then she reached forward to terminate the video conference.

Wardle had just finishedbreakfastathis desk andwas contemplating a second espresso when the emergency channel flashed up on his screen. Another call from Beijing. Not the embassy but an OD wrist tab. He waited for the encryption software to kick in.

"Brightwell, is that you again?"

"No, Mr Director, it's Gopal. We've lost her, sir. We've damn well lost her."

"What are you talking about?"

"Rabten and I. We got split up from Freda inside a Chinese government building. She had hidden herself in a crate and—"

"I spoke to her only half an hour ago. She's safe in the British Embassy."

"Thank goodness for that. Rabten, you hear that? Freda's OK. Look out! Behind you."

Wardle was about to reply when he heard a scuffle at the other end of the line. "What's going on there?"

"Sorry, Mr Director, we had to get out of sight. We left the government building in rather a hurry. Hiding in a damned ugly part of the city. Rabten is just dealing with some muggers."

"Stop messing about and get on with the mission. Get yourselves to the export agency – they've been instructed to offer you every assistance in transporting you to the North Korean border."

"What about Freda, sir?"

"She's heading back to Britain."

"So just Rabten and me? To find this missing warhead and take out the terrorists? Isn't it a job for the Hereford mob?"

"Can't risk the SAS. If they get spotted, the North Koreans will think it's an invasion. They have plenty of warheads left. Start lobbing them around Asia, maybe even across the whole world if their missile technology's up to it."

"Should we try to get some help from the Chinese, instead of sneaking around?"

"Not sure I trust them. They might try the invasion option if they think there's a warhead on the loose. Besides, you two are not exactly popular with the Chinese authorities after what you did six years ago. Let's hope the MSS haven't cracked our codes, eavesdropping on this."

"So where do you suggest we start looking?"

"Just get near the border. Somewhere full of tourists. And wait for further instructions."

25

───

South Korean Civilian Control Line

A truck pulled up at barriers that marked the entrance to the last few kilometres of South Korea. The pick-up had big off-road tyres and an open bed behind the cabin. The driver was Park Shi-woo. He lowered the window and reached inside his dusty windproof jacket. The passenger handed over his document too. The uniformed guard inspected the ID cards while a colleague checked the equipment visible at the back of the truck. A grunt and a nod were all the driver got as the guard handed back the IDs. The barrier was raised. A man with stripes on his sleeve came out of the control office next to the barrier.

"They employing school kids these days?" He shook his head and bent down towards the driver's window. "Don't forget to check in with us every four hours. And you need to be back here by sunset."

Shi-woo nodded and closed the truck window. He looked across to the east. The dark blue sky had faded to milky white towards the horizon. Clouds were tinged with pink. He smiled as he slid down into a lazy driving position and stamped on the accelerator. In the rear-view mirror, the fence and gate disappeared behind the dust kicked up by the tyres.

"This is pretty cool," said Ryu Min-jun, the man in the passenger seat, as he slurped from a battered aluminium camping bottle. Unspoiled countryside stretched away on either side of the road. Before long, it felt like they were the only two people on the planet. "When was the last time you got this close to the DMZ?" asked Shi-woo.

"Huh, can't remember. About ten years ago, some big school trip. Barely allowed out of the bus. Not like this."

"There must be dozens of teams all along the border doing the same thing as us."

Min-jun grinned. "Imagine if it was us that found one…"

"A tunnel? No chance. Last one of those was in 1990. Fifty years of looking and only four ever found."

"Yeah, but the North is acting really weird right now. Maybe they've started a new one."

The driver shook his head. "Don't hold your breath."

"If you're so sceptical, why bother volunteering?"

"Ahh." Shi-woo smiled and wiggled his eyebrows. "Got me a camera hidden under the spare tyre."

"You what? You're going to photograph the DMZ? You know that's illegal. And potentially lethal. If the North have any snipers watching—"

"I'm not photographing that. I'm here to capture the wildlife."

"Yeah, right." The truck bounced on its suspension as they went over a large pothole in the crumbling road. Some water spilled out of Min-jun's drink bottle and dribbled down his leg. "Watch it."

"Think about it. The DMZ has had virtually no human contact for decades now. Nature reclaims its own. Endangered

species. Red-crowned cranes, moon bears, even Amur leopards."
Shi-woo was counting off species on his left hand. The steering
wheel slipped as they went around a bend in the gravel and the
car slid momentarily.

"We'll be an endangered species if you don't keep your eyes
on the road."

The truck stopped in a clearing next to a hill. Thick forest
surrounded them. Shi-woo wondered what they would look like
if he could launch a video drone from here. Like ants on a bare
patch in a dark green rug, maybe. The men went to the back of
the vehicle and lowered the tail gate. A selection of digging
tools, camping gear and some more unusual items waited for
them, under a tarpaulin covered in fine dust from the journey.
Shi-woo reached for something that looked like a metal
detector, with an extra-large head, and clipped a foldable spade
onto his belt. Min-jun grabbed a box that had headphones and
two pads attached via wires.

"Right, here's our grid," said Shi-woo, spreading out a map
on the bonnet of the truck. "I'll do geo-phys on A1-A4, while you
listen in B1-B3."

"OK." Min-jun started walking into the trees, heading for the
brow of a low hill.

"See you back here in a couple of hours," Shi-woo shouted.
A couple of birds broke cover from the woods behind him. He
watched as they climbed into the pale dawn sky. Shi-woo bent
down to unscrew the spare tyre and fetched his camera from a
hidden recess. Slinging it around his neck, he set off for his
sectors.

. . .

Min-jun had just finished studying civil engineering at university. Soon he would be applying for jobs. Not soon enough, according to his parents. Final exams had been tough. He was going to enjoy the summer before stepping onto the corporate ladder. The call for volunteers – to help look for new 'tunnels of aggression' – had been too exciting to turn down. Min-jun knew his way around a listening device and had been paired up with a bossy archaeologist. Min-jun wished he'd been allowed to drive the jeep. But still. Getting this close to the De-Militarized Zone... the stuff of legends.

He had covered sector B1 already and had descended from the hillock. There was a stream that ran through B2 and Min-jun headed there next to taste the water. He took off his headphones and enjoyed the near-silence of the surrounding trees. A gentle breeze played across the leaves and a fish broke the surface of the stream with a pop. The air smelt so fresh, it was like somebody had given him a third lung.

As Min-jun bent down to drink at the water's edge, he heard something that made him freeze. There it was again. A deep snuffling noise, and a sound like claws raking the ground.

"OK, Shi-woo, very funny. You can come out now." The snuffling and scraping stopped.

"You can't have finished your sectors yet."

Something in the trees on the other side of the stream growled.

A low, lingering snarl.

Min-jun stood up and backed away from the water. "I'm not scared, you know."

A shadow emerged from the trees opposite Min-jun and solidified into a black bear. It sniffed the air and reared up on its hind legs. There was a crescent of white fur on the bear's chest. Min-jun's bladder emptied itself, soaking into his trousers and socks. He screamed and ran for the truck.

· · ·

Park Shi-woo took a sip of beer from his bottle and shook his head. "I can't believe you got that close to a moon bear. Lucky so and so."

Min-jun shuffled in his spare trousers, looking down. His face reddened slightly. "Didn't feel that lucky at the time."

Shi-woo leant in closer to his colleague. "I got some nice pictures of two different cranes. Red crowned and white naped. Pretty pleased with that."

They ate in silence for a few minutes. At the various tables there was excited chatter from other teams that had been out that day, searching for tunnels. The room fell quiet suddenly as somebody turned up the volume on the vid screen. The news was showing on the far wall. Everybody turned to watch.

The main story was of their neighbours. The North Koreans were whipping themselves into a fervour, apparently. The authorities there claimed that some outside forces had stolen a treasured relic of the Democratic People's Republic. There were pictures of crowds in Pyongyang's squares, weeping, pulling their hair, burning images of western leaders. The news story switched to blurry, distant pictures of the village Kijong-dong, just beyond the DMZ in North Korea. Loudspeakers were blaring out messages. 'The thieves will be punished severely.' 'Retribution is upon any who desecrate our beautiful, peaceful country.'

Min-jun took a sip of beer. "Told you they're mad. I reckon there's a tunnel being dug right now, ready to launch a new invasion force."

"So, the bear hasn't put you off the hunt?"

"No way. But I'm definitely packing some heat tomorrow. Any bear comes sniffing around will be sorry it messed with me."

Shi-woo muttered something under his breath as he drank and then looked up. "If you meet another one, please just fire into the air. Don't kill it. OK?"

Two people circled each other across a wooden floor. Each had a long bamboo sword grasped with both hands. A metal grid on their helmets hid their faces from each other. Heavy shoulder pads, a chest plate and thick gloves added further protection. One set of armour was coloured red, the other black. Without warning the person in red took a quick step forward, shouted and smashed their sword down towards their opponent's head. The other person parried with a perpendicular sword then stepped sideways and tapped the other person on the shoulder.

"Don't over commit."

The person in red lunged and shouted again. This time it was a fake attack. When their opponent had raised their sword in defence, a follow-up swipe narrowly missed their ducking head.

"Better attack. Good. Now defend."

The person in black danced sideways then forwards. Their sword blurred as it was raised, lowered, slashed and lunged. Each blow accompanied by an exhorting cry. The first three blows were parried. But the fourth found its mark and the red person fell backwards. Landing heavily, their breath escaped in a hurry. They scrambled to their feet and barged into the person in black, sending them sprawling across the wooden tiles. Before they could get up, red brought their bamboo sword crashing down time and again, until the bamboo split. Then they threw the sword away and took off the grille. It was Mattias Larsson.

The person in black lay there for a moment, recovering from

the assault on her body armour. Precious removed her helmet slowly and got to her feet. "You must learn control."

"Huh," he snorted.

"Look, I know you're mad about losing our mole."

"That imbecile in Overseas Division? He's expendable."

"But what if they get him to talk?" asked Precious.

Mattias walked over to a small table in the corner of the hall. "He knows little." He gulped down a glass of water. "They sell themselves so cheaply these days."

"So... What's wrong?"

"The Heaven Mission. It's taking too long. They're going to get caught."

"They're making progress. Slow, admittedly, but the terrain is tough. Especially during the rainy season. And all the roads are in virtual lock-down. They're travelling by foot now, you know this. Hiking all that way, with the equipment they have to carry."

"Yes, I know. And you know how much is resting on this."

Precious began unlacing Mattias' armour. "I have to admit, I do find the logic behind this mission a bit... fuzzy. I know the oil companies will love it when all the solar panels stop working. But remind me why that's helpful to us."

"Besides the enormous pay check? Look, climatologists reckon global warming has gone runaway, right? Feedback loops multiplying, speeding up the process. Our only chance is to stop the vicious circle."

"And the millions, or even billions, who could die in the chaos?" Mattias shrugged. "The planet is over-populated anyway, using too many resources. If this pares humanity back to a more manageable size, all the better. If the team succeed."

"Relax," said Precious. "Ivan knows what he's doing."

"Tell him to get a move on. And to go to radio silence. We don't want to risk any intercepts."

Precious sighed. She adored Mattias. The man was a visionary. But he had his moods, she wouldn't deny that. He seemed like a petulant teenager at times, even now with all this power and the fate of the world at his fingertips. Precious still remembered the tales of the old kings of Calabar that her mother used to tell her.

They had seemed so commanding at the time, Precious couldn't ever have imagined meeting somebody even more powerful in real life. It was worth putting up with the occasional tantrum.

The villager was standing on the edge of an open-sided hut, watching his stream of piss merge with the rain that ran off the bamboo roof. He finished long before the rain would stop and returned to the group huddled around a small fire. The flames cast a flickering light on the faces of his family and on the ceiling of the hut, chasing away the dark jungle outside.

The meat would be ready soon, his wife had told him. Go get some rice. The man groaned. The rice store was in a different hut and that meant running through the rain and the mud. He looked at his wife and knew better than to refuse.

Soaking wet and sandals caked in thick brown goo, the man bent down to pick up a small sack of rice. A noise from the corner of the hut made him pause. He hated rats and he hated losing precious food to those vermin even more. He slowly reached for the beating stick next to the bags of rice and moved towards the back of the store. He raised the stick above his head and never saw the blade slip between his ribs as a hand was clamped over his mouth. The man slumped to the floor and the killer slipped out into the storm with a bag of rice in each hand.

The rest of the mercenaries were waiting for Julio. They were trying to stay dry under a tarpaulin covered in camouflage netting. As he ducked into the bivouac, Julio shook the rain off his hair and the sacks.

"Watch what you're doing," said the woman nearest him.

The man at the back of the tent, Ivan Jenkins, looked up. "Any trouble?"

"A little."

"How little?"

"Some guy came into the store at exactly the wrong time. I thought they were staying dry in the other hut."

"And?" asked the leader.

"He was going to find me, so I silenced him. No problem." Julio made a stabbing motion with his right hand.

"Yes, it is a problem. Because the family will report the death and the authorities will be under instruction to investigate anything unusual right now."

"Oh."

Ivan shook his head and pointed to the woman. "Tomkins, take Julio back and finish the job. Then hide the bodies, OK?"

"All of them?"

"What do you think?"

"Yes, sir." She pulled out her pistol and fitted a silencer to it. "Come on, Jules. And don't forget your spade."

Ivan went back to studying his map. Hurry up, the last message had said. As if he wasn't pushing them hard already. And radio silence from now on. So, they were on their own. He closed his eyes for a moment and thought about what he would do with his share of the prize. And then shook himself out of the dream. Not yet. Not until the job is done. Heaven Lake awaited them.

26

———————

Kiruna, Sweden

Sim Atkins had arrived in the new town earlier that morning and had already spent a couple of hours just wandering the streets near the centre. His backpack was starting to weigh heavily on his shoulders as the temperature rose. He caught his reflection in a shop window. Sweat was glistening in patches on a face that still looked alien. The pores on his remoulded contours were not yet open. Sim was about to head to the house where he would be staying when he noticed the old red church and its unusual bell tower.

At first, he thought it was rust, but as he drew closer Sim realised that they were wooden buildings, painted red. And the sun was accentuating the dramatic hue. The bell tower sat in front of the church. Its base was a pyramid, and sitting on top was a cube, supported by stilts that reached halfway down the sides of the pyramid. The walls of the cube consisted of a series of pillars with lattice work between them. Sim could just make out the bells and the wooden beams inside. On top of the cube, the bell tower continued upwards with an onion-shaped minaret.

Sim stood for a moment admiring the craftmanship. It dawned on him that the town must have dismantled this old monument, moved it a few of miles down the road and rebuilt it in new Kiruna. Were the locals especially religious? Or was it just a deep respect for tradition and heritage? Moving home was unsettling. Sim smiled at the perfect aptness of the word for a community whose faith in the very ground beneath them had been taken away.

The church clock clicked onto midday and the bells in the tower played a short tune before sounding out twelve strikes. Only a few hundred yards beyond the church was the house where Sim would be renting a room for the month. There was a carport to one side of the building, occupied by a modest vehicle that had been plugged into a power socket. The front yard was covered in gravel, with a variety of potted plants scattered at random. It reminded him of his parent's passion for pottery. Sim felt his boots scrunch on the gravel and then climbed the steps to the front door and rang the bell.

A lady with silver hair and reading glasses halfway down her nose answered the door. She peered at Sim over the glasses and beckoned him to enter. Sim couldn't help noticing that while the left arm holding the door open looked normal, the arm she had used to guide him inside was half the width and shorter, like the withered branch of a tree. She tucked it behind her torso as she saw Sim staring.

"Boots off at the door please," she said in accented English.

She introduced herself as Mrs Andersson and showed him around the ground floor, explaining which rooms he could use and which were private. His bedroom upstairs was a comfortable size and airy even if the décor looked rather shabby. She explained that she had her own bathroom, but that Sim would be sharing the bathroom on the landing with any tourists who rented out the third bedroom. He filled in his details on the home hub, including his new name, Lucas Trent.

"Do you want me to feed you while you stay?" she asked, looking at his stomach. "Fatten you up a bit?"

Sim smiled. "Not sure about the hours I'll be working yet, Mrs Andersson. Best to say no for now, until I know my routine."

"Hope you'll not be coming back at all hours of the night, Lucas, disturbing me and the other guests. Not to mention the neighbours. This is a very respectable street."

"Message received and understood, Mrs A. I'll be good as gold."

"Hmm, we'll see about that. And it's Mrs Andersson, not Mrs A if you don't mind."

She gave him a key to the house and left him to unpack. Sim hid some of his special equipment with his clean underwear and attached a small device to the new keyring. As he went to put his toiletries in the bathroom, he stopped for a moment when he saw his reflection. He stared, tracing his fingers over the new curves and shadows, trying to learn and accept his altered reality.

Sim headed back towards the town square wearing his augmented reality glasses and watched as people passing by were tinged green in his lenses. The glasses had been loaded with the known personnel of ESCO. There were simply too many for Sim to memorize. But any member of staff who came into view would register in the facial recognition software and show up as red in Sim's glasses.

He turned to cross the road. A cyclist was approaching him. The man's body turned red in Sim's field of vision as a name appeared in tiny writing next to the bike. An idea occurred to the British agent and just as the cyclist was about to pass in front of him, Sim stepped out into the road. The cyclist slammed on their brakes, swerved to go around him and skidded. A car coming from the other direction slammed into the bike and the cyclist was thrown onto the bonnet. Their helmet cushioned the initial impact and as they rolled, their arm smacked into the windscreen. There was a loud crack and a howl of pain as the man continued to roll, falling off the far side of the car.

The driver leapt out as Sim rushed across the road.

"I'm so sorry, I didn't see you," said Sim. His stunt had worked a little too well. Sim tried to assuage his guilt with thoughts of the Swedish car's autonomous emergency braking.

The cyclist sat up, cradling his right arm. "Din jävla..." He drew in a deep breath, wincing before he could finish his curse.

"He came out of nowhere," said the driver to the people who had gathered to see what was happening. Close up, Sim's AR glasses showed that the ESCO worker was a communications expert and had been working there for a couple of years. Sim stepped back into the crowd as a person with medical knowledge offered to help.

Sim found the local arbetsförmedling office near the Stadshus. He glanced up at the thin metal clock tower, glinting in the sun. The public employment service office was quiet and Sim did not have long to wait. He explained his situation – looking for a temporary post – and said that he would prefer an international company whose primary language was English. The man on the other side of the desk asked for his qualifications. Communications expert. The man shook his head and said there were no vacancies fitting the bill right now, but if one came up he would be in touch.

Sim gave his contact details and stood up to leave. "You never know, I might get lucky."

Later, he returned to his rented accommodation, weighed down by some new hiking gear and an expensive SLR camera with a variety of lenses. There was a message waiting for him as he logged into the encryption and communication app on his roll tab. The note was from Wardle, explaining about a potential link between ESCO and the casino in Kiruna. He put on a smart jacket and a pair of chinos, then went for a simple dinner in the town centre. He listened to the wide range of languages being spoken at the restaurant while he picked at a not-very-Scandinavian lasagne verde. By the time a large portion of Tiramisu had been devoured, the street lights had started to outshine the late evening sun. Sim wandered over to the *Golden Antlers* casino and put on his augmented reality glasses.

As he entered the large two-storey building, Sim passed under a sign that looked like the inverted arches of a McDonalds restaurant. He couldn't remember the last time he'd had a McFlurry. The grin of past memories was quickly wiped off his face as a security guard put his hand out.

"Sorry, sir. You can't wear those glasses in here."

"Pardon?"

"No AR devices allowed in the casino, sir. House rules are very clear about that." The guard pointed to a set of regulations on a sign next to the entrance. "Happy to look after them for you, sir. They'll be perfectly safe in our cloakroom."

"But I'm short-sighted. How will I see?" Sim could see some customers walking past him and staring. He didn't care if he was making a fuss. He needed those glasses.

"Don't worry, sir, not the first time it has happened. We have plenty of pairs of varying strength. Sure my colleague will be able to find one to suit you. If you wouldn't mind stepping this way." The guard placed his hand on Sim's shoulder and guided him towards a desk without waiting for Sim's agreement.

Sim handed over his special glasses, was given a fob to reclaim them later, and then was asked about his prescription. He made up some negative number and pretended that they were just right when he tried them on. Finally, he was allowed to enter the casino hall. He took off his useless borrowed glasses and stuffed them in a pocket. Sim stood, looking around the bright, loud area, thinking about how he could possibly identify the ESCO employees without his AR glasses. There must have been at least one hundred people visiting the casino that night.

"Shit."

Sim wandered the main hall, watching the glazed faces of people playing the slots. It was an oddly hypnotic combination of coins clunking into slots, barrels whirring and the beeps of losing symbols, broken up by the occasional cheer and louder clunk of coins being disgorged after a winning row. He stood next to a roulette wheel and glanced at the expectant faces. Sim never understood the appeal of roulette. Just like the slots, the odds were clearly against the punters. Only slightly so, but enough. No skill involved to tip the balance in the player's favour. As long as enough customers played the table, the house would always win. A young woman in a shiny dress squealed when the ball landed on her corner at eight-to-one. There had to be occasional winners to keep the hope alive. He shook his head.

He moved on to the blackjack tables and sat down to watch a man accumulate an impressive stack of chips. After a few more hands, the man gifted a small chip to the croupier and exchanged the rest of his stack for several high-value tokens. Sim watched as he wandered off to the cashier near the back of the hall. An idea formed and Sim went to order a drink. He took the tumbler of vodka, a serviette and pen and settled into a seat with a good view of the cashier's desk.

Over the next hour or so, Sim watched carefully for people coming to cash in a big win. He made a quick description of each person and tried to watch whether they left straight away or hung about in the bar afterwards. He noticed four winners – three men and a woman – had gathered around a table in stages. Once all four were there, the cork of a champagne bottle was popped and glasses were charged.

After the second bottle of bubbly had been consumed, Sim was still nursing his vodka and beginning to feel tired. He was about to order himself a coffee when the group stood up to leave. He followed at a discreet distance and watched them climb into a driverless taxi outside. Sim made a mental note of the taxi's number and then went back inside to reclaim his AR glasses.

He wandered back to his rented accommodation. Too cloudy for moonlight or stars and the road that his landlady's house was on had few street lights. It never really got pitch black at this time of year, but Sim still managed to bash his shin on a ceramic pot. He swore loudly as he stumbled in the gravel and a cat screeched as it darted out from some shadowy den. Sim noticed a light flick on upstairs in the house. He glanced at his watch. 2am. Not a good start to his tenancy. He wondered if Jason Bourne had ever had to fend off a punctilious landlady.

27

S im was dreaming of Scotland when the buzz of his phone intruded on the scene. He stretched out an arm to wrap around Rosie and grasped at thin air. The phone buzzed again. He blinked as he tried to focus on the screen. *Shit, nearly noon.* A vacancy had come up at ESCO. Just a temporary one. A communications worker had broken his arm and collarbone yesterday and would be laid up for a few weeks. What a stroke of luck. Could Sim come in for an interview tomorrow, the employment agency worker had asked. Sim got dressed and headed into town.

Once his stomach had been sated by a plate of sausages, smoked cheese and scrambled eggs, Sim set off to find the garage that looked after the driverless taxis in Kiruna. It was a short walk to the east of the centre, just off one of the main roads. A mechanic was working under a vehicle that had been raised up on trolley jacks. Sim bent down to ask where the manager was and a greasy hand appeared, pointing a wrench towards a room at the back of the garage.

Sim knocked on the half-open door.

A woman sitting at a desk looked up. "Yes?"

"Sorry to bother you, but I think I lost my wallet in one of your cars last night."

"Don't think anything was handed in. Hang on. Wilma!" the woman bawled the last word out across the garage floor fighting the noise of an axle grinder that the mechanic was now using. "Wilma!" There was no response. The woman tutted and picked up the phone. She punched one of the buttons and waited. "How many times have I told you not to listen to music when you're on reception?" she said after the ring tone had been replaced by a voice. "Got a man here who says he lost his wallet last night." She placed her hand over the receiver and looked up at Sim. "What time? Where?"

"Just before 2am, I was dropped off at the casino. It was the big black driverless cab. The one with the advert on the side for the Northern Lights safari."

The woman relayed the information and waited again. She looked up and shook her head. "Definitely nothing handed in."

"Oh," said Sim trying to look crest-fallen. "You couldn't tell me who the customers after me were, could you? Maybe they picked it up by accident. Perhaps a reward would jog their memory?"

The woman shook her head. "Can't do that. Against company policy."

Sim extracted a banknote from his pocket and flattened it out on her desk. "Like I said, I'd be happy to offer a reward."

The woman squinted and then spoke into the phone. She listened to a response and scrawled something down on a piece of paper. She slid the information over to Sim and then placed her hand over the money.

As Sim was leaving, he noticed that the grease monkey had appeared from under the vehicle and was taking a break outside.

A cigarette was pursed between purple coloured lips.

Another woman. At least the company's moniker made sense now. Venus Taxis. Sim walked over and nodded towards the car on jacks.

"Never liked electric motors myself. Too fiddly when something goes wrong," he said.

"Don't get much choice these days," she replied, still staring off into the distance.

"Got a nice two-cylinder petrol bike back home."

The mechanic turned to look at Sim. "You after a cigarette, or something?"

"No, no, nothing likely that. But actually. Yes, there was something. You know that big people carrier you have? The driverless one."

She nodded.

"I want to play a prank on a friend of mine. He'll be hiring it soon for a stag party. I wonder if you could modify the driver's seat? I'll pay, of course."

"Modify in what way?" She was squinting at Sim by now.

Sim pulled a piece of paper out of his pocket, with a sketch on it. "Think you can do that?"

The mechanic took the design and looked at it for a moment before smiling. "Yeah, should be easy enough. Stag party, huh?" She dropped her cigarette butt and ground it into the tarmac with her steel-toed boots. "Four hundred euros. Up front." She held out her hand. Sim hesitated and then reached inside his jacket, counting out some notes.

"For that price, I get it done by tomorrow evening, OK?"

Mrs Andersson had made some stew to feed an American couple who were staying at the house and Sim was allowed to have the leftovers. Straight after supper, he set off for old Kiruna wearing his new clothes. In his backpack he had a sleeping bag, a tripod and two zoom lenses as well as a flask of hot coffee. Around his neck was the new Pentax and its wide-angle lens.

The bright sunshine had faded long ago. All the colours were blanched like a printer running low on ink as Sim hiked the few miles west. He glanced at his watch – near midnight. The roads were clear and so was the sky. The mosquitoes seemed particularly hungry and Sim spent half the journey slapping his hand ineffectually against his neck or ankles. The crescent moon was visible in the half-light, just above the eastern horizon. Sim stopped to set up his tripod and used the biggest zoom lens to photograph the celestial body.

He thought of the people he had left behind at Moon Lab One. Elsa, Lin, Yvette. How were they getting on? His chest tightened as he thought too of the corpses still up there. All the workers killed by Doctor Payne. But most of all, Sim thought about his dead son. He realised that he had not thought about James for several days. Pre-occupied with his operations and his mission. But the grief had not diminished. It had merely been stored up, waiting for something to trigger the flood of emotion. Sim discovered that his new eyes could produce tears. He squatted down, wrapping his arms around his shins and rocked to the rhythm of his sobbing.

The skies had darkened a little further by the time Sim collected himself. He had a job to do. He wiped his eyes and gathered his equipment. It was gone midnight by the time the headquarters of ESCO came into sight. Sim could see the peak of the Kiirunavaara and its lob-sided profile. He walked a little closer to the perimeter fence of the security company's grounds and set up his tripod again. This time the lens was pointed at the ground, not up in the sky.

Sim watched the security gate for half an hour. He had snuggled into the sleeping bag to keep warm and had nearly finished the flask of coffee by the time he heard a vehicle approaching. The camera clicked away as the truck was halted next to the barrier and the driver showed some ID to the guards. The vehicle was allowed through.

Sim made notes on the perimeter patrols. And then looked up as another vehicle approached the gate. Sim could not see a driver, but it was a large people carrier with four or five passengers across two rows of seats. As the car was let through the barriers, Sim could see the taxi licence plate. The camera clicked. He would check the details later but it looked like the same one from the casino. He prayed that it was.

Then a noise off to Sim's right, from behind one of the crumbling old houses. Sim quickly swapped out the memory card and panned his camera around to the mountain peak He started taking lots of pictures, pretending not to notice as a pair of near-identical guards approached him.

"What you doing here?" asked the first. "At this hour?" said the second.

Sim looked round at them. "Oh, don't mind me. Just taking some photos of the Kiirunavaara. Did I pronounce that right? New here, myself. They're supposed to be arty. You know, with the milky way in the background. Punters love these ones. Put a limited-edition sticker on a sixty-by-forty and you can sell 'em for five hundred euros."

"You don't say?" Tweedledum came closer and peered at Sim's equipment. He poked Sim's rucksack with the end of his automatic rifle. "This is a restricted area. Not safe to walk around here, 'specially at night."

"Oh, right, nobody told me," said Sim.

"We're telling you," replied Tweedledee. He pulled a walkie-talkie from the back of his belt and relayed a whispered message.

Tweedledum smiled. "Don't worry, we'll give you a lift back to town. Just to make sure you don't get lost on the way back."

"Oh, don't need to go to all that trouble just for me," said Sim. "We insist."

On the drive back, Tweedledum (or was it Tweedledee?) flicked through the pictures on Sim's camera. Would the guard notice that all of the moon and mountain pictures had been time stamped within a few seconds of each other? Sim held his breath and smiled when his camera was handed back. The vehicle dropped off Sim back at his landlady's house, after 1am. As he got out, one of the guards threw the rucksack and sleeping bag out through an open window. The car started to drive off.

"What about my tripod?" Sim shouted.

The car's brakes squealed and the tripod was ejected, clattering to the ground. Sim went over to pick it up as the car zoomed off. One of the adjustment handles had broken off. Sim collected his belongings and scrunched across the gravel to his front door. He noticed that an upstairs light had come on again. He crept upstairs to his bedroom and downloaded the high-resolution pictures from the hidden memory card onto his roll tab.

28

Sim grabbed a cup of coffee from the kitchen as the clouds began to part and the sun emerged. His stomach rumbled as the smell of leftover bacon and toast invaded his nostrils. The look on Mrs Andersson's face told Sim it would not be worth asking for a late breakfast. He drank his americano in silence. After analysing the pictures from his midnight walk, Sim wrote up a progress report for Wardle. He went out to buy a tie.

As he got dressed for the interview, Sim's fingers fumbled with the new tie. It had been a long time since he had worn one of these. And, if he was being honest with himself, there was a nervousness to his movements. He had to decide whether to take any of the Overseas Division special equipment with him. It might help him out of a tight spot but, if discovered, would terminate his job prospects, perhaps with extreme prejudice. Wardle's disguise for Sim might fool them, but finding his pockets full of secret-agent kit would not. At least the employment agency knew he was going to ESCO – it would be hard for the company to cover up if Sim went missing.

He pocketed his new keyring and went downstairs to wait for the taxi. Mrs Andersson saw him looking smart and nodded, with the faint hint of a smile on her face. Maybe the first one Sim had seen from her. *Clothes maketh not the man, Mrs Andersson.* The taxi arrived before Sim verbalised his inner cheek.

The interview went remarkably well. Sim was banking on the guards from the midnight patrol being off duty around lunchtime. And although he had to pass through an iris scanner on the way into the building, the disguise seemed to be working. The person who interviewed him, a black lady who introduced herself as Ms Osundare, was patient and gentle with her questions. Sim did not have to bluff his way through the technical part of the interview. His degree in satellite communications was more than enough.

Precious stood up and offered Sim her hand. "Congratulations, Mr Trent. You have the job."

"Oh, wow," said Sim. "That was quick."

"There are some extra forms I need you to fill in. Basically, the post is just for a month, while Mr Karlsson recovers from his accident."

"Sure, yes, that's fine."

"Why don't you spend the rest of the afternoon here, familiarising yourself with the offices. I'll get one of your new colleagues to show you around." She tapped on her wrist band and spoke into it. "Linnéa, can you come to conference room three, please."

Sim was given a tour of the facility, much like Captain Hamilton had been a couple of weeks earlier. He had already studied the feedback the captain had sent to Wardle, so had a rough idea of the layout of the base. Sim was shown the information nerve centre where he would spend some of his working day. It would be his responsibility to make sure all the news feeds were optimised, dealing with any outages. Double-checking stories for fake accounts.

Linnéa seemed pleasant enough as they strolled around the offices together. Sim watched her carefully. Either she was a very good actor, or she had no idea about the shady side to this whole operation. Assuming that the mission wasn't a complete wild goose chase. He was shown to a desk and given login details for the company's intranet.

"You'll need to register your retina with the central database, just for security purposes. They're very careful about cyber-crime here, of course." Linnéa smirked. "Would be rather embarrassing if a company like this got hacked, wouldn't it?"

Sim tried to smile as he prepared to lean into the retinal scanner. This was the real test for whether Wardle's disguise was going to fool these bastards. Sim blinked a couple of times and then held his eye as wide open as he could for a few seconds. An orange beam played across his eyeball. There was a flash and a beep.

"OK, all done, Lucas." Linnéa's desk glass pinged and went red. "Looks like you have your first assignment." She swiped two fingers across the screen and Sim's new desk glass showed him the details of an issue that needed fixing.

The next two hours passed quickly. Linnéa never let Sim out of her sight and was continually looking over his shoulder at the programming on his desk glass. It was time to go home.

"Come, I'll walk you out," she said.

Djeez, talk about a limpet. Sim was beginning to worry that he would never get a moment to sneak around the offices. If Feinberg's intel was correct, the Terror Formers would be striking soon. Sim had to make fast progress. *Might need to stir things up.*

"Pretty sad to hear about that pop concert in Brazil," said Sim, referring to one of the stories that had dominated the social media feeds all afternoon. "Which group has claimed responsibility?"

"I think they all did in the end. Not even sure what they are trying to achieve any more. Still, if there weren't any terrorists, maybe we wouldn't have any clients, right?"

Sim stared at Linnéa's face. "I guess so."

"See you in the morning, Lucas."

Back at Mrs Andersson's house, a message from Wardle was waiting. Tensions were rising further in Asia. An American aircraft on patrol over the Sea of Japan had been shot down. The North Koreans denied it at first, and then said the aircraft had drifted into their airspace. The Americans were moving a second carrier battle group to the region. Gopal and Rabten would be in position soon, waiting to infiltrate, once they had something specific to go on. There was no time to lose. Sim ordered a taxi for midnight.

Wardle went for a walk along the corridor of OD headquarters. Pacing always helped him to think and was good for his blood pressure, as his doctor kept reminding him. Fishing was what he really needed to calm himself down but, somehow, he doubted that was going to be an option any time soon. He stopped outside David Feinberg's office and went in without knocking. The Israeli IT expert was slumped over his desk.

"Feinberg! What the hell do you think you're doing?"

David sat up suddenly, looking around the room without focusing. His dark hair was sticking up on one side of his head, and matted to his cheek on the other side. He wiped the drool from the edge of his mouth and sniffed. Then managed to focus on his boss. "Oh. Err, sorry, sir, must have dozed off. Is it morning yet?"

Wardle looked around the room. No windows. No clock even. "You been here all night?"

"A lot of the best TF traffic seems to happen overnight."

"Any progress?"

David yawned and rubbed his bloodshot eyes. "It's quite paranoid. There's a lot of discussion of stocking up on supplies. Hunkering down. You know, like they've all got prepper's disease. Or, they know something."

Wardle sat down next to David. "Fits with the idea that they're hoping to trigger world war three with this stolen warhead." He wondered if he'd have time to get to his wife if the missiles started flying. He took his glasses off and rubbed his face. The roll tab on David's desk – the one that was hooked into the Terror Former's communication lines – buzzed and the screen came on. A brief snatch of a pop song played. "What was that?"

"Oh, it's weird. That melody seems to have become their theme tune. Attached to every message from central command."

"Play it again."

David pressed some buttons and a few beats sounded. "Again."

The same snatch of notes.

"I know that tune. From a long time ago." Wardle closed his eyes and hummed the notes. He hummed them again and added a few more notes. He hummed it a third time, adding a falsetto 'Ooh baby.' "Memory like a sieve, these days. Don't ever got old Feinberg."

David's hand went to his throat, a faint bruising still visible where the rope had dug in and squeezed his windpipe. "Oh, I intend to, sir. Only one thing worse than getting old."

"Hmm?" said Wardle looking off into the distance. "Not getting old."

Wardle hummed the tune and started singing as his eyes closed again.

David started to smirk but straightened his lips as his boss' eyes flashed open.

"Belinda Carlisle. Heaven is a place on Earth."

"Never heard of it," David replied.

"1980s. When they knew how to write a song. And Belinda... well she was hard to forget."

"Any of this relevant, sir?"

Wardle's eyebrows creased. "I don't know. You tell me. And don't fall asleep again. Take some stim pills if you have to. GR8 need something to go on."

Wardle was in a first-class carriage on the high-speed train down to London, reading through his briefing notes for the hearing. The steward had just brought him a macchiato. Wardle counted drinks off in his head. Fourth coffee of the day and it was barely past three o' clock. He looked up as golden fields of wheat whipped past his window. He'd be reminding the committee about the crop virus later on that day. His wrist tab buzzed. It was Feinberg. He pressed on the tiny screen and raised his wrist towards his mouth.

"Hang on." He told his bodyguards to secure each entrance to the otherwise empty carriage. "OK. Go ahead."

"It's about that song, sir."

"I'm trying to prepare for a grilling by the Joint Committee, Feinberg. This better be good."

"I can't guarantee anything. But there's a mountain right on the border between North Korea and China. It's a sacred site for the North Koreans."

"And?"

"The mountain is a volcano. One that's laid dormant for centuries. Last time there was a massive eruption, it formed a huge crater and over time that filled with water to form a lake."

"Get to the point, dammit."

"The lake, sir. It's called Heaven Lake."

"Hmm." Wardle looked out of the window. "Not much to go on, but OK let's assume it's the target. Why would the Terror Formers want to blow up a sacred lake?"

"Right on the border between two trigger happy states? Could cause mayhem. But like you said a few days ago, sir, it doesn't seem like the TF's style. Of course, if they placed the bomb on the bed of the lake and cracked open the caldera chamber... we could be talking about an eruption of epic proportions."

"Go on."

Feinberg breathed deeply down the phone line. "An eruption of that scale would fill the atmosphere with ash. Enough to cool the planet by a couple of degrees for a few years or more. We're talking worldwide crop failure. Oh, and forget about any solar panel output. You know how much we rely on those, right?"

The train's motion rocked Wardle back and forth.

"That sounding more like the Terror Former's modus operandi, sir?" asked Feinberg.

PART III

And hast thou slain the Jabberwock?

29

North Korea

The mercenary turned to his companion as his boot disappeared into ankle-deep mud. "If I see another ditch filled with mud, I think I'm going to scream."

"It's rainy season, what did you expect?"

They stopped to shift the pole onto their other shoulders. The heavy cargo swayed at the sagging mid-point. "Don't these people know how to build bridges?"

"Not ones we're allowed to cross." As the other mercenary replied, his foot slipped on the greasy bed of pine needles. The cargo thumped on the floor before he could regain his balance.

Ivan turned around. "Quit your chinwag and concentrate on carrying the bloody payload, OK?" He walked back to the two chatter-boxes and bent down to look at the cargo. He opened the thick cloth bag and took out a spherical lump. Even in the dim light of the pine forest it caught the sun, radiating a warm glow from its white gold surface. The leader tapped a couple of buttons on a small screen that stuck out near the top of the ball. He nodded. "Jones, Humper. You're up next. These two dingoes are on point for the rest of the day. Let's see if they can learn how to keep their gobs shut for a few hours."

Ivan strode up the slope to resume his position at the front, while the two recalcitrant soldiers drew their guns and disappeared off to one side of their colleagues. Jones and Humper humped.

Seven men and a woman sat around the small gas fire while it heated their water. The faint whiff of butane mixed with the musty aroma of damp clothing. The two mercenaries on point had failed to bag any wildlife for supper, so it was hard rations again. Tough to swallow without a drink. And Ivan knew that a hot drink was good for morale, especially when trench foot was starting to set in. The chances of anybody airborne spotting this tiny fire through the heavy canopy were very slim and they were a long way from any villages.

The leader removed his boots and socks, looking at the blisters. He found the worst of the lot and tried to dry the skin before applying a plaster. He pulled at the bruised nail of his left middle toe, wondering if it would come off before they were done here. He looked up and saw others also inspecting their feet, the murmur of discontent almost inaudible.

Once everybody had their tin mugs full, Ivan raised his cup. "Right, lads. We're onto the final straight now. This is where it gets tough. Once we've picked up the diving equipment, there'll be extra to carry. And the mountain will be crawling with tourists and guards. Remember, this is a pilgrimage site for the locals. We'll have to do the last few miles at night. Full camo-gear, proper silence." He turned to look at the two who had already been punished earlier that day.

"How far is the cache, sarge?"

"About ten clicks west of here." He smiled. Delivered a few

weeks ago, right under the noses of the North Koreans. He had to hand it to the Chief, Larsson knew how to plan an operation. He bit into the hard biscuit and chewed it for a minute and then slurped his tea. He tried to smile to the rest of the group as he swallowed the tasteless mash. He really could murder a curry right now.

Breakfast rations were the same as supper. A mug of hot tea and a work-out for the jaw. It was only the sun's rays filtering through the canopy from the east that told the difference in meal times. Ivan's socks had refused to dry out overnight. The team was still grumbling about conditions. They weren't a bad lot really, he thought. The hijack operation had gone as smooth as clockwork. But this had been a long yomp, through terrible terrain, at the worst time of year. He'd seen action in Africa several times during the world war for water but at least there you could drink plenty during the day and cool down at night. There is something particularly demoralising about being continually damp. Eating away at your foundations, like water's effect on old brickwork.

Humper broke wind, pulling the leader out of his morning meditation. Jones looked at his neighbour. "Ahh, mate, that is rancid. No way I'm going behind you in column today. Christ. Talk about chemical warfare."

Ivan stood up and pointed to six of the group. "Right, you lot are going to head to the cache today, while Sing-song and me go scout the mountain. We'll meet you at the cache. Tomkins, you're in charge of the rabble. I'll expect a full inventory and check of the equipment by the time I get there."

· · ·

Ivan and Sing-song stopped for lunch on the edge of the forest. A cold drink and a handful of chocolate-covered peanuts was the sum total of the meal. No fires this close to other people. The leader shivered as a cold wind blew down from the mountain. The pair hunkered down under some camouflage netting. As Ivan glanced through binoculars, five kilometres of open terrain sloped gently upwards to the 9000-foot summit of Mount Paektu. Off to their left was a winding road. An hour passed by. There were a few buses, full of passengers, that climbed the twisting path and a handful of jeeps, carrying soldiers of the North Korean army. The sun was close to its zenith. Wispy clouds cast faint shadows on the ground, but that was all. It would be impossible to cross this open ground during daylight.

Ivan checked something on his wrist tab. "Shit. It's only a couple days past full moon. With no clouds, this place is gonna be lit up like a wedding cake. But we can't wait much longer. Pray for some rain, Sing-song." He clapped his companion on the shoulder.

There was a noise off to their right. A pair of soldiers was approaching, machine guns slung over their shoulders. Sing-song drew his silenced gun and took aim.

Ivan pushed the gun barrel downwards and whispered. "Zero body count. Not yet." He dragged the camouflage net over their heads and waited while the soldiers drew closer.

When they were within twenty metres, one of the soldiers put his hand out and said something in North Korean. Sing song's hand twitched on his gun. One of the guards walked up to a tree and peed against its trunk, whistling a merry tune. The stream of urine seemed to last forever as the two mercenaries lay under their cover, trying not to move, breathing quietly. Finally, the soldier was done. A quick shake of the leg and the pair moved on, not giving a second glance to the lump of green netting.

As the Koreans disappeared from view, Ivan sneezed and wiped his nose on a sleeve. "God, that man could piss like a horse. What do they drink, these guards?"

The howl of a wolf pierced the black shadows. The replies of its pack echoed off tree trunks. Ivan and Sing-song were pleased to locate, at last, the rest of the squad. The pair were very hungry and tired, having covered twice as much ground as the others that day. As the leader approached and shone his light on each of the team's faces, he could see something was wrong.

"What happened?"

"Boss, it's not our fault."

"What isn't?"

"The equipment's not there."

Ivan took a deep breath, trying to control his anger. "You couldn't even follow a simple set of co-ordinates? Bloody Nora. Do I have to do everything around here? Somebody get Sing-song a drink while I go find the cache."

Tomkins followed him into a darker part of the forest. "Boss, you don't understand..." She jogged to catch up.

Ivan turned towards his pursuer. "I don't want to hear it." He stomped off again. He re-appeared ten minutes later, still stomping. The sight of that empty hole in the ground, the camouflage netting off to one side and plenty of tramped-down vegetation around the cache told its own story.

The leader sat down next to the small gas fire. "Where's my brew?" He snatched it off Humper and stared into the flames.

This mission just kept getting worse. He couldn't call for a new drop of equipment, not without breaking radio silence. And even if he did, the delay would be unacceptable. Larsson had been clear about the deadline. Without diving gear, they couldn't get the bomb in place. And they couldn't blow up the warhead on the surface of the lake, that might not get the job done. He took a bite out of his hard rations and reached for his

Babel app. First light, they would go and talk to some locals. And screw the body count this time. Getting back their equipment was all that mattered.

Mattias Larsson's ears were burning. Not because somebody, on the other side of the world, was talking about him. The pain was very real and very deliberate. Precious Osundare was pouring hot wax from the tip of a candle onto his earlobes. He yanked on the handcuffs that secured him to the bed.

"Now, now Mattias. Relax. Embrace the sensations. Let them send little sparks to all of your extremities." She held the candle upright and moved it over his naked body. She stopped it over his left nipple and tipped the candle, letting a few drops of molten wax fall onto his chest.

He writhed again. And smiled. "This is the worst part."

"Oh, we both know that's not true," said Precious moving the candle lower down his body.

"Not this. The mission."

"I'm not going to play if you're not going to concentrate."

"It's all the waiting around, during radio silence. Hoping to hear the confirmation. Not knowing which day it will be. Or whether they've been captured. The plan might be in ruins."

Precious shook her head. "Jenkins is your best soldier. He'll get it done."

"Any other news?" he asked.

She arched an eyebrow and poured hot wax over his crotch.

He bucked up and down on the mattress. "Will you fucking stop doing that?"

Precious sucked her teeth and threw the candle across the room. "ESCO operations are all fine. As always. Don't I look after everything?" She rubbed her splayed hand over his torso and pulled at a piece of wax that had hardened on his skin.

"Who was that man I saw you interviewing the other day?"

"Just some temp we need to help cover the comms stuff for the next few weeks."

"A bit unnecessary given what's about to go down, isn't it?"

Precious unlocked the handcuffs. "What I am thinking is, it will look pretty suspicious if ESCO operations cease the moment the bomb goes off. We don't know how long we'll have to wait, do we?"

Mattias sat up and rubbed his wrists. "You know I don't like using temps."

"Take it easy, we're keeping close tabs on him. Besides, he cleared our security check. And you should know how impossible that is to fake."

"Alright. Fine. What about the Yellowstone bunker?"

"The brochures went out a fortnight ago." Precious smiled. "Got all the richest clients worried about the caldera in the national park. We've had five acceptances already, despite the price tag."

"The ultimate insurance policy. Who wants to be the richest dead person on the planet?" said Mattias.

"More than enough to cover our costs. And it adds a plausible cover to our miraculous survival of the forthcoming shit storm."

"Construction on schedule?"

"Of course, we're already stocking up."

"I want to inspect it all myself. Tonight."

Precious sighed. "OK. I'll let the pilot know. Take off in a couple of hours."

"Just enough time for the rest of my session," he said pulling her down onto the bed.

30

───────

Kiruna, Sweden

The driverless taxi pulled up outside Sim's house just as his landlord's clock was chiming midnight. He crept downstairs, not daring to turn the lights on and fumbled with the door lock. A third night in a row, not getting any sleep. He popped a stim pill in his mouth as he closed the front door as softly as possible. He made sure it was the right vehicle and got in the passenger's seat at the front.

It pulled away and headed for the random address Sim had requested. Once around the first corner, Sim leant across and unzipped the cover on the driver's seat. Beneath, where there should have been foam, springs and heating coils, there was a compartment. It went down through the bottom of the seat, making it just big enough to fit a small person. The mechanic at Venus Taxis had done her job.

Sim shifted over from the passenger seat to the defunct driver's seat. It was not uncommon in driverless cars for all the original controls to have been left in place. Sometimes the owner wasn't sure it they would enjoy being driven everywhere.

Sometimes it was simply left as a back-up in case the automated software ever malfunctioned. Whatever the reason, Sim needed to clamber over the gearstick and squeeze his legs past the steering wheel while the taxi negotiated the junctions and traffic lights of Kiruna. Finally, he was in place and managed to zip up the cover from the inside. He tried to get comfortable kneeling on his ankles, which were being pressed into the cold metal floor of the vehicle.

The taxi arrived at its destination and asked for Sim's wrist tab for payment. Shit, he hadn't thought of that. The vehicle had pulled up near the centre of town. There might be people watching by now. He unzipped the cover a few inches and poked his wrist out, hoping it would get close enough to the machine's payment reader. There was a beep and the taxi's voice confirmed the transaction. Sim drew his hand back into the cover and waited.

His feet were numb by the time the vehicle moved off for its next customers. The mechanic had left a tiny patch of gauze near the top of the seat cover to help Sim breathe. He could just make out the street in front of the taxi and was relieved to see the vehicle pull up outside the *Golden Antlers* casino. After a few minutes, Sim felt the vehicle's suspension react as several people got in the back of the car. He could smell the alcohol almost straight away. As the rear doors slammed, Sim heard the passengers shuffle into place across the two rows of seats.

The vehicle spoke: "Six passengers. All heading to ESCO headquarters, yes?"

"Yeah, yeah, same as always tin-man."

"Hey, wait, did he say six?"

"Shit, there's only five of us. Damn machine can't count none."

"Must be dodgy operating software, some cheap knock-off version."

A German woman's voice cut in. "Or Vindows 11." There was a burst of laughter.

"Would sirs or madam like the windows open?"

"Hell no, tin-man, just drive. Just drive."

There was silence for a few minutes. Sim tried to keep his breathing slow and soft, bracing himself against the inside of the seat as the taxi negotiated the junctions leading towards the main road and onwards to Old Kiruna.

One of the passengers started speaking again. "I ain't ever getting tired of casino night."

"Best part of the job, ja?" said the female comedian.

"Cruising the tables, picking one with a smug-looking guy who's up a load of chips. Then watch his face as I clean up, at his expense."

"Got to hand it to those croupiers, I still don't know how they fix it."

"It's all in the dealing shoe, man, I'm telling you."

"I don't care as long as there is plenty of drinking. Prost!"

"Hah, well said Frida, well said."

Sim's heart skipped a beat as, for a moment, he thought his old OD partner was in the car. It didn't sound like her, for sure. Must be just a coincidence. He wondered what she was doing right now. And then he wondered how long this journey would last. The cramp in his feet was excruciating.

When the taxi pulled up at the entrance to ESCO headquarters, Sim had to fight the urge to shift his weight or sit up slightly to alleviate his ankles. The bright lights of the security gate contrasted with the darkness of the countryside between the new and old towns. Sim hoped that the mechanic had used a heavy gauze to cover his tiny breathing hole. Would it show up under the guard's scrutiny? He held his breath.

Sim could hear a window being lowered in the back of the car.

"Frederick, my man. Got the night shift again? We been working too, brudd."

The other passengers giggled.

"Very funny. Hold on, the vehicle's claiming six passengers. I only count five. You got a stowaway?"

"Course not, Freddie. Just a stupid error by the computer."

"I better check the boot," replied the guard.

"Lighten up, Herr Frederick. You want to give us Germans a bad name?"

"Boring, boring, boring Fred," chanted the others.

Sim heard a click as the boot was opened and then clunked shut again.

"Alright, you lot, keep it down. Before I refuse you entry." Cue for theatrical shushing, louder than the talking.

"Bunch of idiots," said the guard as he raised the barrier and let the vehicle pass.

The vehicle drove forward again. The lights of the security gate faded as the taxi weaved between dark old houses. The shadows receded once more as they approached the main building. The taxi dropped off the inebriated passengers at the front entrance to the headquarters. It sounded more like they were poured out of the car. Sim shifted his weight off his ankles but stayed out of sight. The vehicle did not move off and Sim realised it was waiting for him to disembark too. He had to think of something before the guards came to investigate the stationary car.

"I left something back at the Casino, can you take me back there please," he said in a low voice to the onboard computer.

"Compliance." The vehicle pulled away.

Sim unzipped the cover and as the car passed through the shadows of a decrepit house, he opened the driver's door and tumbled onto the ground. He had tried to leap, but his leg muscles would not react after being squeezed for so long into that tiny space. Fortunately, the car was not going fast. Sim rolled a couple of times in the gravel and came to rest up against the crumbling sidewall of an abandoned home.

He lay there for a moment, wiggling his toes to get some blood pumping again, listening out for the signs of any approaching guards. When he sure there was none, Sim got up and half running, half crouching, he made his way through the shadows. He glanced at his watch. Nearly 2am. The base was quiet. He got as close as he dared to the front entrance of the main building and watched. Nobody. He took a tiny collapsible telescope out of his pocket, pulled it open and scanned the building. The night vision picture in green showed another door, on the far left, hidden in darkness.

Sim hesitated before using his new ESCO security pass. Even if it worked, somebody surely would notice the strange hour that he was entering HQ. He did not have much choice. Trying to hot-wire his way in might take too long and could easily trigger an alarm. He would have to come up with an excuse if somebody stopped him and started asking questions. He brushed the dirt off his clothes and ran a hand through his hair.

Sim pressed his card up against the sensor on the door and waited for it to turn green. For a moment nothing happened. He tensed, ready to sprint back into the shadows if an alarm started flashing. The panel changed to green and he pushed the door open, letting out a long breath.

Sim had memorised the layout of all the subterranean layers of the headquarters as best he could. But even after Captain Hamilton's briefing, and Sim's introduction to the place yesterday with Linnéa, it was confusing. Especially using this side entrance. There were still big gaps in his knowledge. Blank spaces on the map, like the sea-faring explorers of old had to navigate. *Here there be monsters.* Sim nodded to himself. It took nearly an hour to orient himself properly. Partly because of the labyrinthine nature of the corridors and stairways but partly because Sim was still keen to avoid meeting other staff.

He descended to a couple of levels below ground and made his way to the laboratories where the biological work was being done. If ESCO was caught up in the new Ebola strain and had been responsible for the attack on Moon Lab One, surely there would be evidence here. Sim could see a light on. Even now, 3 o'clock in the morning. *Damn.* He sneaked as close as possible to the observation windows and darted a quick look into the lab. Just one person. Man or woman? Hard to tell with the protective mask covering their features. The scientist had their back to the gallery and was looking down at a petri dish.

Sim's hand hesitated, with his ID card hovering next to the door panel. There were no excuses for a junior comms analyst to be visiting the labs, especially at this hour. If he went in now, he would have to subdue whoever was under that mask. And then his cover would be blown. There would be no turning back. But what choice did he have? It might be his only chance of getting the evidence to nail these bastards to the wall. He wanted justice for his son.

He pressed his ID card against the reader and waited for it to turn green. Nothing happened. He tried again. Still nothing. *Shit. There must be different levels of clearance.* He wondered about breaking in, but then heard somebody approaching from down the corridor. Sim hurried off in the opposite direction to think again. He pressed himself flat against the wall in a darkened recess and suddenly felt a wave of fatigue hit him. He yawned and reached for another stim pill. He couldn't remember how many of these he was allowed to take in one night. The department's medical officer had given him some warning about over-dosing but not with any sense of real peril. Sim had not been concentrating back then and was struggling to do so now.

He decided to retreat to the safety of the office where he was supposed to work. He would have to hack his way into the filing system. Other experts at Overseas Division and GCHQ had already tried. But not from here, inside the building, with a staff login. Surely that gave him a fighting chance. He passed a drinks machine in the corridor and grabbed a can of coke. Just like an all-night online gaming sesh, he thought to himself. Shame he couldn't order in pizza.

Sim sat down at his desk and logged into the system. He pulled out a cord from his wrist tab and plugged it into his desk glass. He delved into the servers on the ESCO intranet. Heavily password protected. But the software on his wrist tab made short work of most of these. He opened up dozens of files at random hoping for a eureka moment. None. Half an hour wasted.

Sim took a slurp from his can and decided to focus on all the most recent files. There was an extra layer of security on a folder labelled YB. It had been created only a few weeks ago. About the time that Sim was up on the moon and James was... Sim sniffed and took another big gulp of coke. The screen went blurry for a moment. He blinked a few times and the poor vision passed. It took even longer for the code to break into this section of YB files. Once in, Sim began reading.

He glanced down at his watch. Another forty-five minutes gone somewhere, it was well after 4am now. He shook his head and began reading again. Yellowstone Bunker. There was a bunch of corporate bullshit about this being the ultimate insurance scheme. This place was bomb-proof, nuclear-fallout-proof, disease-proof and isolated to boot. Not even on any maps.

No marauding mobs trying to muscle in on this sanctuary if the world started falling apart.

Sim looked at how much clients were being asked to pay for a lifetime guarantee of entry and indefinite stay in the safest six-star hotel in the world. He whistled. *Why are they building this now? So they can release a pandemic? Use this new Ebola strain to wipe out humanity?* He still needed proof of their involvement with the disease.

He found out where this bunker was. An island in between Norway and Svalbard. Bjørnøya. Maybe one of Wardle's other agents could check it out while he finished this mission.

Sim woke up when his slumped body pushed the empty coke can over the edge of the desk. He sat up quickly and wiped his mouth. Rubbing his eyes, he realised that Linnéa was in the office too. Standing still, just watching him with a puzzled look on her face.

"You've been here all night, yes?"

The adrenalin pumping around his body had forced him wide awake instantly but Sim pretended to yawn to give himself time to think. He hunched his shoulders. "Just wanted to make sure I was on top of things. Understood all the systems."

"I'm impressed. But." She looked him up and down. "You might want to freshen up before we get stuck into the day's routine. I'll get us some coffee."

Sim tried to brush the remaining dirt off his trousers as he went for a shower. He wondered about asking Linnéa for help. Maybe she had no idea what went on here, behind the scenes. She had sounded so proud of the company when she'd showed him around the day before. Maybe she would be appalled if she knew the truth and would offer to help him. Could he risk telling her the truth? As a desperate last effort, maybe.

Back in the office, he tried engaging Linnéa in more conversation, asking about her education and her route to working at ESCO.

"I did social media studies at university. I thought it was going to be so cool, so relevant. What a waste of time. How do you say in English, empty?"

Sim thought for a moment. "Vacuous?"

"Yes," said Linnéa. "I wanted to do something good, something useful. I thought social media was supposed to help society. Here, I can keep people safe."

"Only if they pay, right. What about the masses who can't afford it?"

"That's a pipe dream, Lucas." Linnéa shook her head. "When will I ever get the chance to help that many people?"

"You never know. You never know," mumbled Sim.

31

———

Freda was fiddling with her control panel, trying to get the window blind on her business class seat to raise. The plane was taking her from Beijing to London. She looked out through the tiny portal, trying to figure out whether the route would take the aircraft over the Russian prison that had briefly held her, Rabten and Gopal. She glanced back at the video screen in front of her. For a moment she thought she heard Sim telling her about which films he liked. A replay of a conversation on a plane many years ago. She gripped the armrest and squeezed her eyes shut. *I can't believe he's gone.* Escaped death in a Himalayan crevasse. Survived a knife through a lung. Several narrow misses up on Moon Lab One, judging from the accounts she had read. All that and then some shithead within Overseas Divisions had betrayed him to the Terror Formers.

She passed the hours catching up on the briefing notes from Sim's investigation into the Ebola attack. Captain Hamilton's aborted investigation of ESCO. The foiled attempt to grab Terror Former ring leaders in the Canary Islands. She looked through the glossy ESCO brochure – the public face of this security company. It claimed a perfect track record at keeping its client safe from terrorists. Not difficult to do if you are also masterminding the Terror Formers. But how to prove it?

She logged into the OD system and thought about the investigation into the Canary Island debacle. She realised that the inquiry had not known about the possible link to ESCO at that point. It gave her an idea. She checked the airport logs for the Canary Islands around the time that the *Club Of Rome* had caught some of the Terror Formers. She focused in on private jets and cross referenced them to arrivals from Sweden. There was one, a Challenger 650, that had arrived from Kiruna airport, landing at the Canary Islands one week before the COR mission. Twelve passengers. It had returned to Sweden the day after the mission, empty. She re-read the investigation into that mission. Ten bodies recovered, two had escaped in hydras. The numbers added up.

Freda looked up a picture of the billionaire founder of ESCO. Mattias Larsson. She stared at the face, memorising every detail. *I'm coming for you, Larsson.*

Freda spent the next hour ordering as many gin and tonics as she could. She poured half of them away once the cabin crew weren't watching, but had a couple to taint her breath. And frankly to steady her nerves. As the plane flew over St Petersburg and crossed the Baltic Sea, Freda flipped out. She started swearing. When a steward asked her to calm down, she pushed him out of the way and ran forward. She bashed on the door to the flight deck. Even started yelling about a bomb on board. An armed Air Marshall magically appeared and pulled a gun on her. Freda was handcuffed. But she had got what she needed. The plane was going to make an emergency landing at Stockholm.

As soon as it touched down, fire trucks surrounded the

airplane and inflatable slides were used to evacuate the passengers as quickly as possible. Freda was bundled into the back of an airport security van. It took half an hour for the interrogators to believe who she said she was and bother to check her ID with the UK authorities.

"Of all the idiotic things to do, Brightwell, this really takes the biscuit." Freda had been allowed to make a holive call to Wardle and the small hologram projection of her boss was conveying the full blast of his fury. "The Swedish government will be sending us a huge bill for that stunt. And if the airline presses charges…"

"But—"

"The auditors are hauling me over the coals already. They're just going to love it when they hear about this. I need you to—"

This time it was Freda's turn to interrupt. Before Wardle could finish his instructions, she terminated the call. If he ever followed up on this conversation, she would claim the Swedes had made it time-limited. Freda did not care about budgets and spreadsheets. She had the link between ESCO and the Terror Formers. Maybe it would hold up in a court of law, maybe it wouldn't. She had no intention of waiting around for some legal battle and the risk of a fancy lawyer protecting that bastard. She had the man in her sights. She went shopping in Stockholm and caught a train to Kiruna.

Freda stepped off the train in a new outfit, carrying some improvised kit. She thought about booking into a hotel, to wait while her body dealt with the jet lag. She needed to be razor sharp if she was going to pull this off. But they would probably be monitoring the local hotel registers. It wasn't worth giving them extra time to prepare. A couple of stim pills would have to do the trick.

She caught a taxi out to the headquarters of ESCO and, when she got to the gate, asked to see Mr Larsson.

"Have you got an appointment?" asked the guard. Freda shook her head from the back of the vehicle. "Sorry, no admittance without a prior booking."

"He'll want to see me," said Freda.

"They all say that."

"Tell Mr Larsson that there's a member of British Intelligence on his front door step and if he doesn't let me in right now, I'm coming back with a dozen fully-armed hydras in twenty-five minutes. We'll tear a nice big hole in his fancy fortress so next time we want to come visit, we won't have to ask snivelling little shits like you. Capisce?"

A hurried conversation on the intercom ensued and the barriers were raised. The taxi dropped Freda off at the front entrance and Precious Osundare was waiting to escort her into the building.

"Welcome, Ms Brightwell. This is indeed an honour to receive such a distinguished guest. If only we'd had some warning we could've prepared you a meal, some entertainment." She ushered Freda into the main atrium and then down some spiral stairs.

"You Larsson's secretary, then?"

"It's a little more complicated than that."

"Oh, I'll bet it is."

Precious smiled with her lips tight. "If you'd be so good as to hand over your gun to Frederik, please. Then we can have a nice civilised chat." Two armed guards had appeared from a hidden passage and stood blocking the way to a conference room beyond.

Freda reached inside her jacket. The guards raised their firearms. "Easy fellas," she said, pulling her gun out slowly and releasing the clip. She flipped the gun around and handed it to the guard on the left. The men retreated and Precious led Freda into the conference room.

"So, I am wondering. To what do we owe this pleasure?"

"I came here to talk to Mr Larsson, in person."

"What I am saying is that this is not possible."

"Lots of things seem impossible, until you try. I'm here to talk about the Terror Formers. About Moon Lab One. About Sim Atkins."

"Was he a colleague of yours? I understand he met with an unfortunate ending quite recently. Such a tragic loss. You were close, once, weren't you? Before he married."

"You seem very well informed about Overseas Division."

"That is our job, Ms Brightwell. Basically, we stay on top of developments all over the world. Protecting our clients. Keeping them safe."

"Sounds like the mafia to me. Protection money? Oldest con in the book. Only you don't bother squeezing the little purses, just the big fat juicy ones, right?"

"Nobody forces our clients to sign up. They're welcome to leave at any time."

"Enough with the bullshit." Freda stood up and moved towards the door.

Precious followed her. "Well, this has been fun. Hopefully not a complete waste of your time. Shall I get one of our drivers to take you back?"

"Oh, I didn't say I was leaving." As Freda reached the door, she yanked a metallic cord from out of her belt. Turning quickly, she jabbed Precious in the solar plexus. As the other woman bent forward, she lashed her foot out, trying to knock Freda off balance. Freda dodged the attack and wrapped the cord around her neck. Precious gasped and tried to get her fingers between throat and cord. She kicked out backwards with her heels, but Freda was too quick.

"I think Mr Larsson will see me now," Freda whispered into her victim's ear. She maintained the pressure on Precious' throat but did not tighten it further. The woman was not asphyxiating, not yet. Freda could hear her rasping breaths. She dragged Precious out into the corridor outside the conference room.

Two guards appeared, maybe the same two who had taken Freda's gun from her. They raised their guns and aimed. Freda made sure Precious was between her and the guards. "Stand down," she shouted.

Another man appeared from a side passage. Freda recognised him at once. Mattias Larsson. "Stand down, or what Ms Brightwell? What will you do if my men refuse to cooperate?"

"She dies."

"Really? It takes more than a few seconds to crush somebody's windpipe, you know. Even with a steel cord like you're using. Our research suggests fourteen seconds, minimum. Plenty of time for the guards to shoot you."

"The cord's just holding her in place. The poisoned tip concealed in my bracelet is what's going to kill her. Unless I get some cooperation right now." Freda pulled a bit tighter on the cord. Precious gasped and her fingers trapped under the cord began to bleed.

Mattias turned to look at his guards. In a mock whisper, loud enough for everybody to hear, he said. "She's bluffing." He turned back to face the British agent. "Go ahead, Freda. Once you've killed Precious, let's see how far you get. We have the whole thing on camera. 'Mad woman kills at ESCO headquarters. Guards have to use deadly force to protect rest of staff.' I can see the headlines now. Won't look good for Director Wardle, will it?"

Freda squeezed the cord again as she stared into Larsson's eyes. And then she let go. Precious threw the cord down, turned around to face her attacker and punched Freda in the stomach. It was Freda's turn to double-up. The guards rushed forward and used the cord to bind her wrists.

"So basically, you were going to let her kill me?"

Mattias looked at his partner, deadpan. "Precious, really. We have the most advanced lab in the world right beneath our feet. Developing every conceivable antidote. How much danger were you in?"

Precious sucked air through her teeth.

Mattias approached the British agent. Freda yanked on the cord around her wrists and kicked out. One of the guards hauled back on the wire, while the other crashed a baton into the back of one of her knees. Freda collapsed to the floor, head bowed low. Mattias bent down and lifted up her chin until she was looking into his face. "This does seem all very rash of you, Ms Brightwell. You're normally so calm and rational. At least that's what your OD assessments keep saying. Of course, I've not read them all... Maybe something has upset you recently? It couldn't be related to the death of a certain Sim Atkins, could it?"

Freda pulled her chin away from his hand and looked sideways as blood dripped from her wrists where the cord had bitten deep. "It must have been painful when he chose Rosie McDonald over you. Even more so when he said yes to Elsa Greenwood on Marinus." Freda hauled herself upwards. She lowered her eyebrows, pursed her lips together and tried to burrow her gaze straight through the forehead of her tormentor.

Sim was heading out of the building. Exhausted after just a couple of hours sleep. Plagued by indecision about Linnéa, whether he should confess his true purpose in being here in the hope that she would help. All he had to show for the break-in at night was the information about a hidden shelter in the middle of the Norwegian Sea. He needed to relay that information to Wardle as soon as possible. But was it enough? He doubted it.

He'd been walking along with his head down, watching his feet, in a semi-trance. A noise in the corridor up ahead made him look up. A woman was being frog-marched away by a couple of guards. He squinted and then shook his head. *Must be seeing things. I've got Freda on the brain at the moment. A nosy journalist?*

He remembered he had left something on his desk. He jogged back to the office, all the while wondering about the woman he'd just seen. *It couldn't have been, could it?* He pushed open the door to his office.

"Linnéa? I just saw a woman being escorted out of the building by a couple of guards. Practically dragging her off. You don't know what's going on, do you?"

She looked up from her screen. "Hmm, could be an industrial spy, though they tend to try hacking in these days. Probably just some journalist poking their nose around. Trying for a scoop. You'd be surprised how many we get."

"What will happen to them?" Sim asked.

"Oh, just driven back to town. Put on the first plane out of here, I expect."

"That's all?"

"What do you think we are? A bunch of thugs?"

32

—————

S im ran out of the building towards the main gate where a vehicle was waiting to be let out. It looked as though there were two men in the front seats, but no sign of Freda. The barriers were just being raised as Sim got close. Before the vehicle pulled away, he heard a muffled cry and a thump from the boot of the car.

One of the guards at the gate spotted Sim. "Oi! Where do you think you're going?"

"On an errand, need to pick something up from town." Sim flashed his staff card to him.

"New, aren't you? Planning on walking?" The guard kept walking closer, finger resting on the trigger guard of his machine gun.

Sim tensed, ready to leap at the man if he came any closer. He couldn't afford to lose sight of that car.

The guard reached into his pocket and tossed a key to Sim, nodding towards some cross-country motorbikes off to the side. "You can borrow one of our patrol bikes, mate. But make sure it's back by six, alright?"

Sim grinned at the man. "Sure. Thanks." He jumped on the

nearest bike, gave it a kick start and span it around with a squeal of the rear wheel. He revved the engine and zoomed off as soon as the guard had raised the barrier. Sim tried to remember his way back to the main road. He hunched himself low over the handle bars and opened the throttle even more. He caught sight of the car just as it was leaving Old Kiruna, pulling out onto the E10. But instead of turning left towards the new town, the car went right. Sim followed, pulling out in front of a large truck that slewed as the driver slammed on the brakes. Lights flashed in Sim's wing mirrors as he accelerated.

Sim was still trying to blink away the dazzle of the truck's headlights when he saw the car pulling off the main road again. Left, towards the mining operation. On the near side of the Kiirunavaara peak there was a big wedge-shaped chunk missing, as if some giant had buried a hatchet into the side of the mountain. To the left of the indentation, a gentle slope. To the right, a steep incline and then a plateau. The low evening sun cast long shadows over the left-hand face of the peak. There were some buildings up on the plateau, set just back from the edge. Sim could see steam rising from a few of them.

The car followed a trail around the back of the small mountain. Sim tailed at a distance. There was a train track leading off to the west. It seemed to start inside the large hill, though Sim could not see the hole where it disappeared. On this side, there was a steep slope up towards the buildings on the flattened peak. Sim saw sections of a twisting road that led up to the processing plants. But the ESCO car stopped short of that. The two men got out. Sim threw his bike on the ground and lay flat. Damn this evening sun. The whole side of this mountain was bathed in a warm orange glow. How was he going to get close?

The driver opened the boot of the car and gestured with his gun. A woman struggled out, hands tied behind her back. No doubting it now, it was Freda. Her strawberry blonde hair was much longer than he remembered, tied into a tight plait. But even now, she still held herself with such poise. She probably had some cunning plan to get herself out of this. That would be just like her. But Sim wasn't going to test that theory. His fists clenched as the guards pushed her towards the hill.

One of the men began to climb the slope, while the other prodded Sim's old partner in the back with the barrel of his gun, getting her to follow the first man. Sim waited until they had gained some height and ran over to the car. He crouched behind it while the other three continued their ascent. As he watched them climb, Sim searched desperately for a route up that would not be in plain sight of the guards. "Fuck." There was absolutely no cover at all.

He ran back to the bike, hauled it up and started the engine. Sim raced the bike around the curve of the mountain, until the sun's rays were casting oblique shadows across its face. He drove off the road and began to climb the slope, bouncing over the rutted surface and skidding on loose scree. He had lost sight of the guards and Freda but that meant they could not spot him either. Sim just hoped that they were heading for the industrial complex. If they shot Freda halfway up the slope... it didn't bear thinking about.

Even on a motorbike, the hill was hard work, avoiding the boulders and the deep ruts. Sim regularly rode his Triumph Sprint around the sinuous roads of Sutherland, but it had been many years since he had been dirt-biking. The old skills were there, rusty perhaps, but urged on by Freda's peril he was remembering them fast.

When he got near the peak, Sim left the bike and covered the last two hundred metres on foot. Crouching low, he could see the three people just nearing the peak too, a little to his right. Straight ahead was a series of buildings, all laid out along the same North-South axis. The first few formed two sides of a triangle and then several behind followed in a row, as if the whole grey complex described the outline of a ship. The impression was continued by an orange conveyor belt that was feeding rubble into the heart of one of the buildings halfway down the ship's hull, like a gangplank.

The thugs were leading Freda towards the nearest building. There was a rough-cast car park between them and the building. As they started to cross it, a miner appeared in dirty overalls. The thug behind Freda threw his hand over her mouth and dragged her behind one of the parked cars. The other one ducked behind a closer car and raised his gun. The miner did not see them, too busy trying to light a cigarette while admiring the amber sun, low in the sky. After a few drags of nicotine, he got into a beaten-up black car and headed down the hill.

Sim had crept closer to the man guarding Freda, while their attention had been fixed on the miner. But he was not quite close enough to spring an attack by the time the worker had left. The thugs continued to frog march Freda towards the nearest building and Sim's chance had gone, for now. At least he had more cover, from the cars, containers and outbuildings that dotted this part of the industrial complex. The noises from the machinery masked any sound Sim was making on the gravel and the guards were watching for movement from the buildings ahead. He stayed close, hoping for another chance to strike.

In the distance, Sim could see more workers entering and leaving buildings at the far end of the processing plant. He noticed the men guarding Freda were proceeding more cautiously too, by now. They made their way to a door in the side of the first building. It looked like a fire escape. There was a window next to it. One of the guards stared through the glass for a few seconds. He raised his gun and smashed it into the window, butt first. After clearing away the shards, he climbed through the opening. A moment later, the door was opened from the inside and Freda was pushed into the building.

Once the door had clicked shut again Sim ran up to the window and crouched below it. He listened and then poked his head above the sill. The others were already at the far end of the room. Sim could see many crates stacked along the walls, some on pallets that were covered in shrink-wrap. There were a couple of tool boxes on work benches off to the right. Sim was trying to figure out what he could use as a weapon, when the door at the far end of the room opened and another miner appeared. The noise of loud machinery beyond invaded the silence.

The man stopped when he saw the two guards and Freda. He shouted something in Swedish and pointed at their guns. One of the guards replied, signalling with his hands that he couldn't hear what was being said and beckoned the man forwards. Sim wanted to shout out a warning, but knew that he had to stay hidden. As the miner came closer, Sim saw one of the guards grab hold of the restraints on Freda's wrist. The other guard reached behind his back and pulled a knife from his belt. As the miner leant closer, the guard plunged the knife into his neck and clamped a hand over the man's mouth. The door swung closed and the machinery noise was cut off.

"Huh, maybe we can ditch this body with hers," said the killer, nodding his head towards Freda. "Industrial accident, right?"

"Yeah, nice one."

They moved through the door and as soon as they were out of sight, Sim vaulted in through the broken window. He ran up to the work bench and found a hefty wrench. He was about to dash off in pursuit of Freda when he noticed a small cardboard box next to the tools. It had some English written on the box. 'Pelletized samples.' He flipped the lid open and saw dozens of greyish purple balls. They were like rough-cast marbles, only about a centimetre across. Sim tipped the box into his pocket and ran for the door.

The next room was much longer than the previous one. Sim could feel the floor thrumming through the soles of his boots. A machine in two sections, connected by a conveyor belt, ran the length of the room. The first unit, nearest Sim, resembled a huge tumble dryer and the noise coming from it was painful. A cylinder, on its side, was rotating but held off the ground by stanchions at either end. Inside, something was grinding away. He shook his head, trying to think. Beyond this machine there were three smaller cylinders, perpendicular to the large one. They seemed quiet and still.

The two guards and Freda were near these smaller cylinders. They had dragged the dead miner across the room, but stopped pulling now. The two men looked at each other and one said, "This will do."

Sim had run out of time. Ducking behind the large cylinder he pulled a couple of metal marbles from his pocket and threw one at the guards. The ball clanged into the machine they were standing next to, causing them to look up, startled. Sim threw again, this one catching a guard on the side of his head.

"What the fuck was that?" The guard rubbed the mark where he had been hit and started walking towards Sim's hiding place, clicking the safety off his machine gun. Sim retreated around the end of the cylinder. As the guard got to the end of the machine, he failed to notice the balls that Sim had quietly scattered across the floor. The guard's foot came down on two of the marbles and slipped. Not enough to topple the man, but his arms flailed as he tried to maintain his balance. Sim leapt out and brought the wrench crashing down on the man's head. It missed, but crunched into his collar bone. Sim heard something snap and the guard howled with pain. The machine gun fell to the floor. Sim swung again with the wrench, this time from left to right and it smashed into the man's face. The guard collapsed to the floor. Sim bent down to pick up the machine gun but before he could grab it, a burst of bullets thudded into the cylinder next to him. He dived for cover.

Sim tried to reach around the corner for the gun, while staying hidden behind the machine. As his arm poked out, another burst of bullets. One of them nicked his sleeve. A burning sensation whip-cracked up his arm. Sim yanked his arm back and wrapped the fingers of his left hand around the wound. It was a deep cut, slicing open his forearm, and would need bandages. But he did not have time for that. At least the bone was intact, he could still use the arm if he ignored the pain.

Sim scrambled to the far side of the cylinder and crept along the room towards Freda. He held the wrench in his left hand now, and had the few remaining pellets in his right hand. Blood from his wound was dripping into his palm, mixing with the rough marbles. He heard the guard start to walk towards his fallen colleague. The footsteps ceased. Sim realised he would be a sitting duck if the man climbed across the conveyor belt and came down this side of the room. Just in time, Sim dropped to the ground and rolled under the large cylinder as the guard did exactly that. A hail of lead rang out against the end wall.

Sim rolled out from under the cylinder into the side of the room he had started on. Freda was standing there, hands still tied behind her back. The bindings seemed to be looped around something, because she was struggling but not able to leave that spot. Her eyes widened as Sim ran up but she did not speak. Her forehead creased as she stared at her rescuer. The makeshift handcuffs had been hooked onto a protrusion from one of the three smaller cylinders. Once Sim had unhooked Freda's bindings, the British agents retreated to the end of the room.

The guard appeared at the far wall. He squeezed the trigger on his gun, aiming at the pair as they ducked for cover. There were only two shots, both pinging into the wall next to them. And then the noise stopped. The guard looked at his machine gun and swore. He gave his colleague's body a flick with his boot. No reaction. He knelt down to pick up the second machine gun and started walking slowly forwards. He had a clear sight of both doors. Sim and Freda were trapped.

Crouching there, Freda noticed some Swedish writing on the three cylinders that she could not understand but a symbol that she did. Underneath there was a large red stop button and next to that a green switch. As the guard came closer she flicked the switch. The three cylinders began to hum. The gun flew out of the guard's hand and clanged into the side of the cylinders. Sim's wrench also was yanked from his hand and stuck to the machine, magnetised. Freda leapt out from behind the cylinders and aimed a roundhouse kick at the guard as he tried to pull his gun away from the machine. Her foot caught him in the lower back. He gasped in pain and turned to face his attackers. Sim circled around so that the guard had two opponents coming at him from different sides. He was much taller and broader than either of them. Sim threw an uppercut that the guard dodged easily but the distraction was enough. Freda landed a kick to his head and the fight was over.

"There's some cord in the other room, I'll get them both tied up before they come around." He jogged off while Freda stood guard. As soon as he had them tied up, he ran up to Freda and gave her a hug. "It's so good to see you again."

She stood there, not returning the embrace. "Err, thanks for rescuing me. But... do I know you?"

"It's me, Freda. Sim." She shook her head.

"I've had some surgery as a disguise."

"Prove it."

Sim lifted up his shirt to reveal the scar that ran between a pair of ribs on his left. Freda's fingers tracked the milky white line and then her arms wrapped around him, squeezing tight.

"Wardle told me you were dead, the shithead."

Sim felt tears wetting his cheek as they stood there for a moment, not caring about anything else in the world.

"When Tom tried to poison me, Wardle figured it would be best to keep my survival a secret from the TF. And that meant keeping it a secret from everybody." Sim stood back, allowing Freda to dry her eyes. "Rosie's twelve weeks gone and thinks she's a widow now."

"Rosie's pregnant? But I thought Elsa had your child."

"My life got complicated after you left." Sim paused. "Why did you leave?"

"I thought I was over all this." Freda lowered her eyes. "Poor Rosie."

"Things aren't much better for Elsa. I don't seem to bring much luck to the women in my life. You sure you want to stick around?"

"Ha, I thought I was the unlucky one. Funny thing is, I came here to avenge your death."

Sim smiled. "I think we may have blown my cover at ESCO."

"We're running out of time to stop the nuclear warhead," said Freda. "I don't think we have time for the subtle approach any more. What did you find out?"

Sim explained about the secret base.

"Maybe we can break into ESCO headquarters and send a signal to the terrorists with the bomb. Make them think the mission is being aborted."

"If we can get back inside. Disarm all the guards. Hack into their systems." Sim shrugged. "Seems like we're in it up to our again. Come on. I've got a bike waiting outside."

33

———

North Korea

*I*t's funny how a human face becomes unrecognisable when it's upside down. Ivan was staring at a naked man, strung up by his ankles on a crude set of gallows. *The human brain is good at recognizing people from a distance, sideways on, even just half a face. But flip them upside down and nothing. Just not programmed to do it, I guess.*

The first man they had strung up had suffered a stroke or a seizure and had died even before the questions had started. The mercenary leader shook his head at the stubbornness. *Somebody in this crappy village must know the whereabouts of the dive equipment. Why won't they just tell us?* He looked around at all the pathetic specimens his team had corralled into the centre of the village. Most of them seemed malnourished. Hadn't even put up a fight. *So why won't they talk?*

Ivan knew that his Babel app was working. He could see it in their faces. The villagers were listening to him. And it must have been somebody in this hamlet who stole the kit. There isn't another settlement around for miles. Not surprising when he saw what a wretched living they must make off the land around here. Hundreds of miles from Pyongyang. Scratching out just enough food from the few fields the mercenaries had walked through to get to the village. Poor soil, no irrigation and ploughed by man or buffalo as far as he could tell. He couldn't see any signs of power cables or solar panels. *How do people live without electricity these days?* And he was pretty sure from the smell that toilets were just a hole in the ground to these people.

Ivan lashed out at the inverted prisoner with the back of his hand. The man groaned and his body swayed slightly from the force of the blow. The leader was struggling to contain his anger. Not just at the tight-lipped people but at their government for forcing this miserable existence upon them, for making them so paranoid that the threat of torture held little power over them. But anger would not get answers. And he needed that equipment.

One of his men returned from searching around the village, clutching a car battery and some lead wires. Ivan showed the battery to his prisoner. Some of the villagers who were being forced to watch began to whisper to each other.

He turned around to look at them all. "Anybody got anything they'd like to say before I attach these probes to his bollocks?" Nothing. He shrugged and clipped the wires onto the battery.

The man's eyes opened wide as the first wire's bulldog clip bit into his flesh. "Please. We don't know who took it. Whatever you're looking for. It wasn't us."

Ivan hesitated for a moment. The voice sounded genuine enough. But some people are just good at lying. He'd cracked some tough nuts in his time. Hah, he smirked at his own little joke. These nuts are not for cracking. Frying, maybe... He clipped the other wire in place and listened to the screams as the suspended man writhed in agony. He turned to look at the other villagers.

Most had shut their eyes or turned away, some were holding hands over their ears.

Still no confession. He unclipped the wire and breathed deeply as the screams subsided to a whimper. "Cut him down."

He was going to have to try something worse. Walking towards the rest of the villagers he selected a girl. Not yet old enough to be physically different from a boy, but the long hair and skirt gave it away. He tried to drag her to the front, but the girl's mother clung onto her, crying and shouting something his Babel app was struggling to translate. He nodded to one of his colleagues who forcibly separated mother from daughter. The mother would not give up. She kicked and gouged at the soldier until the butt of his machine gun smashed into her face and she dropped to the ground.

The leader thought about the best way to leverage the girl. String her up like the others? He doubted it would make much difference. The mother might have talked but now she was unconscious, thanks to Humper's heavy handedness. Was the father amongst the crowd being forced to watch? He wasn't sure.

A thought struck him and Ivan asked his colleague where the car battery had come from. He left the girl in the hands of another soldier while he went to investigate. A room at the back of the biggest and least-decrepit building in this village. The battery had been attached to a large radio set. Its antenna reached up to the ceiling. A pair of headphones lay on the table next to the radio. He grabbed the headphones and yanked their cable from its socket.

Returning to the assembled villagers he held the earpieces aloft. "Are you all fucking spies or something?" They all shook their heads, like naughty schoolchildren. "Then what the hell are these for?"

One man stepped forward nervously, glancing at his fellow villagers. "Please. We listen to news. Chinese news. BBC world service. Not allowed in our country." The other villagers nodded but kept looking at their feet.

"Oh, give me strength." He pulled out a knife and held it to the girl's throat. "Where is my bloody dive equipment?" he shouted. The girl squirmed under his grip and the blade nicked her throat. Some blood trickled along the blade, wetting his knuckles.

One of the other mercenaries came forward. "Sarge? Do we really have to do this?"

Ivan switched off his Babel app. "I'm not missing out on the biggest pay dirt of my life. Do you fancy swimming into the middle of a freezing cold lake in your skivvies? Diving down to check for netting without any scuba gear?"

"Can't we get some more kit flown in?"

"We don't have time for that. Besides, we're on radio silence, remember."

"But—"

A wrinkled man with grey hair ran out from behind one of the buildings clutching an ancient gun. The mercenary leader looked up. "Bloody hell, is that an AK47?" He stood watching for a moment before realising that the old villager was raising it to fire. He held it awkwardly and squeezed the trigger. The gun flew out of his hands but some bullets found their mark. The mercenary closest to him had been slow to react, like his leader, puzzled by the absurdity of the attack. His face creased in puzzlement as blood seeped through the front of his shirt and he dropped to the ground. The other villagers started screaming and ran off in different directions. Some of the mercenaries started shooting indiscriminately.

The old man turned to flee. Ivan ran towards him, impeded by the people running in different directions and the bloodied bodies he was leaping over. He pointed at two of his squad and shouted. "You two, stay with the package. Everyone else, get after the old git!"

The mercenaries were struggling through the forest, trying to keep up the pace demanded from their leader. They had lost one of the team to the old man. He was surprisingly fast for somebody who looked like he'd been around during the original Korean war. And he had refused to talk. By the end, death had been a merciful way out of the pain. The other villagers had shown the soldiers where he had lived and it had not taken long to find his secret treasure. He had obviously been a hoarder. Attractive bird feathers, skulls of tiny animals and smooth, coloured stones festooned his home. And under a dirty rug, beneath the floor boards, there was a compartment. Along with another AK47, some ammo clips and a grenade, they had found some jewellery, a jerry can of petrol and their diving equipment. Even the villagers seemed surprise. The soldiers had buried their comrade, smashed the radio and left the villagers to clear up the rest of the mess.

Now the mercenaries had an additional load and fewer shoulders to share the burden. Ivan insisted on setting off straight away, even as the moon crept out from behind broken clouds. Not much moonlight penetrated the canopy and their head-mounted torches lost their potency as battery charges dropped. Tired legs stumbled in the gloom as mud and roots sought out more victims. The sky was brightening a little by the time they reached the edge of the forest. Back to the spot where Ivan had first surveyed the approach to Heaven Lake. Too late to make a dash across the open ground now. He knew the men were too fatigued and the sun's rays would soon be lighting up the eastern slopes ahead of them. They made camp and ate the food they had commandeered from the village. Ivan allowed a small fire to be lit. The team still grumbled about the tasteless pulp.

"At least it's not hard rations again. Looks lads, you'll be able to afford five-star cuisine soon enough. We'll bed down here during daylight. Tonight, we finish the mission." He raised his mug of tea in celebration. *I won't need you lot for much longer.*

On the other side of the Chinese-Korean border, Gopal and Rabten were being driven by a woman from the export agency. They had needed to stay low for a couple of days after the debacle at the hyperloop terminus. Once their new IDs had been sorted, the agency had kitted them out for the mission and assigned them a handler. It was a long drive, but the woman insisted on doing it all herself. Five hours straight, both before and after lunch. Rabten had complained about the long gap between meals on the first half of the journey, but had shut up once they had bought extra snacks during the lunch break just west of Shenyang.

Gopal tried to read as many briefing files as he could, but looking down at a screen while the car was in motion was not good for his neck or for travel sickness. He stared out of the window, watching the crop fields of Eastern China slip by. After he had helped foil the Gangotri plan, he had often wondered about the water situation here in the driest, most densely populated part of the country. The crops looked healthy enough. Perhaps the Chinese had found another solution.

The agency driver was annoyingly chatty. Gopal could understand why she needed to do something to help stay alert during such a long journey. But at first Gopal had been trying to read and Rabten, when he wasn't stuffing his face, had been trying to nap. Actually, napping was not a bad idea. The driver had finally taken the hint when she saw Gopal pretend to nod off as well. And who knew what they would need to do when they got to the border, or when they would next get the chance to sleep? Gopal did not feel guilty at all.

Once they left the G11 highway and got to the end of the S26, the quality of road quickly deteriorated. By the time they pulled up outside the Changbai Mountain Tianchi Hostel, the track was more dirt and gravel than tarmac. There were plenty of hotels among the trees here, and the driver reminded them how popular this place was with domestic tourists. The agents unloaded the kit and thanked the driver for getting them here so efficiently. They checked in under their new false identities and retired to the room. Gopal made contact with OD headquarters. Wardle explained what Feinberg had figured out. About Heaven Lake and what a bomb at the bottom of the lake might do. Not just to the revered site, but to the whole planet.

"I'm sending you a full technical debrief on the warhead you'll be dealing with. There's an idiot's guide to defusing it, if you get there after the thing's been primed. Even Rabten should be able to follow that."

Rabten appeared in the background of the vid conference and bowed, clasping his hands in prayer.

"But let's suppose the TF do get there before us. How are we going to find and retrieve it from the bottom of the lake?"

"I have a stealth Hydra on standby, with a special package. Just send the word as soon as you are on the lake shore. But make sure it's at night. We still haven't managed to make these things invisible yet."

"Understood, Mr Director," said Gopal, glad now for the bit of sleep he had managed in the car.

"And listen, fellas. I know you've been through a lot in the past two months. But I'm counting on you. This is the big one. I know you can pull through for me. For all of us."

"We won't let you down."

They spent the next hour taking it in turns to have a last decent wash for a few days and packing the kit into a pair of rucksacks. Most of it was basic camping gear. Who knew how long they would have to hide out next to the lake waiting for the terrorists to show up? There were a couple of grenades each, but these were concealed within eating utensils. Gopal's kukri could just about pass for an elaborate camper's knife and the surveillance equipment might be mistaken for the kit of an over-enthusiastic bird-watcher or nature photographer.

The hunting rifle would be harder to explain, but Gopal was not going to take on a bunch of crazed terrorists armed with just a knife and Rabten's martial art skills. The gun was lying on the bed, gleaming after a thorough strip down and clean when somebody knocked on the door, declaring 'room service' in mandarin. Gopal was in the shower oblivious to the danger. Rabten was already in his light-absorbing stealth cloth, inspecting the mini-bar in their room for food. Not paying attention to where the rifle had been left.

A woman unlocked the door from outside and bustled in just as Rabten came over to block her entrance. She looked at his black outfit and then glanced past the advancing figure. Her eyes opened wide as she saw the weapon on the bed. "You cannot go hunting here. This is a nature reserve."

Rabten shook his head, trying to explain in his basic mandarin. "No, no, it not like that. We no hunters."

"What you going to use it for then?" Her voice was rising in tone as her eyes opened even wider. She turned to leave, but Rabten hauled her inside and slammed the door shut.

"Gopal, get in here, quick. I think we have a problem."

The woman screamed as the naked ex-Gurkha ran out of the

bathroom. Rabten clamped his hand over her mouth and kept it there even as her teeth sank into his fingers. Blood oozed out of the bitemarks while Rabten did his best to suppress a scream of his own.

They gagged the maid and tied her up in the bathroom. They tried to re-assure her. They weren't going to hurt her. They would be leaving soon and she'd be discovered in the morning. Rabten asked her where the snacks for all the mini-bars were kept and, taking her keys, he went to retrieve some. He came back with a bag load of confectionery.

Gopal put his hands on his hips as the monk returned to the room. "She doesn't need them."

"For us. We'll need to keep our energy up." Rabten drew a packet of nuts from the bag, shaking it. "And they come in handy-sized packets."

"Alright, the nuts and chocolate bars, yes," said Gopal. "But you're not making me eat those disgusting olives."

They had a final hot drink and waited until the hotel complex had gone quiet, then slipped off into the night. They had a few miles of uphill hiking to do. And they needed to get to Heaven Lake well before dawn. It was the kind of place where Chinese tourists got up at 4am so they could enjoy the first rays of sun coming over the North Korean side of the mountain. The agents needed to call in the Hydra and get themselves concealed before there was any risk of being spotted.

Gopal shook his head as Rabten opened the first packet of nuts by the time they had reached the end of the hotel drive.

34

Kiruna, Sweden

Sim was enjoying the feeling of Freda's arms around his waist as they rode the bike back to ESCO headquarters. That thought was followed immediately by a pang of guilt. Rosie. Alone in their home, mourning a death, creating a life. Sim twisted his head around a little and shouted into the wind. "Any ideas for breaking back into the base?"

"We could try *The Great Escape* technique," she yelled back.

"We're trying to get in, not out."

"You must know the film. It's a classic. Steve McQueen jumps his bike over the barbed wire."

Sim smiled. He'd missed her film references. One day he was going to get around to catching up on all these 'classics'.

"Ride parallel to the fencing and look for a slope you can use as a ramp, then just rev it like crazy."

Sim shook his head. "You're crazy."

But he could not think of an alternative. Even if his cover had not been blown yet, and his staff ID still worked, how was he going to smuggle Freda into the base? When they got close to the headquarters, Sim gave the main gate a wide berth and started circling the outer perimeter looking for a suitable incline. He found one about halfway around the fence. They waited behind a ruined house while a guard conducted a perimeter search.

Once the guard was out of the way, Sim turned to look at Freda. Neither of them had helmets to wear. "You sure about this?"

She nodded. Sim lined the bike up, revved the engine and let go of the brake as Freda squeezed his waist tight. The bike's wheels span in the dirt before it darted forwards, gaining speed as it hit the bottom of the slope. It was still accelerating as they reached the top of the incline. The bike took off and arced through the air, just clearing the barbed wire fence. Freda's weight at the back of the bike held it level instead of coming down nose first. Both tyres hit the ground hard.

Sim could feel Freda falling sideways. Her grip was threatening to pull him off too, but he squeezed his thighs tight around the bike and they just stayed on. The bike was still travelling at speed and Sim did not dare turn the wheel while their balance was so precarious. The front wheel hit something half buried in the dirt. The vehicle stopped suddenly as the suspension fork snapped. Sim and Freda went hurtling over the handlebars and rolled in the gravel. The motorbike's engine screamed for a moment then cut out. Silence.

Sim blinked and coughed. He spat out a mouthful of shale. There was blood in his saliva and both his hands were covered in lacerations. He wasn't sure if his ribs were intact, but it hurt when he spat and when he breathed. Freda was lying motionless, one arm resting across his back.

"Freda?"

A groan. Sim rolled over and gently lifted her arm off him.

He wiped her hair away from her face. The left cheek had been scraped raw, but he could see she was breathing, thank goodness.

"C'mon, sleepy head. No time for a nap yet." He pulled her upright and held her shoulders while she blinked and slowly came around. Sim turned to look at the bike and could tell that vehicle was going nowhere any time soon. "Can you walk?" Freda looked at him as if he were speaking a foreign language. "Have you broken anything?"

"Yes."

Sim scanned her limbs. Nothing was obviously askew.

"Yes, I can walk." She propped herself up on all fours, then stood and swayed for a moment, before starting to walk in the wrong direction.

Sim grabbed her hand and told her to wait while he covered up the wrecked bike. He led Freda towards the side entrance he had used less than twenty-four hours ago. Sim's ID card still worked and the pair of agents slipped inside without any guards noticing them. Sim turned to look into Freda's eyes. "You OK now?"

The real Freda smiled back and nodded. "You look a bit like Steve McQueen with those contacts, you know?"

"Come on, my office is this way. There's somebody who might help us."

As they stepped out into a long corridor an armed guard appeared at the other end. He called out when he saw them. "What's going on here?"

Sim whispered to Freda, "Pretend you've got handcuffs on." He pushed her towards the guard. "I caught this one in the grounds. Must have escaped from the other guards, somehow. Taking her back to see the boss. Reckon she might be dangerous."

The guard looked down at the filthy clothes the pair were wearing. "Put up a fight, did she? You need a hand?"

"What, and share the glory? You're alright, no thanks, mate." Sim pushed Freda past the guard, not waiting for a reply. He whistled once they were around the corner with no signs of the guard following them. "Down these stairs and first left."

Linnéa looked up from her desk glass when Sim entered the room. "What's going on? Who's this? Isn't she—"

"I followed the guards, Linnéa. They weren't taking her to the airport, they were going to shoot her and dump the body at the mine."

"Nonsense." Linnéa stood up and reached for something under the far end of the desk.

Sim held up his hands. "Please, just hear me out. Before you sound the alarm. You ever wondered how ESCO always manages to stay one step ahead of the Terror Formers? Why the company needs so many armed guards? So much research into toxins? Chemical warfare?"

Linnéa shook her head. "What are you implying? I've never seen anything untoward."

Sim held out his hands. "I'm not accusing you, but surely you must have had some doubts."

She looked down. "I don't understand. How could you know?

You've only been here a couple of days."

Sim looked at Freda who just shrugged. "We're British intelligence, trying to capture the most dangerous terrorist on the planet. Mattias Larsson. He's the mastermind behind the Terror Formers."

Linnéa smiled and shook her head. "Rubbish."

"The laboratories here. They're not just for developing antidotes.

Biological weapons too. They've created a new strain of Ebola."

Linnéa's hand moved away from whatever alarm button she had reached for earlier. "Show me some proof."

Sim told her about Jember Abdi and the mass grave they had found in the Turkish village. A photo of the ESCO haz-mat suit found at the scene. He told her about the stolen nuclear warhead. And he showed her the files he had uncovered about the secret shelter built by Larsson, ready for the apocalypse.

"I can't believe it. I've been working for those bastards? All this time?"

Sim placed a hand gently on her shoulder. "Don't feel so bad about it. Every secret service in the world has been trying to trace them for years. Slippery gits."

"What can I do to help?"

Linnéa had used her security clearance to gain access to all the ESCO files on the system while Sim had explained a little more of the background to his mission. "What am I looking for?"

"Information about the mission to steal a nuclear warhead. And while you're at it, anything about the bio weapons program. Are they planning to unleash it again?" said Sim.

Linnéa scanned through directories, sub-folders. Wage bills, HR records, accounts. "Nothing obvious."

It was taking too long. Freda kept looking out into the corridor. "It must be here somewhere," said Sim.

"Wait. I have an idea." Linnéa accessed the floor plans of the headquarters and displayed them on the desk glass. She scrolled through a couple of pages of schematics and then pointed. "Look. This section here. It's completely self-contained. Only accessible via Larsson's private apartments. Even has its own electricity supply and communication links. That's where it will be. It must."

Freda came away from the office door and nodded. "How are we going to get in there? Way too many guards to get past."

Sim rummaged around on his desk and found the keys to his rented bedroom. His landlady already hated him. Losing the keys would be just one more item on his list of misdemeanours. He fingered the special fob that he had attached to the keys. "I have a plan. But we're going to need to get suited up."

Twenty minutes later, the explosives in Sim's keyring blew a hole through the outer wall of the laboratories. Linnéa was already climbing the stairs that led to the main atrium and the front doors of the building, waiting to hear the detonation.

She got to the top step and coughed loudly when the noise of the blast had died down. As soon as she had the guards' attention, she collapsed onto all fours. "Explosion. Gas," she rasped.

One of the guards ran towards her, while another punched the alarm system. Sirens started going off throughout the complex. A voice was relayed over the intercom. "All personnel, a gas leak has been detected. Please leave the building immediately. This is not a drill, I repeat, this is not a drill."

Sim and Freda, wearing full haz-mat suits, climbed in through the newly created entrance to the laboratories. Three lab workers were lying dazed on the floor. The agents tied them up and searched through the ice-cold storage units as the workers regained consciousness. Even in the freezers, the cover-up was complete. Phials labelled as antidotes, serums, vaccines. Sim had no way of telling if these glass tubes held death or salvation. He took a few with interesting labels and carefully wrapped them in a cloth, stuffing the bundle into a pocket.

He jumped when Freda tapped him on the shoulder and once he was facing her, she shouted through her Perspex mask. "I've rigged a gas leak. It should blow in a few minutes. Let's head for the inner sanctum."

"What about the lab technicians?" Sim looked at the three people who were sitting on the floor, their hands behind them.

He could see the fear in their eyes. Maybe they were the same as Linnéa? Kept in the dark by a brilliant cover-up?

Freda walked up to them and kicked one in the butt. "On your feet. If you want to live, walk out of here and don't look back." She pulled the woman upwards by the lapels on her lab coat. "Got it?"

Sim and Freda kept the suits on in case any heroic guards had decided to stay behind, but all they found was a dropped machine gun. Freda tried to give it to Sim, but he pushed it away.

"You always were a better shot than me," he said, remembering their very first time together on the shooting range.

Sprinting through the corridors, trying to recall the schematic Linnéa had shown them, they were sweating inside their rubber suits by the time they reached the entrance to Larsson's private quarters. Even here, the guards had disappeared. Freda ripped off her face mask, breathing deeply and then peeled off the rest of her suit. Sim did the same. He used his OD wrist tab to crack the code on the lock.

Freda grabbed the handle and pulled the machine gun in tight to her body. "You ready?" Sim nodded and ducked to one side of the doorway, grasping the long screwdriver Linnéa had given him. He had lost count of the number of times he'd approached a fight without being armed properly.

The door swung open and Freda rolled forward into the room beyond, scanning the area from side to side with her gun. Nobody. Just a living room. A well-furnished one, admittedly, with a nice view of Kiirunavaara. But hardly the centre of an evil empire. Sim had expected more torture devices, or bad taste at least.

Freda walked up to a foot cushion and kicked it across the room. "Where are these fuckers?"

They moved through the apartment methodically. Tipping out drawers from the desk, pulling books from shelves, opening kitchen cupboards. Sim found himself an automatic pistol and some dubious sex toys in the bedroom. Drawers were already half open, clothes were strewn around the floor as if Mattias and Precious had left in a hurry. The British agents broke into a corridor that led to some stairs spiralling downwards into darkness. Sim pulled out his torch and went first.

At the bottom of the stairs an unlocked door led through to some sort of command centre. There was a console in the middle of the room, with a banked desk glass, surrounded by several small monitors, and on the far wall a giant screen. A pair of headphones were synched to the left-hand armrest of the chair and there was a pair of motion detector gloves at the end of the other armrest. The small screens were filled with messages, location information, targets and dates. This was definitely the Terror Formers' nerve centre.

A few seconds after Sim had entered the room, the giant screen flickered into life. A familiar face appeared on the screen. Mattias Larsson settled himself into a chair and put on some headphones. He spoke into the mic and a second later, his voice filled the command centre.

"Greetings to you. I see you've found my little secret. Miss Brightwell. You really are quite difficult to kill off, yes? Like the cockroaches, huh?"

"There's only one vermin in this conversation, Larsson," she replied.

"Ahh, the famous British wit. Of course. Now, don't tell me. Two British agents, one is Freda Brightwell. Could it be that the other is Sim Atkins? Come back from the dead? Deceiving our security clearance? I have to congratulate you, Mister Atkins. That is no mean feat."

Sim stared at the screen. He gazed into the eyes of the man responsible for his son's death. A heat spread through his body as his breath quickened. "I'm coming to get you, Larsson. You're finished."

"Ooh, I'm getting goose bumps down my spine. So macho. That must be what Miss Brightwell finds so attractive."

"Call the bomb off. You don't need to start world war three, Larsson," said Freda.

"Too late for that. The men have had their final instructions. Nothing can stop them now."

"We'll see about that." Sim started tapping away at the keyboard, hoping to break into the Terror Formers central command system. "Well, you know where to find me. Don't leave me waiting too long, will you?" He sighed. "It was such a nice place to live. Pity."

Mattias smiled for the camera one last time and then leant forward to switch it off at his end.

The giant screen went blank and the room seemed very dark again. Freda grabbed Sim by the hand and pulled him towards the spiral stairs. "Come on!" They sprinted up, around and around until their thighs burnt with lactic acid and their lungs were screaming for mercy. At the top of the stairs, they ran along the corridor. When they were back in the lounge, Freda sprayed the window with a burst from her machine gun. The glass pitted and cracked but refused to break.

"Shit!"

"Keep going," said Sim dashing for the door out of Larsson's apartments. There was a rumble from deep below them and a moment later a cloud of smoke billowed out of the corridor that led to the spiral stairs. Sim paused for a moment. "Is that it?"

"Let's not wait to find out," said Freda and they began to run for the main doors.

35

North Korea

Ivan kept looking up at the sky. The sun was just disappearing behind the summit of Mount Paektu. Soon it would be dark enough for the team to cross the open land that led to the lip of the crater and then down within it, to the lake. But only if the Moon stayed out of sight. Turning to his left, the leader could already see a pale three-quarter Moon, clearly visible in the last of the daylight. If there was no cloud cover, they would have to either risk being spotted on the approach to the lake or wait it out another 24 hours. The food was getting low and the team was getting restless. He knew they were behind schedule and Larsson was not a patient man.

He ordered the gang to have one last hot drink. Recent meal-times had been half-rations, trying to stretch out the supplies. But he let them eat a full portion this time. There was a long night ahead of them.

They packed up the camping gear, raked the ground with branches to hide evidence of their presence and hefted the equipment one last time. The sun's descent had left nothing but a faint smudge of orange across the top of the mountain, as if the volcano was warming up, ready to erupt. Some clouds began to appear, blown in on a chilly breeze. It was now or never. Ivan surveyed his squad and nodded.

The banter that usually accompanied hikes or mealtimes was completely absent. The mercenaries kept their mouths shut and their eyes on the slope ahead of them. The leader glanced upwards at the clouds as often as he scanned the horizon left and right for signs of movement. The channels that slowed their progress were big enough to hold a torrent of water but at this time of year contained mere rivulets.

The burden of the warhead was frequently swapped between soldiers. It was the only way they could carry the 100kg load while maintaining the pace set by their leader. There was no path to follow while the gradient was getting steeper and rocks under foot were becoming smaller and looser as they neared their destination. The Moon was almost directly overhead, occasionally peeping out from behind the clouds, as they reached the top of the crater lip. Half a mile to their left was the official summit of Mount Paektu. At last the mercenaries could see their goal, Heaven Lake. It was far larger than Ivan had imagined. He had studied the map of the region before the mission began, of course, but numbers on a map don't always convey a sense of space. The Chinese shoreline was four or five kilometres away. Somewhere in the middle, an international boundary cut the lake in half.

A break in the clouds allowed beams of moonlight to flood the crater with silvery light. Ivan ordered his men to drop flat. He lay there admiring the huge expanse of water. Despite the stiff breeze on the lip of the crater, the lake's surface was quite still. A reflected Moon gazed out of the water at him and he could see why this place was revered as a holy site.

Soon, it would be remembered for different reasons. But first they needed to get down the inner slope of the crater. There was a gentle slope to their left that would be quite easy to descend, but it passed close to the only buildings on the North Korean shore. The route straight down from their current position would minimize the risk of being spotted, but would increase the risk of a fall. Ivan decided that they would have to abseil. Slowly. If the warhead was dropped and damaged now, after all their efforts... No, he wouldn't let that happen.

While they found a suitable anchor point and set up the ropes, the leader dispatched Tomkins and Sing-song towards the building. They were instructed to disable any surveillance equipment that might be scanning the shoreline of the lake. Zero contact with any guards. Lethal force only if absolutely necessary. The two people he had chosen were quick and small. He was sure violence would not be needed. Not yet.

Humper, on the other hand, was going to do what he did best. Making sure the warhead came down the slope in one piece. His footing slipped on loose scree. The bomb smacked into his kneecap. He held his arm against his mouth and muffled a cry of pain into the crook of his elbow.

When they were all at the bottom of the slope, Ivan began to change into the diving gear. He checked the breathing apparatus and the volume readings on the tanks, leaving the flippers to one side. Then he waited until the other two members of the team re-joined them.

Humper and another soldier carried the warhead to the water's edge while the leader inflated a raft that he would use to carry it out into the middle of the lake. The mission briefing had been clear. If the bomb detonated on the surface of the water, there was a

had to take place on the bed of the lake. Ivan still could not quite believe how deep it was. Over two hundred metres. That was way beyond the range of an amateur diver like him. He had read of experts setting records beyond that, but they had been using special gas mixes and a lifetime of experience.

He told his team to stay out of sight on the shoreline and wait for his return. A couple of them seemed puzzled that nobody was accompanying him on the raft, but the leader pushed off and began paddling before they could ask why. They wouldn't have liked the answer.

Ivan made slow progress. The raft sat deep in the water and he only had a small paddle to propel the cumbersome craft. The lake was so large that from its surface it was hard to tell when he was in the middle. He was running out of time if he was going to make it back to the forest before dawn. Here would have to do. He switched on the breathing gear, fitted his mask and rolled backwards into the water. He swam down a few metres, scanning the water with an underwater torch that he held in his left hand. He descended a little further, just to make sure there were no nets and came back to the surface.

Scrambling back into the dinghy he took off his mask and tried to breathe some warmth into his fingers. He set the timer on the warhead, not for twenty-four hours like his team expected, but for just eight hours. Minimizing the risk of discovery. It might be enough time to get away. But if it wasn't, well, his wife and children had been promised a place in the Bjørnøya sanctuary. Their future was secured.

Ivan put his mask back on and rolled into the water once more. This time, his left hand held a knife. He punctured both sides of the craft and watched with satisfaction as the warhead slipped below the surface, wrapped in a deflated rubber dinghy. He began to swim for the shore. Everything had gone according to plan. He wanted to smile and celebrate. But he had one final task to accomplish, and he wasn't looking forward to that at all.

· · ·

The leader chose Humper once again for his particular attributes. After he had changed out of the diving gear, Ivan called the big guy over to him. Never the sharpest member of the team, it seemed to take Humper's brain a second or two to register the blade that had slipped between his ribs and stopped his heart. Ivan grabbed Humper's machine gun, still slung over the man's shoulder and spun it around to spray bullets into the rest of the team. Most of them fell instantly, too shocked by the attack to react. But Tomkins had dived out of the way and returned fire. Unfortunately for her, the leader had made sure Humper's bulk was between himself and the rest of the team. Humper's body jerked with the impact, but Ivan was safe. He fired again. A short round designed merely to flush out the survivor. When the woman darted towards a machine gun that lay next to one of her dead comrades, the leader was ready for her. And this time he was quicker.

He let Humper's body slump to the ground and checked the rest of the team to make sure they were dead too. He kept telling himself he was only following orders, but the taste in his mouth made clear what his conscience thought of orders. He was about to climb the rope out of the crater when a movement on the far side of the lake, just above the horizon, caught his eye. He grabbed his star-scope and peered across the water. A hydra, in whisper mode. He watched it slow and bank, landing on the far shoreline. Two men darted out from a concealed spot and unloaded something from the cargo hold.

The mercenary looked back at his dead team, suddenly wishing he had not been so hasty. He took a couple of fresh magazines for the machine gun and started jogging around the edge of the lake, hoping he could get there in time.

36

———————

Kiruna, Sweden

Sim had borrowed another bike from ESCO headquarters. The chaos caused by Linnéa's feigned gas leak had intensified when Larsson's booby trap exploded. Everybody assumed that the leak was flammable as well as poisonous. So, escaping had been far easier than getting into the compound. While Linnéa sneaked back into the base, Sim drove Freda back to his rented room in New Kiruna, to fetch the rest of his OD kit. His keys were buried in the rubble so he knocked on the front door. His landlady stood there in her dressing gown, her arms folded across her chest and her mouth a thin crack of malice.

"I know, I know, Mrs Andersson." Sim walked up the steps. "It's not worked out, has it? I'll go and pack my bags."

"She's not coming in," she said, pointing at Freda. Sim shrugged and looked at his partner.

"It's alright," said Freda. "Go get your things while I get in touch with HQ."

Sim squeezed past his landlady and went up to his room.

Freda moved away from the front door and called up Wardle on her wrist tab.

"Sir, we're in pursuit of Mattias Larsson. We believe he's headed for some sort of bunker on Bjørnøya island. We need transport and back up."

"Sorry, who is this?"

"It's me, Freda. I'm with Sim. This is urgent."

"No, I'm afraid you're very garbled. I can't understand a word you're saying."

"This is field agent Freda Brightwell requesting immediate assistance."

"That's impossible. Freda Brightwell went AWOL at Stockholm airport. Overseas Division has been disbanded."

"Because of what I did?" asked Freda.

"All field agents have been ordered to return to headquarters immediately."

"They can't do that," said Freda.

"Now if you'll excuse me, whoever you are, I have work to do. Captain Hamilton is not responding to my requests. He ought to be in Narvik harbour but I can't seem to track him down. I do hope that sub of his doesn't wander off somewhere."

Freda clicked off the call and stared up at the house. Sim emerged with a duffel bag over one shoulder.

"Hand over the keys, if you're leaving," said Mrs Andersson. "Oh, I'm afraid I blew them up." Sim waited while her face moved from puzzlement to shock and then anger. "But you can keep the deposit."

The pair of agents climbed back on the bike. Before they set off, Sim checked his watch. Almost exactly 9pm. "You know, something's bothering me about Larsson's last comment. He said it was a nice place to live, but he didn't blow up his apartment. Just the Terror Former basement."

"That's where all the incriminating information was. Makes perfect sense," said Freda.

"Yeah, but why mention the place to live?"

"I'm not sure people like that ever think things through logically."

Sim glanced at this watch again, even though he wasn't sure why the time was important. Just gone nine. He realised he had not heard the church clock ring out. A sense of dread knotted his stomach. He got off the bike and knocked on Mrs Andersson's door again. She nearly yanked it off its hinges and was about to shout something when Sim got in there first.

"How long have the bells been silent?"

Her anger changed back to puzzlement. She looked towards the tower, the view blocked by a neighbour's house "I remember hearing them last night. But now you mention it, not all day. Why?"

Sim held out his hands. "Just stay indoors, close your windows. And tell the police to meet us at the church." He ran off, not waiting for any more questions.

Sim and Freda rode the short distance to the church. Even if Mrs Andersson had believed him, the police would not arrive for several minutes. Freda picked the lock on the door into the ground floor of the red tower. There were no windows at this level, just a little evening light streaming in through the open door, and a stairway upwards that was faintly illuminated from the floor above.

Sim walked over to the staircase, but Freda held out a hand to stop him.

"Wait. Switch your torch on and check the stairs."

The beam of Sim's torch shone up the staircase. He was about to say all clear, when the last sweep of his light caught something.

A thin wire was stretched across one of the steps halfway up the flight.

"You were right. Sixth one up," said Sim.

They climbed the stairs, carefully avoiding the tripwire. Sim double checked further up the stairs and at the entrance onto the next level up. The tower was pinched narrow on this floor. It was a small square room whose only purpose seemed to be to house the ladder up into the bell room. Tiny windows high up each wall let in a little light. The agents continued upwards slowly, checking for more booby traps. Sim went first. When he reached the top of the ladder his head poked through to the level where the bells were hung. The evening sun flooded in through gauze windows. Sim blinked while his eyes adjusted to the brightness and then he gasped as he looked around the room.

There was at least a dozen gas cannisters, each with a group of small glass phials arranged around the nozzle at the top of the tanks. Wires from each cannister led to a set of batteries in the middle of the floor. The section of flooring around the top of the stairs was slightly higher than the rest of the floor and Sim could see a wire that led from here to the same batteries. A pressure pad, in case the staircase wire hadn't worked. But how to disarm it all?

There was a sound of approaching sirens and flashing blue lights began to illuminate the bells intermittently through the open sides of the tower.

"Plenty of time for the boys in blue to sort this lot out," said Sim with a smile.

"The stairs!" shouted Freda. She slid down the ladder and ran across the floor below to the top of the first stairwell. "Don't move!" Sim heard the police asking Freda some questions from the bottom of the stairs. He was willing to bet a large sum of money that these phials contained some airborne form of the Ebola virus. From this elevation, with these open grilles on all sides of the tower, it was the perfect place to launch a gas attack. Why on earth Larsson would want to kill his fellow Swedes? It did not fit the pattern of other Terror Former attacks. Larsson had been counting on some member of the church setting off the cannisters as they came to investigate the silent bells. Perhaps he had some grudge against the Church?

After a hurried conversation with the Swedish police, they had been allowed to leave. The motorbike got them across the border into Norway. Freda had described her bizarre conversation with Wardle and they'd agreed to go look for the captain. There was no way they were going to abandon this mission halfway through. They were sure the captain would feel the same, if they could find him.

Sim had stopped outside Narvik, just before midnight. The pair of British agents dismounted and looked down into the town. On the right was a marina filled with small pleasure craft. Further away, on the other side of the peninsular, was the larger industrial harbour. A huge conveyor belt was pouring aggregate – Sim guessed it was iron ore from the Kiirunavaara mine – into the belly of a big tanker. Now they had to hope that Hamilton was still somewhere out there in the Fjord.

"How are we going to get in touch with him? If he's gone rogue, like us, he'll probably ignore messages from an OD device," said Sim.

"Hang on. I remember reading the debrief when he rescued that journalist."

"Which journo?"

"You know, the one who helped capture Richard Taylor. Doesn't matter. The point is when she was escaping she used a dating app to project a distress call to any listeners in the local environment. Quite smart, really," said Freda getting off the bike.

"Right. So, you have a dating app on your wrist tab? Your official, agency wrist tab?"

"Obviously not. But you're good with software, with gadgets. You can sort that, can't you?"

Sim got off the bike too and looked around. There was a bench and picnic table in the lay-by. He got out his roll tab and spread it on the wooden surface. After tapping away for a few minutes, he called Freda over to look at the message he had prepared.

'Disavowed members of Wardle appreciation society seeking new *Endeavour*. You provide the transport and we'll provide the destination.'

"Hmm, disavowed. I like that. Sounds all *Mission Impossible*," said Freda.

Sim smiled. "Do I get to be Tom Cruise?"

"Wait. After six years, you finally got one of my film references? It's a miracle."

"Course I've watched the *MI* series. Required viewing for a teenager who wants to become a spy, no?"

Two hours later they were on board Captain Hamilton's submarine, heading for Bjørnøya. The captain was tucking into a substantial breakfast while the two British agents relayed the events over the past two days.

Freda was watching Hamilton add rounds of buttered toast to his fry-up. "You're not related to Rabten, are you?"

"Who?" asked the captain, between mouthfuls. "Never mind."

"How many fighting men do you have on board?" asked Sim.

"About a dozen men and women. If I leave just a skeleton crew on board the ship."

"That will have to do. It's clear we can't ask for

reinforcements," said Freda.

"What do we know about this bunker they've built on the island?"

"Linnéa was keen to prove she hadn't been working for the terrorists. So, before we came on board, I asked her to send me the schematics of the place," Sim said. "We'll need to surface to check my wrist tab for messages. Assuming she managed to recover them from the ESCO files."

The plans were waiting for Sim on the surface of the Norwegian Sea. He stood on the bridge, admiring the design of Hamilton's vessel. It seemed equally at home whether above or below the waves. But definitely faster on the surface. Hydrofoils had emerged from the side of the hull and the boat was now skimming the surface at 40 knots or more.

Grey clouds dominated the horizon and the sea had little colour to give except white-tipped waves. It was like one of the monochrome views from the windows of Moon Lab One. Sim remembered watching a rocket launch from the observation desk with his son, James. The pitch of the boat through the foaming waves was nothing compared with the lurch of Sim's heart. He thought too of the colleagues he'd left behind on the Moon. If this bomb went off, they might just be in the safest possible place. How ironic.

Finally, the files were downloaded and he went below. Sim, Freda and the captain were standing around a 3D projection of the underground bunker that had been built on Bjørnøya.

The captain rubbed his chin. "Looks pretty robust. It's even got an inner sanctuary, just in case either entrance is breached."

"There's a weakness here," said Freda pointing to the air-vents that led from the surface down to the shelter and inside the core part of the base.

"Bound to be monitored, or booby-trapped," said Sim.

"If the captain and his team attack through the underwater

entrance, hopefully they can knock-out the systems that guard the air vents," Freda replied.

"Huh," said the captain. "Reminds me of the end of Star Wars."

"Many Bothans died to bring us this information?" said Freda. The captain smiled at her. "Episodes four, six and seven."

"Have you two quite finished?" asked Sim.

The captain coughed. "I don't like sending my team in the front door, but if it buys you some time to get under the radar... Right, full steam ahead."

Sim and Freda caught a few hours of much-needed sleep as *The Endeavour* sailed towards Bjørnøya. When they awoke, Hamilton's soldiers had prepared for battle by donning body armour, Kevlar helmets and respirators. Most of them were armed with stocky assault rifles, though Sim noticed a couple brandishing Remington pump-action shotguns and one with a two-handed hammer.

Captain Hamilton kept scratching his chin. He saw Sim watching. "I vowed not to shave until we've stopped this monster. Why are new beards always so itchy?"

"Think shaving's the least of our worries right now," said Sim.

The captain shrugged. He had an automatic pistol holstered and was clutching a pair of large rubber-handled bolt cutters. He pointed them at Sim and Freda. "We drop you two off at the shoreline, wait for you to scale the cliffs and then, bam. We hit them hard. OK?"

By the time Sim and Freda had waded ashore, *The Endeavour* had already slipped back below the surface. The rocket-propelled grappling hook flew up and gently arced over the top of the cliff. Freda pulled hard. The hook moved a little at first, then held fast. She leaned back, stretching her neck to look along the length of rope. Sim fired his rocket too and the pair of agents began climbing. Even with fall-arrest karabiners to give them occasional respite, the freezing cold rain and biting wind were both taking their toll on shoulders and arms by the end of the climb. Sim flopped to the ground at the top of the bluff, resting for a moment. Freda had reached the top first and was impatient to head towards their target. Up here, the island was a barren wasteland. Grey lumps of striped rock, interspersed with small lakes. In the shadows of the lumpy surface, streaks of snow clung on throughout the summer.

The camouflage cloth of their outfits had adopted a broken grey and white pattern that blended in perfectly.

They made their way to the helicopter landing pad. Inside a small hangar, a helicopter waited with folded blades. There was nobody around. Freda disabled a pair of CCTV cameras. Sim forced open the engine compartment of the aircraft and inspected the machinery. He asked Freda for a leg-up to reach inside. Balancing on her cupped hands, Sim stretched into the housing, and sliced through both the fuel lines. No escape route for the slippery bastard this time.

The entrance to the bunker was not far off. Another pair of cameras was covering the approach. The British agents kept their distance. Instead, they headed to the air vents that were a further 200 metres beyond, tucked away behind an ancient boulder. Freda looked at her wrist tab. "Right on schedule."

Ten metres below the surface of the sea, *The Endeavour* approached the underwater entrance to the bunker. The submarine had accelerated to flank speed. A pair of torpedoes sped out from the craft and detonated on the barrier. The metal gates twisted and parted slightly. The submarine's prow rammed into the wreckage and forced its way through. The captain winced as the remains of the metal barrier scraped the top and sides of the bridge. A tunnel continued on for another one hundred metres or so before opening to a dock above.

The Endeavour broke the surface and almost immediately shook as two grenades exploded on the outer hull. Small arms fire drummed the window on the bridge, but could not penetrate the thick glass. In between shots, the captain could hear the wail of a klaxon, announcing their arrival. The submarine's automated turrets, fore and aft of the control room, swung around and twin barrels burst into life. A stream of bullets homed in on two of the sentries who had been on duty in the concealed harbour. Their bloodied bodies were flung against the wall as the turrets found their mark. The other two guards tried to take cover as the submarine's guns turned towards them.

Fromtheback of *The Endeavour*'s conning tower, a door burst open and the captain charged out. He jumped across to the underground quay while the turrets were keeping the guards occupied. Hamilton poked his head above a crate and then beckoned for the rest of his squad to join him. A scream from one of the guards told of another defender chalked off. But as his squad leapt across from the submarine deck, the last remaining guard fired his machine gun and caught the legs of the man who was carrying the hammer. He teetered for a moment on the edge of the quay.

"We need that hammer," shouted Hamilton. He dove out from behind the crate and scragged the man's bullet-proof vest just as he was about to fall backwards. The captain grabbed the hammer and then the man's body shuddered as another volley of bullets found their mark. His eyes rolled up and blood spewed out of his mouth. Hamilton let go of the man's vest and the body dropped down into the water.

"Somebody taken out that fucking guard!"

Petty Officer Simpson threw a flash-bang and two more of Hamilton's crew darted forwards. A pair of guns fired and then the dockside fell silent. They all ran forward to the door that led to the rest of the complex. The captain smashed the hammer into the hinges of the door. The echo bounced off the walls of the cavern as the shock-wave reverberated along the captain's arms. After a couple more blows, the door gave way. The captain pointed to a man and woman.

"You two, stay here and guard this door. Everyone else, split into pairs and spread out. Cause as much mayhem as possible. I'm off to find the control room." He dropped the hammer and pulled out his pistol. As he ran off down a corridor to his left, he could hear firefights erupting in all directions.

The control room was exactly where Linnéa's schematics had indicated it would be. The occupant was now lying on the floor with a big lump on the back of her head. Hamilton had been unable to switch off the monitoring equipment from the bank of desk glass at the heart of the room. So, he had sought out the main box of cables and opted for a more permanent solution with the help of his bolt cutters.

As his team re-grouped, the captain counted heads. Seven plus him. Five people lost. But the base was now theirs. The occupants were either dead or tied up. All except two. One of his crew had seen a white man and a black woman retreating behind a huge bomb-blast door. Now it was up to Sim and Freda.

37

North Korea

Gopal powered up the remote vehicle that the hydra had delivered to them. The stars had disappeared and the sky above the eastern rim of the crater was beginning to brighten as he carried the drone to the water's edge. The pair of agents checked the video feed and control unit. The instructions explained that the RV would submerge and hunt for the missile warhead by itself. Honing in, using radar and a host of sensors tuned into electrical currents, metal objects and radioactivity. In theory, Gopal and Rabten would be able just to sit back and wait for the miniature submarine to surface a couple of hours later, carrying the bomb. Which was a good job, because there would be a bus load of tourists heading their way soon, hoping to catch the first rays of dawn as the sun cleared the summit of Mount Paektu.

As the ex-Gurkha crouched in front of the control unit, he began biting his nails. The RV had honed in on something almost straight away. But this was near the surface. The video feed had shown some sort of wire mesh but no radioactive signal. And now it seemed as if the underwater drone had snagged itself on the netting. Gopal put a hand in the water to test the temperature and withdrew it almost immediately.

He looked over at his partner. "I don't suppose you fancy a quick dip, do you?"

Rabten shook his head. "Never learnt to swim."

"You're kidding?"

Another shake of the head. "No need at the monastery. Meditation, martial arts and prayer. That's all we did. In between meal times."

"Well, stay alert. And get ready to haul me out when I surface. It's bollocking cold in here."

Gopal stripped down to his pants and, leaving his clothes and rifle on the shoreline, waded out into the lake. His breath came in big gulps. His feet slipped and stumbled painfully on the small stones at the water's edge until they became numb with cold. He waded a little further and finally re-gained control of his breathing. Gopal dove forwards and began to swim. The control unit had given him a rough idea of where the RV was stuck. But it wasn't going to be easy to judge the distance, especially with the water trying to turn his brain into an ice cube.

Rabten watched his partner swimming out. Once the bobbing head had become difficult to spot, he switched his attention to the RV control unit. Tiny screens relayed a murky underwater picture. He assumed the lotus pose, listening to the sound of local birds welcoming the imminent dawn. His breathing and his heart rate slowed. A heron landed close by and Rabten had to resist the temptation to turn his head and watch.

There was a noise behind him and the bird took off with a flurry of wings. Rabten rolled to one side, ducking behind a rock as a spray of bullets ricocheted off the pebbles he had just been sitting on. The RV control unit jumped across the shingle, finishing upside down, a cracked and fizzing wreck.

Rabten picked up a fat, round pebble and flung it across the shoreline. Another spray of bullets followed the noise and he was able to scurry across a little further, now hiding behind a large boulder.

"I know where you are," a voice shouted. "Why don't you come out and surrender?"

There was a pause as if the man was expecting Rabten to acquiesce. The ex-monk crouched there in silence looking around the edge of the boulder as much as he dared.

"This doesn't have to end in violence, you know."

Rabten peeped out a little further and a bullet zinged off the boulder just in front of his face. If only the man would come a little closer. Maybe Rabten could dive out and grapple him to the ground. But not from this distance. The man seemed in no rush, holding his ground. The grenades were out of reach. He would be mowed down if he tried to make a dash for those.

Rabten was running out of ideas, his back resting against the boulder and looking out to the lake. He noticed that his partner was swimming slowly back towards shore. Rabten bent down to pick up a dozen pebbles and began lobbing them roughly in the direction of the armed man.

"What's this? Sticks and stones, eh? You'll have to try harder than that, mate."

Rabten threw some more, this time standing up a little straighter and exposing his arm above the boulder. Another burst of bullets. One of them went through the fleshy part of his hand. He gasped in pain and sat down quickly, trying to squeeze the wound shut. Blood oozed out between his fingers. He grabbed more pebbles with his left hand and started throwing those. Using his wrong hand, the trajectory and aim was feeble.

But he had to keep distracting the man while Gopal swam to shore.

The stones he picked up were getting smaller as he ran out of natural ammunition lying near the boulder. The blood from his wound was making them slippery and difficult to throw. He was tensing himself for a suicidal charge at the man when a single shot rang out, reverberating off the sides of the crater rim.

Rabten peeped over the top of the boulder and saw the other man writhing on the ground. The monk ran forward and kicked away the gun. But Ivan Jenkins was not finished yet. The mercenary leader hauled himself to his feet and pulled a large knife from his belt. Rabten could see that the man was hobbling and blood was seeping from a wound in his left leg.

The knife flashed in front of Rabten's face. But he just grinned. Now the odds were more even. Both of them injured. One armed with a knife, the other a White Crane martial arts expert. Rabten's foot lashed out and kicked the other man's injured leg. It buckled and there was a howl of pain. Ivan's face contorted. A snarl of anger, but his eyes darted from side to side and Rabten could see the fear in them.

The mercenary made a clumsy lunge with his knife. Rabten easily dodged to one side, grasping the man's wrist. He twisted and jammed his own bloodied hand into the elbow, pushing it in the wrong direction. Another yelp and the knife fell to the ground. Rabten let go and Ivan's right arm dropped lifelessly to his side. He started to back away as Rabten advanced. A yoko geri kekomi kick thrust Rabten's heel into Ivan's chest and he toppled backward into a heap.

Ivan tried to roll over. Rabten hovered next to him, wondering whether to knock him unconscious with a strike to the head, but not sure if they might need to question him. The pause was just enough time for Ivan to reach into a pocket and slip something into his mouth. He groaned and then rolled onto his back as his face become bright red. His mouth began to foam and his spine arched upwards as if the earth beneath him was too hot to touch. He collapsed back down and the bubbles coming from between his lips ceased.

Rabten felt for a pulse but could find nothing. Then a groan from the shoreline and he remembered his partner. He rushed over and pulled a freezing cold Gopal from the edge of the water. The man's arms and fingers were so rigid, Rabten found it hard to prise the hunting rifle from his grip. He tried to dry off his partner and wrapped him in blankets. He rubbed Gopal's limbs, trying to get the blood flowing again, even though the movement was causing agony in his own wounded hand. Gopal's teeth were chattering uncontrollably. And all Rabten could do was press his body against his friend, trying to share his own warmth. He offered to light a fire, but Gopal refused. He whispered, in halting snatches, that they had to stay hidden until the bomb had been brought to the surface and disarmed.

By the time the RV surfaced, Gopal's teeth had stopped chattering. But his limbs felt no warmer. Rabten was starting to shiver too.

"Come on, Gopal, stay awake. Look, the drone has found it." He slapped his friend's cheek but got little response. As the RV nuzzled into the shoreline, Rabten laid Gopal down, covering him up as much as possible, and went to recover the bomb. It was so heavy, he could barely drag it onto dry land.

Rabten rummaged in his pockets and pulled out a crumpled piece of paper. The idiot-proof instructions for disarming the warhead. He read them carefully and completed step one, removing the outer case. There inside lay the ball of white gold, surrounded by explosive charges and a timer. The read-out was counting down. Forty minutes to go. Thank goodness for that.

Step two of the instructions told him to key in a code to access the timer's controls. He did so, but nothing happened. He re-read the instructions and repeated the step. Again, nothing.

His fists balled tight. Looking across, he saw his friend's eyes were already closed. There was no way Gopal was going to be able to help. Idiot-proof instructions and Rabten couldn't even manage that. He felt so slow, like his mind was wandering through thick fog. He tried to stay calm. He shook himself and went to fetch his wrist tab. *HQ will know what to do. Plenty of time...*

38

Bjørnøya

On the surface of the bleak island, Sim and Freda hunkered down, trying to stay out of the biting wind. Just inside the air vents aperture, they could see the faint red glow of a laser grid that monitored the secret way into the bunker.

"Were we fast getting here, or are they being slow?" Sim asked. "Give him time," said Freda.

Sim peered down into the duct for the eighth time. As he was watching, the red lights went out. "Right, let's go."

They removed the grille at the top of the duct and fastened ropes to the rock next to the hole. Freda insisted on going first and she began to abseil down. Progress was slow because every jolt to the side of the metal tube reverberated. She prowled down the air vent like a cat stalking a bird backwards. After about twenty metres, the light from above was beginning to fade. The duct split in two at this point. Freda stopped.

Sim, a little higher up, was just about to ask which way when his wrist tab beeped. A message from Wardle. Good timing, he thought. He clicked the screen off and put it into silent mode.

"Will you stop messing about," Freda whispered through gritted teeth. There was a noise coming from the branch on the left, and then something from the right-hand one too. "We need to split up. Take them by surprise. I'll give you ninety seconds to get into position, OK?"

Freda disappeared around the bend on the left and Sim lowered himself down the right-hand tube. The duct levelled off and became horizontal after another few metres, so Sim unclipped his carabiner. He slid along until he reached a vent into one of the rooms. Peering through, he saw the top of Larsson's head. He wasn't sure, but there did not seem to be anybody else in the room with the Swede. Sim glanced at his watch. He did not have time to unscrew the covering so he levered himself above it and jammed his feet down as hard as he could.

The cover gave way far more easily than Sim had expected. He fell through the opening and landed awkwardly onto the floor, ten feet below. His grip on the pistol came loose and it skittered across the polished tiles. Larsson turned around and put his foot on the gun as it slid towards him. He bent down just as Sim jumped up and threw himself at the Swede. Larsson staggered backwards, unable to pick up Sim's pistol. But he brought his fists crashing down onto Sim's back and knocked the wind out of him.

Sim released the hold on his opponent and rolled to his left, momentarily disoriented. Where was the gun? Sim looked up. The room had a big leather sofa opposite a screen that dominated one of the walls. The pistol might have ended up underneath the settee. Larsson stood opposite him and raised his fists, smiling. "Sim Atkins, I presume?"

Sim advanced and jabbed with his left fist, connecting with

Larsson's mouth. The Swede felt his lips and looked at the blood on his fingers. "You punch like a girl."

Sim swung with his right hand, harder, but more obvious. Larsson swayed backwards and the punch missed his face. "Your people should be grateful for what I'm doing." His right foot lashed out and connected with Sim's thigh. The leg buckled for a moment, but as Larsson's guard dropped, Sim pushed off with his left leg and punched the Swede in the belly.

Larsson gasped and doubled up, backing away. He stood up and smiled again. "That bomb is the only we're going to stop run-away global warming. You must know that by now. Your egg-heads must have crunched the numbers."

"And don't worry about the millions who will die?" asked Sim. Larsson had backed into a pool table and felt behind him. His fingers gripped around a cue. He whipped it around in front of him and held it like a sword. It was Sim's turn to back away, glancing around for a weapon to defend himself.

"Kill millions, to save billions? Of course, that's a trade I'll make any time," said Larsson, swishing the cue inches from Sim's face.

"What about the moon base? What would destroying that have achieved? Just for fun, was it?"

Larsson shrugged. "We should be colonizing the moon, not raping its resources. It's not like many people died." He raised the cue above his head and brought it crashing down. Sim managed to put his forearm up and block it. The end of the cue broke off and Sim felt something crunch inside his arm. But he did not feel any pain. Instead his whole body felt hot and stretched like an over-inflated balloon as his mind filled with pure anger.

"One of those was my son, you murdering fuck." Sim darted forward, grasping hold of the broken end of the cue even as his hand filled with splinters. Sim yanked the cue forwards and as

Larsson lurched towards him, unwilling to let go of the weapon, Sim smashed his forehead into Larsson's face.

Sim pulled back, slightly dazed, but when he looked up he could see Larsson clutching his nose, blood dripping freely between his fingers. "That hard enough for you?"

"I had no idea there were children up there. What sort of place is that to bring up a child?" said Larsson.

"And the Turkish children you experimented on? To perfect the virus. Go on, pretend you didn't know about them as well?"

Larsson dropped his hands and grinned. He licked the blood from his lips, savouring the taste. He reached down to his boot and pulled out a thin handle. At the push of a button a blade appeared. Larsson waved the knife towards Sim. "OK, I'm bored now. This conversation is over. You can surrender or die."

The door next to the giant screen burst open. Freda advanced into the room, her gun raised. "Drop it, Larsson."

Sim looked across at his partner. Her bottom lip was bleeding and he could see that she was limping as she advanced into the room. Something had slashed across her abdomen, cutting her clothes, but hopefully not her stab vest.

Larsson dropped his blade. "Ahh, Ms Brightwell. You seem to have bested my Precious. Not an easy thing to do. Congratulations."

Freda hobbled further into the room, keeping her gun trained on Larsson. "You alright, Sim?"

Sim bent down to pick up the discarded knife. "I will be soon." His knuckles turned white as he gripped the handle and brought the tip of the blade up to Larsson's throat. He held it there for a moment. "On your knees."

Larsson obeyed and Sim pulled the man's head back by his hair. The vein in Larsson's throat pulsed and his Adam's apple bobbed up and down a couple of times. Sim closed his eyes for a second, remembering the moment when his son's life had slipped away from him. All because of the bastard kneeling in front of him.

He opened his eyes and flexed his fingers on the knife handle. He pressed the blade against Larsson's flesh. A single drop of blood appeared where the tip was resting.

"Get your hands off him!"

Sim turned his head towards the noise. Precious Osundare staggered into the room, one hand clutched to a bloody wound in her belly. She held a knife in the other hand and flung it at Sim. Time seemed to slow down as Sim was caught between killing Larsson and defending himself. The knife was tumbling through the air, end over end, heading inexorably towards his chest. Freda reacted first. Her arm flashed out and she knocked the blade out of the air as it passed in front of her. She winced as the blade nicked the fleshy part of her palm. And then she turned to face Precious, firing twice. One whistled past, missing its target but the other found its mark. The woman's head jerked as the bullet passed straight through her left eye and blew away the back of her skull. Her limp body dropped to the ground.

Sim had let go of Larsson and the Swede rubbed his neck. "That is a pity."

"You expect us to show you any pity?" asked Sim.

"I meant, it's a pity for Freda. Precious doesn't fight fair."

Sim looked at Larsson for a moment, eyebrows creasing in confusion. And then across at Freda as she gasped and doubled up. "Freda? What is it?" Sim pushed Larsson to the ground, face down and lashed his hands together with some cord from his belt. Freda collapsed to the floor, writhing in agony. She closed her eyes then re-opened them wide, staring at Sim. It looked like she was trying to speak, but her facial muscles were not cooperating.

Sim turned to Larsson and kicked him in the stomach. "What's happening to her?"

Larsson rolled over onto his back, grinning. "Right now, the toxin that Precious uses on her knife is working its way through Freda's nervous system, shutting down muscles. Soon it will reach her lungs."

"Shit." Sim kicked Larsson again. He bent down to cradle Freda's head. Her breathing had slowed already. Her mouth was changing colour, bluish-purple like a gothic shade of lipstick. But her breaths remained shallow and infrequent. She looked up at Sim. He could see the pain and fear behind her eyes.

And then a thought struck him. He reached inside his jacket and pulled out the tubes he had retrieved from the ESCO laboratories. His hands shook as he carefully unwrapped each one, reading the labels. There was a *truth serum* and a hallucinogenic concoction. The third one listed some chemical compound and included the word 'antidote'. Sim didn't know if it was the right sort, but he popped the top off and poured the tiny portion of liquid into Freda's mouth. He sat her up and tilted her head back slightly, encouraging her to swallow. By now, she was completely floppy and Sim could not hear any more breaths.

"Come on, Freda. You can do it." The blue tinge to her lips had spread across her face and neck by now. Her skin was cold but damp with perspiration. Sim laid her down and pinching her nose, he breathed into her mouth, watching for the rise of her rib cage. He did it again.

"Antidote or not, her heart's going to give way any minute now." Sim looked across at Larsson, who was sitting up, hands still tied behind his back but a look of smug satisfaction on his bruised face. "Shut the fuck up." Sim gave another two rescue breaths. He knew there should be some improvement by now. He felt for a pulse but got nothing. He stood up and ran through the inner sanctum of this bunker. He untwisted the big lock on the inside of the blast door that separated this section from the rest of the base.

The captain was waiting for him on the other side.

"Freda's been poisoned. I think she's gone into cardiac arrest. See if you can find a defib unit." Sim dashed back to his partner, without waiting for a reply from Hamilton. Back at Freda's side he began CPR. Chest compressions and a breath. Repeat. Repeat. He could hear feet running about behind him and then somebody shouted their success. Chest compressions and a breath.

The medic from Hamilton's crew knelt down next to Freda, opposite Sim, and ripped open her top. The small box that was going to save her life was placed on the floor by another person. They were cutting into Freda's stab vest, stripping away her layers. "Careful," said Sim as the blade they were using threatened to slash across her skin. He felt a hand on his shoulder and turned to see the captain standing over him.

"They've got this, Sim. Give them the space they need to do their stuff."

Sim paused. He nodded, wincing from his own wounds as he stood up. He turned away and tried not to listen to the pair of Hamilton's crew, fighting to save Freda's life. Instead, Sim's eyes focused on Larsson. His mouth began to froth as the anger inside him tried to find a way to vent itself, like a pressure cooker looking for a release valve. Sim walked across to the captive, picked up the knife and once again held it against Larsson's neck. The smiled disappeared from the man's face at last.

Sim thought of all the moments he had wanted to avenge his son's death. To get revenge, not on Yusuf, the man who had carried the disease to Moon Lab One. But on the person who had instigated the whole plot. The person who had ordered his goons to kill Freda, and maybe at last had succeeded. The person who was trussed up in front of him, like a bird for the slaughter house. And then another image entered Sim's mind. His wife, Rosie.

Pregnant, thinking she was a widower. He ached to get back to Scotland, to explain the deception, to ask her forgiveness. He wanted to be a proper husband, a decent dad. How could he if, deep down, he knew he'd killed a defenceless prisoner? His grip on the knife handle relaxed and then tightened in rhythm with his heart beat. He stared into Larsson's eyes.

"Hey, Sim?"

A voice made him drop the knife and turn with tears in his eyes. Freda. He knelt down and hugged her. She was pale and cold, wrapped in a blanket, but it was her. Back from the dead. He squeezed his eyes closed as he rubbed her back.

Freda looked at his wrist tab, inches away from her face as Sim's arms stretched around her. "Didn't you get an urgent message from Wardle?"

"Oh crap, yes." Sim let go, and tapped on the tiny screen. His eyes opened wide as he read the words scrolling across. "We need the code to the bomb. Rabten can't disarm it without the code."

"You're not getting it from me," said Larsson.

"We'll see about that," said Sim, reaching for the test tube labelled truth serum. "Captain, get *The Endeavour* back to the surface. We need to send a very important message halfway across the globe. Now, open wide, Larsson."

EPILOGUE

The Endeavour was heading back towards Britain. They had managed to transmit the code to Rabten in time and the bomb had been disarmed. The look of defeat on Larsson's face when they had received this news helped to dissipate Sim's anger. At first, he had been disappointed with himself for not being able to kill the head of the Terror Formers. Now, things had changed. He would never stop mourning his son. But maybe he could focus on cherishing the few days they had spent together on the Moon, instead of letting rage eat away at his memory of James.

The last they had heard, Rabten was still very anxious about Gopal. Hypothermia had set in by the time the bomb had been disarmed. Before he had slipped into unconsciousness, the Gurkha had insisted that they should stay hidden from the Chinese authorities, in case their interference cost Rabten the chance to deactivate the timer.

Freda was still very weak from the effects of the poison. The medic on board *the Endeavour* hooked her up to a heart-rate monitor, and insisted that she rest for the whole journey back to Britain.

Sim barely left her side, but the captain was a frequent visitor to the sick bay too. "That was a close thing when you went all Mary Elizabeth on us," said Hamilton.

Freda thought for a moment and then her eyebrows raised and she smiled. "At least we didn't have to rely on aliens to save the day."

"Hah, Aliens. Cameron. Nice one," the captain replied with a wink.

"What are you two on about?" asked Sim.

"Just a film joke," said Freda.

"You two speak a different language, you know that?" said Sim. Freda and Hamilton just smiled at each other.

The Endeavour was allowed to dock at Faslane, the Royal Navy's submarine base in Scotland. Standing on the bridge, Sim was surprised to see that Captain Hamilton's eyes were moist as his boat manoeuvred to the quayside. Freda leant over and whispered to Sim how the captain had been thrown out of the navy and had even been hunted by his ex-colleagues not that long ago. Hamilton had admitted to Freda how much he had longed for a chance to restore his reputation and return with character unblemished. While she was telling Sim this he could see her looking over at the captain, with a gleam in her eye.

When they landed, Sim was eager to set a date with Freda for when they could meet up again. He needed to get back to Rosie as soon as possible. But afterwards, when things had calmed down, he didn't want to lose touch like last time. Freda's response was lukewarm. She needed to spend some time with her dad, after all these years. But there was more to it than that. Sim couldn't help noticing the frequent long chats she was having with Hamilton too. He couldn't begrudge his partner a happy ending. Good luck to them, he thought. Wardle arrived at the dockside.

"Any news on Gopal, sir?" asked Sim.

"He's fine. Apparently, the Chinese authorities saw Rabten's fire almost as soon as it was lit and rushed Gopal to hospital. Where he's making a full recovery, minus a digit or two."

"They've not been arrested, have they?"

"Quite the opposite. Once the authorities realised what they were doing, what the pair had prevented... Well, feted as heroes by all accounts."

Freda had wandered over to listen. "Hope they gave Rabten a slap-up meal in his honour. He'd have liked that."

Wardle was beckoning for Sim to join him. Sim looked at Freda and jerked his head towards the captain. "Not the only one who likes his food. Why don't you take Hamilton for lunch. I know a great place not far from here."

Freda strolled over to the captain as Wardle pulled Sim to one side. "We need to talk. About how to handle Rosie."

"What's to talk about? I'm going to see her right now."

"Slow down, Sim. That might not be wise. It's going to be quite a shock. And in her state, maybe we should find a way to break it to her gently."

Sim felt tired as he digested Wardle's suggestion. "I guess you're right. But how long?"

"Let's leave it a week. Give your hair a chance to get back to normal. You can ditch the contacts. And I'll see if the surgeon can do something to help break down your facial implants."

Seven days dragged by. Sim kicked his heels in a private hospital just outside Birmingham. Finally, Wardle showed up in a big limo with tinted glass. They drove up to Dornoch together.

Sitting in the back of the car, Sim asked about Overseas Division's future.

"The accountants have already made up their minds. We're being shut down."

"But surely this mission has just proved they still need us. How can they put a price on saving the world?"

Wardle shook his head. "Never as simple as that. As usual, the glory is getting shared out. The CIA is taking credit for capturing Jember Abdi and obtaining the link to ESCO. The Chinese insisted that they be the ones who return the warhead to North Korea. Apparently, they're using it as a means to gain some trust and re-open channels of dialogue. So, we can't claim that we found the bomb in case it upsets the delicate machinery of the diplomats."

"That is so messed up. What about our jobs?"

"Don't worry, I'll put in a good word for you with the other agencies. Maybe a desk job this time? Now that you've got a little one on the way, eh?"

Sim smiled and then felt his stomach churn as he thought about meeting up with Rosie again. Ten times worse than a first date. But more important than how he felt, he just wanted to make sure that the shock didn't do anything dangerous to her and the baby.

The car pulled up outside their small home on the outskirts of Dornoch. One of those days in late August when the sunlight seemed just right. Not too harsh and bright like June, or feeble and watery like the rays of winter. Sufficient to let everything radiate its true colours. Sim stayed in the car while Wardle knocked on the front door. It opened and there was Rosie. Her face a little more worn and a little rounder than last time he saw her. But his bonnie lass.

Wardle said something to Rosie and her face creased in confusion. Wardle put his hand on her shoulder. Her hand went to her mouth and tears gushed out. She bent down and then stood again, flinging her arms around Wardle. Sim pulled the handle of the car door and stepped back into his old life.

As the leaves changed colour, Rosie's belly continued to swell. Sim would meet up with his old boss, every so often, to go fishing together. It still felt weird calling him Alan, but Sim was getting to know him better. Alan's enthusiasm for fishing was starting to rub off on Sim. The midnight sessions on the silvery Tay were helping Sim to overcome his heartache whenever the Moon shone through. Often the conversation would turn to their colleagues. Freda had decided to explore the oceans with Captain Hamilton. No doubt continuing to swap old film quotes.

"I thought she said she was homesick," said Sim.

"Freda's one of those people with Wanderlust. Like a yoyo, Sim. They have to return home from time to time, but to come alive, they need to be in continuous motion."

Gopal and Rabten had set up a hostel in Kathmandu, offering guided tours of the Himalayas and helping tourists enjoy the majesty of their country. If he could persuade her, Alan was going to take his wife hiking there next year.

But what Sim enjoyed most of all was lying on the sofa with his ear pressed against Rosie, listening to their unborn child and feeling the little movements. Rosie often ran her fingers over Sim's face, tracing out the bumps and contours that remained from his disguise. After the mid-term scan, they discovered that they were having a baby girl. Sim had known straight away what he wanted to call her and Rosie had agreed: Luna.

Standing in the middle of the garden, Sim heard the grandfather clock strike 2am. He was looking up at the full Moon, thinking about Yvette and Lin, the scientists up at Moon Lab One still striving for a breakthrough on clean energy. Down on Earth, the Terror Formers' network had been busted open. The clean-up would take years, but they were winning. For the first time in a long while, Sim was feeling optimistic about the future. Rosie waddled out into the garden in her pyjamas, looking gloriously round.

"What you doing out here? It's freezing," said Rosie. Sim just shrugged.

"I thought you'd run off on another mission. Come back inside, yer daft bugger."

Sim smiled and put his hands on her bump and knelt down to kiss it. "I've never going to leave you two again." There was a kick from inside that made him jump.

"She's a fighter, just like her daddy," said Rosie. And that was when the contractions began.

ACKNOWLEDGEMENTS

Well, this has been quite the journey for Sim, Freda and me! Who knows whether we'll hear from the agents again but, for now, I'm done with their adventures. It's time for a new challenge. What that might be, only time will tell. Watch this space...

Thanks first and foremost to the gang at Bloodhound Books for breathing new life into this trilogy. Tara Gladden's editorial work made a huge difference to the quality of this trilogy, with her keen eye for detail and with structural changes that have improved the flow of the story.

Thanks also to my family and friends for their support in this change of career. I haven't dyed my hair or bought a sports car, so I'm not sure if it counts as a full-blown mid-life crisis. But your time and encouragement has helped enormously.

Most of all, thanks to you, the reader, for sticking with *Overseas Division* through thick and thin. I hope you have enjoyed the highs and lows of the whole plot. Feel free to drop me a line to let me know your favourite (or least favourite) character and scene by using the 'contact me' button on my website. I'd love to hear from you.

A NOTE FROM THE PUBLISHER

Thank you for reading this book. If you enjoyed it please do consider leaving a review on Amazon to help others find it too.

We hate typos. All of our books have been rigorously edited and proofread, but sometimes mistakes do slip through. If you have spotted a typo, please do let us know and we can get it amended within hours.

info@bloodhoundbooks.com

ABOUT THE AUTHOR

David was born in Cheshire but now lives in Berkshire with his picture-book-writing wife and story-loving daughter. After 25 years of working in the city as an economist, David turned his attention to writing. He attended the Faber Academy in 2014 and has since written three climate fiction thrillers (the Gaia trilogy). He joined the Society of Children's Book Writers and Illustrators in 2018 and has written numerous children's stories since then, some of which might eventually make it to print! He is a regular panellist on Radio Berkshire's monthly book show.

David loves reading, especially adventure stories, sci-fi and military history. Outside of family life, his other interests include tennis, golf, surfing and board games.

Find out more at https://davidbarkerauthor.co.uk or follow him on Twitter: @BlueGold201

www.ingramcontent.com/pod-product-compliance
Lightning Source LLC
Chambersburg PA
CBHW050754190726
48285CB00005B/1663